DEATH ON A GREEN

ALEC PECHE

GBSW PUBLISHING

ACKNOWLEDGMENTS

For my editor, G. M. Meyer, thank you for saving Angela from becoming a ditzy blonde when she is actually a smart brunette! I'd also like to thank Kim for helping me as a second reader. Your assistance in preventing opportunities to distract my readers through my choices of improper grammar, poorly selected adjectives, or typos is much appreciated.

As the reader might have guessed, the author had the pleasure of living in Green Bay for a decade in between stints of living in northern or southern California. It's a great city that I hope you get to visit someday.

PROLOGUE

*T*he patient was fine, but the surgeon had barely made it to the closure of the surgical incision. The two men were alone in the locker room. They had just finished changing into their street clothes from the green sweaty scrubs that they had both had on for the past five hours. One of the men looked tired having just provided anesthesia while worrying about both the patient and the surgeon operating.

"You just made it to the closure. What would you have done if you couldn't have finished this surgery?" asked Doug.

"What do you mean? I was fine. I could have continued another hour. My work is just more complicated than yours and requires deeper concentration," boasted Bradley.

"You paused several times during the surgery as if you had forgotten what your next step was. The surgical technician was holding out the appropriate instruments and you were not taking them out of her hands. The patient was under anesthesia for thirty minutes longer than the other five surgeons doing this exact same procedure."

"That idiot surgical tech was handing me the wrong instruments - that's why I wasn't taking them out of her hands. As for the extra anesthesia time, I was being more careful than my fellow surgeons, and I take my time sewing the incision shut. I try to reduce my patients' scars."

"Those are all excuses. You know you barely avoided making several serious mistakes."

"You know I don't want to work with you anymore. I am going to request the office schedule any other anesthesiologist but you for all my future cases."

"My peers worry about working with you. If you get sued for surgical technique, then they likewise get named in the suit. They don't want their names dragged into court with yours. I am going to request the medical staff office do a quality review of your surgical outcomes."

"Are you threatening me?"

"No, just giving you advanced notice of what I plan to do. You and I have worked together for more than ten years and you know that going behind people's backs is not my style. I am really worried about patients under your care. I don't know what your problem is. I don't know if you're ill, if you have an alcohol or drug problem, or if you lost your confidence in the operating room, but your surgeries are getting more dangerous with each passing month. You're a different surgeon than you were a year ago. I wouldn't allow you to operate on a family member and if that is my opinion, I should be concerned for the patients served by this hospital."

"Let me put you on notice that I am going to report you to the medical staff office for causing a hostile work environment in the operating room. Your threats are interfering with my concentration. I'm going to ask them to review the quality of your work."

"That is fine. I always welcome an evaluation of my anesthesia technique. Maybe I'll learn something that will make me a better physician."

Doug looked at Bradley while he made these last comments. He could figuratively see steam coming out of his ears and if his eyes had been a laser like what they used in the OR, he would have been blinded by now. He placed a hand on Bradley's arm and asked, "Are you okay? You look un-well."

Bradley shrugged his arm away from Doug's hand and said, "Just get the hell out of this room and out of my life. You'll regret if you report me to anyone. I am a brilliant surgeon and how dare you say otherwise." He finished the last sentence nearly yelling at Doug.

Doug could see he wasn't reaching Bradley, so he dropped his dirty scrubs in the laundry basket and picked up his satchel to leave.

Bradley tossed a parting shot at him, "You'll regret that you ever brought this conversation up. You can't tell lies about me. I am a brilliant surgeon."

Doug didn't say anything, he just closed the door gently on the locker room and walked away thinking about his next steps. Next to delivering bad news to a patient or their family, the next conversation he hated to have was about another physician's performance. It had been his experience that they couldn't see the poor performance on their own and thus each time he had such a conversation it usually brought up anger and denial. Unlike medical school where you had evaluations in terms of tests or physician Specialty Boards where you had to take a test and stand before your peers to discuss your knowledge, once you finished your medical training there was no regular ongoing evaluation of your skill and knowledge. Bradley was from the old school. When he graduated and took his Boards, it was his for life so there was no recertification every five to ten years. Thus his skill had not been evaluated in almost thirty years by a group of his peers. He had been grandfathered in as an older surgeon and did not have to get re-Boarded. He would give Bradley a week to take action on his own now that he had planted the seed. Doug would also make sure he wasn't paired with him for any upcoming surgeries in the week ahead.

He approached his car thinking about the week ahead. It was Friday night and he wasn't on-call for the week-end. On Monday, he had taken the day off to participate in his favorite golf outing. He enjoyed the outdoors, the chance to play golf, an opportunity to support one of his favorite charities, and just the general tone of this particular outing. It was fun, and really non-competitive which was a good thing given all of the alcohol that was served throughout the course. He also enjoyed the competition of hitting close to the chicken wings chafing dish plugged in on the fairway, the wooden cow, or the bar stool. It was important to have a sense of humor when golfing.

Bradley was still sitting in the men's locker room in the surgery department. He needed to check on his patient and speak to the family to tell them all was well. Because of his stupid argument with Doug, he had to sit here and get his temper under control. He was going to have the surgical tech written up for a poor performance, and then he was going to move on to Doug. He had checked the schedule and knew he had three days to figure out what to do about him. Taking some deep breaths he stood up to go speak with the family, and then he was going to head home to spend some time thinking about his comments. Why had Doug said such things? He was the best surgeon at this hospital. No patient had died under his care and if he was taking longer, it was because he was more careful and his wound closure was better than anyone else. He scoffed at Doug's words in his mind, closed the door on those thoughts and entered the surgery waiting room to shake the hands of his patient's family.

CHAPTER 1

 ill Quint had been in Green Bay for three days of the week that she had planned to spend there. She was visiting her friends - Angela, Jo, and Marie who all made the city their lifelong home. Wisconsin was beautiful in the spring. There was an air of optimism that everyone had made it through another cold winter. The daffodils had come and gone and now the tulips were exploding in a rainbow of colors. It was also unfortunately windshield bug season. A driver would drive down the highway seemingly in a small pebble hail storm, and instead it was big bloody bugs committing suicide against a car's windshield. Yuck, they even made it hard to see through the glass to the world beyond.

On this visit she had been to one of her usual favorites - Highland Howie's bar which served the best Friday fish fry and bacon cheeseburgers on earth. Jill, a resident of California, couldn't find perch in her home state. A staple of Wisconsin Fish Frys, the perch loved the Great Lakes. The term 'fish fry' in the Midwest originated with a meal eaten on Fridays during Lent especially by Roman Catholics. Fortunately, Highland Howie's served it year around on Fridays as well as a few other days of the week.

She had also updated her sports wardrobe with a visit to the Packers Pro Shop. As a team owner - Jill owned her one share of the Green Bay Packers stock - she needed a full range of green and gold items. She was fair skinned, with green eyes and thick blond hair; her coloring meant that some shades of green and gold looked awful against her skin. However, she had a full closet of Packer clothing, so no new clothing was needed. This year she was looking for a new flag to run up the flag pole of her winery in California. The hot sun of the central valley of California had a way of fading green and gold to lime and lemon after two years of flying during football season.

They had lunch with Angela's mother who was a wonderful cook. She had organized countless celebratory and funeral luncheons for her church and could put together a wonderful meal for three or three hundred just as easily. Jill would hit a cheese store just before she left to get cheese curds, a by-product of cheese-making that you could only find in the dairy state. Curds were generally supposed to be eaten within twelve hours of manufacturing to get the squeak when chewed, but her family was fine with day-old curds simply because of their novelty.

Yesterday, Jill and her friends had bicycled from Green Bay to Greenleaf stopping along the way at a winery to taste their varietals. Jill's day job was that of vintner and she operated a part time forensic pathology consultancy that provided both a second opinion on the cause of death as well as a private detective-like service to assist families and law enforcement in determining the murderer. She had been glad to be off her bike as she had yet to find a comfortable bicycle seat. Sipping wine at a local vineyard gave her posterior a rest and allowed her to observe the tasting room. Her own vineyard, Quixotic Winery didn't have a wine tasting room yet; she solely sold her vintage to local liquor stores. She planned to add a tasting room in one to two years. First she wanted to make sure she could handle the production process for making high quality wines. Then she would expand her acreage of grape vines and thus her production. She also examined the wine label on the bottles. Her boyfriend, Nathan Conroy was a world class wine label designer and she seemed to find his labels everywhere. He had remained in California where he and his cat Arthur, were dog sitting Trixie, her Dalmatian. Soon they had been back on their bikes, a wine bottle in their backpacks riding towards the D & G Restaurant for ice cream.

Today promised to be a great day. Jill had timed her visit to coincide with this particular golf outing as it was her favorite. The friends had also golfed two days earlier in the style of girlfriend golf - no one kept score, they walked with a pull cart to burn calories, Angela wore no shoes, and the conversation kept going even while they swung their clubs. Their styles and scores were the polar opposite of Tiger Woods, after all, could he gossip while he swung a club? Probably not.

It was at this golf outing during previous years that she had been introduced to gelatin shots and the skill it took to hit a chicken wing cooker in the middle of the fairway. She hadn't yet figured out if the alcohol from the gelatin shots and margaritas affected her golf game in a positive or negative manner and given the fact that there was really no need to play well, she suspected she would go through life without an answer to that question.

Turning into the golf course parking lot Jill said to Angela, "Looks like we beat Jo and Marie to the parking lot, no surprise there - Jo is always late."

"Jo still has thirty-five minutes to get here prior to the start of the outing. She'll be here by then," replied Angela giving her a look that said 'chill-out'. "What a beautiful day! You can see the sun starting to stream through the trees as the fog and morning mist is lifting. Beats having to take cover from the occasional rain storm!"

Jill tried to relax, but it wasn't in her nature. So instead she took a look around the parking lot studying everyone's clothes and gear. Jill's theory was the more elaborate the golf outfit and the larger the golf bag, the less likely people were to be fun to play with. They took the game far too seriously. She had played one course that required a caddy and wow, was that intimidating. They had even made Angela wear shoes.

Jill lifted the borrowed set of clubs from Angela's father out of Angela's car trunk. Marie, Angela, and Jo were all five feet nine plus, and Jill was a full half a foot shorter. That meant she couldn't often use clubs or bikes from them as she was simply too short for the equipment. She leaned against the car, shoving her blond hair out of her eyes as she put her golf shoes on and then they both headed to the clubhouse. Jo was more of a natural redhead and Marie and Angela were brunettes. Of course their present hair color had more to do with science than Mother Nature. Jill was the heaviest of the four and Marie the thinnest, with Angela and Jo falling in between. They were all active in their lives - walking, running, cycling, and swimming. Leaning their golf bags against a rack, they walked in to pick up their registrations.

"Looks like we have cart fourteen-A and we're starting on hole fourteen," said Angela reading their registration packet. "Let's go dump our clubs into the cart and then return to the clubhouse."

"Sounds like a plan!"

Jo and Marie were just entering the registration area when Angela and Jill were exiting the clubhouse. After exchanging hellos and grabbing the additional registration packets, they all exited to put their bags into the golf cart and the four friends stood around examining their packet's tchotchkes and what food and drink were at each hole.

"It's the usual prizes closest to the pin on two holes, farthest from the tee, closest to the chicken wing warmer, the bar stool, and the wooden cow," said Jill with relish of the competition ahead. She had occasionally won the longest drive, but never did well on closest to the pin.

"Which holes have the gelatin shots and margaritas?" asked Marie clearly with her priorities in the right place.

"Shots are on ten and the margaritas are on two," read Angela aloud.

"They gave us this boxed lunch, but I would rather have some of the chicken wings on the first hole," declared Jo.

"I have never had the wings. Do they have wet wipes to get the sauce and grease off your hands before you touch the clubs?" asked Jill.

"They have a box of wipes just behind the cooker," replied Angela.

"Is the lid locked down? I would think some drives would knock the lid off the cooker," suggested Jill.

"Yes, it is latched," laughed Jo. "You think of the strangest questions. It would not occur to me to worry about a lid."

"Well, I don't want flies or bees entering the cooker. They'll either die on the wings from the heat or leave behind some fly disease. No thanks!" Jill exclaimed.

"Ok, I think you two should ride together so you can continue this fascinating conversation," observed Marie. "Angela and I will ponder a much more difficult question such as are margaritas better blended or on the rocks."

Just then a gentleman with a portable paging horn stepped up to the line of golf carts. He welcomed everyone, gave a fabulous weather forecast, noted food and drink highlights, and then sent everyone off to their holes. The golf outing was very popular and there were two foursomes starting at each hole. They would spend a fair amount of time waiting for other golfers to clear out of the way, before they could hit at each tee box, fairway, and green. Oh well, there was plenty of food, drink, and conversation to keep them occupied.

They soon arrived and introductions were exchanged with the other foursome. Angela, who seemed to know everyone in Green Bay, of course, knew two of the golfers in the other foursome. There were three men and a woman in the group and they felt sympathy for the woman who would hit from a different tee box than the guys. It could be disruptive to conversations. She was soon catching up on their lives. Angela and her foursome were designated to go first. Likely, this was a good thing as they could chat while they were driving from the tee rather than trying to remember to stay silent while the other foursome went first.

Marie stepped up first and placing her tee and ball in position, swung and drove the ball straight down the fairway about one hundred yards. Jo went next and she drove her ball slightly into the rough on the right side. Angela followed driving her ball fairly close to Marie's ball. Jill went last and she was a feast or famine golfer. Her first drive was a complete miss. She swung at the ball with force and missed contact with the ball, but the swing took her around in a circle. After the laughter of her friends and herself died down, she took a second swing and had a beautiful drive twenty yards beyond Marie and Angela. They all headed towards the rough where they thought Jo's ball had landed and found it quickly. Jo was back on the fairway with her shots for the rest of the hole. It was labeled a par five and they were generally pleased if any of them managed to bogey the hole.

They continued their slow pace to the eighteenth hole and then started over at the first hole. It was a par four and by now, Jill was consistently making contact with the ball. Jo turned her body such that while the ball went to the right it was still on the fairway. They continued to the second hole, a par five, and more importantly, it contained the tent over the margarita mix servers. The foursome had been stuck with beer up to that point. The second hole was so much more pleasant when a golfer had a margarita to serve as aiming juice. All four women achieved bogeys at the par five and then they moved on to the third hole. They stood to the side waiting for the group in front of them to clear the tee box. Then they heard it.

A very loud shotgun blast sounded from close by in the woods. Jill dropped to the grass on the green and yelled, "Drop to the ground now! You're an easy target standing up," and they complied with her order.

Jill looked around her and saw that no-one else was ducking. Perhaps they were used to guns going off at a close range, but she wasn't. It sounded like the gunshot had come from the woods that were adjacent to the green of second hole and the tee box of third hole

Then they heard shouts.

CHAPTER 2

"Oh my god, he's dead," were the words that traveled over the air to Jill, who was still face down on the ground.

"Jill, I think we had better go back to the last green - it sounds like someone was shot there, maybe we can help," Angela asserted to her friends. Beyond the single shot that rang out, they hadn't heard any additional shots.

They all scrambled to their feet and ran towards the previous green that they had all just celebrated on. There was a man lying there, face up with a bullet wound almost between his eyebrows. His three friends were standing around him and one was on his cell phone having called 9-1-1.

Jill rushed over and put her fingers on his carotid artery testing for a pulse. It was thin and slow and the man was clearly not breathing. In five seconds of assessment, she knew the man was already dead and it was just a matter of his heart following his brain to its final destination of death. She put her hand behind his scalp and it came away covered in bloody pieces of bone and brain matter.

Jill looked up at her friends and whispered, "This is very bad, I recommend that we not touch him and wait for the ambulance to arrive. We don't want to start CPR on him."

Looking over at the other three golfers, one of which had just finished puking in the woods she asked "When will an ambulance be here?"

"There is a fire station close by - it should be just another minute," replied the woman.

Jill looked over at them and said, "This is a very bad bullet wound to the head, his heart rate is slowing and we could do CPR. Do any of you know how to do it?"

One of the men must have heard the caution in her voice and he asked "It looks very bad. It looks like you have his brains on your hand." The other gentleman turned away to puke again.

"I would guess you are correct about that. I am a forensic pathologist. I worked in a crime lab for many years. I am not trained in trauma or neurosurgery. All I do know is that I saw a lot of these types of injuries at the medical examiner's office."

They could hear the ambulance and fire trucks getting closer. She wondered if they would drive out on the course. Marie had thought to call the golf course's office and warn them that the ambulance would be arriving. A few more seconds went by and no one suggested they start CPR. They could now see a golf cart leading the fire truck, police car, and ambulance over to the green. They needed the little golf cart to direct their path and avoid any water or creeks that the vehicles would get stuck in. Jill leaned down and checked the pulse and found none. She was glad she could leave any further action in the paramedic's hands. They ran over to where the man was laying on the green with their supplies.

Jill said, "I am a physician - a forensic pathologist. His pulse has stopped and he has a grievous bullet wound to the brain."

The paramedics hooked him up to their equipment transmitting the results to the local base station. Everyone at the scene seemed to be of the opinion to do nothing.

"Are you a licensed physician in the State of Wisconsin?" asked the paramedic.

"No, I am licensed in California. I don't know your medical examiner rules and policies in this state so I don't believe I can pronounce him for you."

"I am waiting for the base station to confirm we do nothing here at the scene, and instead send the body to the coroner."

No sooner had he said that, when word came from the base station to go ahead and pronounce him dead.

The paramedic did just that and he and his partner had a discussion with the police on next steps. Green Bay averaged one murder a year, almost always a domestic disturbance. As the shooter had not come forward with smoking gun in hand, this would be a true investigation of the murder. As an afterthought they passed a box of wipes over to Jill and she was able to get the blood and brain matter off her hands. Six wipes later she felt better about her hands, although she would still wash them before she touched food.

Angela had been quiet the whole time, and suddenly, Jill remembered that she had been a friend of the victim.

"Angela, I'm so sorry that you lost your friend. Can you tell me what you know about him?" probed Jill.

"It's really very shocking to join a friend at the beginning of a golf match - one that you haven't spoken to in maybe two years and then two hours later they are shot dead less than fifty yards from you."

By now all the women had encircled Angela and were giving her support.

"What was his name?" asked Marie.

"Doug Easley. He was anesthesiologist at Our Lady of Guadalupe Hospital. He was an absolutely beloved physician. He worked long hours providing anesthesia, agreeing to work over-time to take care of a patient's pain or to assist a surgeon with a last minute tumor removal. You know that most patients can't tell you who their anesthesiologist is, but they knew him which tells you what a great communicator he was," said Angela suddenly overflowing with thoughts and words about Doug. "I even took their family portrait three years ago when his twin daughters were entering middle school. I assisted his daughters in achieving a 'cool look' in the photo. Jill, we need to work on this case for free. Doug would have wanted that and his wife Michelle will want that."

"We'll need Michelle's approval to go forward. I can create a no-charge contract for her to sign. Do you think you can get her to sign it? This will be a terrible day for her, but I would like to get in on the autopsy right away."

"During my photo shoot, I mentioned the part-time job with you and she thought it was so cool. So we won't have to convince her of our legitimacy. As soon as you can get me the contract, I'll go see her and get her to sign it."

"We're going to be stuck here for at least an hour as the police need to take our statements. Afterwards we can go to Office Max in the East Town Mall, and I'll print a copy of the contract and forms for her to sign. I can come with you to meet Michelle, although I think it would be better if you approached her first, but I leave that decision up to you. It would also help if you could take some pictures of the scene - Doug, this green, the woods. I will be setting up a murder board as you know and it would help to have these photos."

"Okay, let me see what I can do with my phone camera. I agree with your thoughts on approaching Michelle and just as soon as we are done here we'll head to Office Max."

"Jill, I have never been on a crime scene before, what do you think is going to happen?" asked Marie. "I suppose the table where Laura Peeters died was a crime scene, but it was not treated that way, while we in the restaurant."

"I have been to many crime scenes as a medical examiner. So the police should leave the body here at the start of the investigation. They should secure this scene and interview each of us separately as to what we heard and saw as well as the three golfers that Doug was playing with. Depending on the size of the detective division, this may take a while to organize. We ought to go sit on that bench over there while they organize. I'm guessing our favorite golf tournament has ended with this tragic event."

They watched a policewoman and a paramedic walk out of the woods close to where they were sitting and where Jill had thought the shot had come from. She was glad someone had taken a look into the woods in case the shooter was still there, but she had doubted they would find anyone as this seemed, in her experience, to be pre-mediated murder. The fire truck had returned to its station while the paramedics leaned against their van waiting for the authorization to remove the body. Meanwhile a whole platoon of police cars had shown up on the scene.

A detective came over to speak with them.

"I hear that one of you is a forensic pathologist," stated a man in a suit with badge clipped to his belt.

"Yes, I am. I am retired from the State of California Crime lab, but I do private consultations on suspicious deaths. Sadly the cause of death here is very apparent. What is your name?"

"I am Detective Van Bruggin," the man said unclipping and showing her his badge and handing her his business card. "If you don't mind I would like to interview all of you separately. Doctor, I would like to start with you. Will you come with me to the tee box on the next hole?"

Jill stood up and gave her friends a look of 'isn't this going to be fun' and followed the detective out of hearing range to the next hole's tee box.

"Can you tell me your name, address, and phone number?" asked the detective, pen and paper in hand.

"I'm Dr. Jill Quint, I live in Palisades Valley, California," Jill followed that with her address and phone number.

"So what is a Californian doing on this golf course?"

"I am vacationing in Green Bay and this is day three of seven days that I plan to spend here. I am on this course for the golf outing and these are my three friends. My day job is that of owner of the Quixotic Winery. Since retiring from the crime lab in California, I have been doing part-time private cases for the past five years. My friends that you will be interviewing also work part-time for me doing investigative work and they live in this city. Over the course of my career as a pathologist, I have roughly participated in over one thousand murder investigations. I also participated in other criminal investigations such as rape, abuse, and under the influence of something. This is the first time that I have been on scene when a murder has been committed. If you would like references for me or my three friends, I can provide them to you from the FBI and the SFPD."

Jill was trying to volunteer as much pertinent information as she could to be helpful to the investigation.

"So short of a detective, you might be the single best person to have on-scene when a murder occurs," summarized the detective.

"Actually, I would go a step farther and say I'm the best person to have on-scene because I can try and save your life after the attempt has been made."

"Touché," agreed the detective. "What did you see and hear today at this course?"

"We met Doug's foursome back at the fourteenth hole where we all started. There were two foursomes assigned to each hole. We were the 'A' group and they were the 'B' group. Angela, one of the members of my foursome, knew the victim and his family. They had a brief discussion before we teed off. We finished the second hole and then had to wait at the third tee box for the group in front of us to finish. This had been the case on nearly every hole we played today. It is a crowded course as this is a popular golf outing. We were all standing around on the tee box waiting for the group in front of us to be far enough down the fairway before teeing off. I bent over, placing my ball and the tee in the grass. As I straightened up, and I heard the gunshot which sounded like it was close by in those woods." Jill described pointing at the woods on the rim of the green. "I dropped to the ground and yelled at my three friends to do likewise. We stayed down but heard no further shots. We then heard conversation drifting up from the green we had just played and it sounded like one of them had been hit by the gunshot. My friends and I stood up and quickly approached the green. I immediately noted that the victim was face up with a bullet wound to the head that I had seen many times on my autopsy table. I approached the victim and could see he was not breathing. I checked his pulse and it was faint but there. I felt the back side of his head to check for an exit wound verifying in my head that this was likely a fatal gunshot wound. By unspoken agreement, we all waited for the ambulance to arrive and it did about two to four minutes after the gunshot. With the aid of the base station and the paramedic assessment, the victim was pronounced dead shortly thereafter."

"Did you move the body while you were doing your assessment?" asked the detective.

Jill stared him down, the answer in her eyes as she said in a clipped voice, "Of course not. His body is in the same position as it was when we approached the green. A gunshot coming out of the woods targeting that man in the head would have produced that body position."

"Just checking. It appeared as though the body had not been moved, but I needed to know that for the record. Did you hear any sounds in the woods before or after you heard the sound of the gun?"

"My friends and I play noisy golf. We continue to converse even as we swing our drivers at the ball. We had some quiet time while the foursome that went before us drove their tee shots. I did not hear anything that registered as unusual. I did not hear the gun get cocked. There may have been the usual noise from squirrels and birds, but I don't remember hearing any sound that was unusual."

"Again for the record, did you have any alcoholic drinks in the past hour?"

With a sigh Jill replied, "I had a beer that lasted me from the fourteenth to eighteenth hole. On the second hole, I had a margarita. I would guess my blood-alcohol would not exceed 0.8 at this moment nor at the time of the actual shooting."

"Thank you. Is there anything I should have asked you that I didn't?"

"You only asked me one question concerning my opinion as a forensic pathologist. What would you ask me if I was the coroner assigned to this case?"

"What gun was used?"

"Given this is a deer hunting region and there had to be some sharpshooting skills, my guess is a Winchester .308."

"Deliberate shooting or an accident?"

"Homicide, deliberate."

"Did the shooter hit the intended target?"

"Yes, Doug was the intended target."

"How do you know that?"

Jill was resisting rolling her eyes, "Because only a single shot was fired. If the shooter had missed, there would have been a second shot. Given the placement of the bullet precisely between the eyebrows, this was a very talented shooter."

"Okay, thanks. You have been very helpful. Would you mind sending over your friend who knows the victim?"

Jill nodded her agreement and left the tee box for the bench where her friends were sitting.

"Angela, the detective wants to speak with you next," and she pointed to where he was standing, writing notes on his computer tablet.

They watched her walk over and then turned to their own conversation.

"What did he ask you?" asked Marie.

"What you would expect - describe what was happening when you heard the gun go off, my name, address, and occupation. Then he asked me a few questions in my role as a forensic pathologist."

"What did you tell him?" asked Jo.

"I don't mean to be rude, but we shouldn't discuss what we heard in case one of us heard something different," explained Jill. "Give your statement to the detective, then we can discuss it between us afterward. I am surprised he didn't give us that warning. Hopefully, whoever is interviewing the other foursome, or maybe I should say threesome, has provided them with a warning."

"Did you tell him we were going to work on this case?" asked Marie.

"No, we don't have Michelle's authorization, so I wouldn't want to mention it until I have a contract in place."

"Ok, I'll follow your lead on that one and hopefully Angela doesn't accidentally mention our intent to do a free investigation. Do you think that they will let us go after the interviews are done?" asked Jo. "I'll need a bathroom soon after the beer and adrenaline rush."

"I'll just ask the officers to excuse us since I could use a bathroom break as well. I am sure the golf course is closed and we can easily drive to the clubhouse in the cart. If they will let us, we should examine the woods looking for clues. That might help us solve the case faster for Michelle's sake."

Jill and Jo walked over to the group of detectives and police officers, trying to avoid looking at Doug who had not been covered up yet. "Detective Van Bruggin is interviewing us; he has already taken my statement. Jo and I need to take our cart and go to the bathroom at the club house," and they continued toward their golf cart.

One of the officers stopped them offering them a ride in a

squad car. Obviously, they weren't willing to let them leave their custody just yet.

"Do you know how to get back to the restaurant in a car? I mean there are some creeks in the way," noted Jill.

"Yes I know how to get there. The course manager gave us a map when we got here with directions on how to avoid hazards."

"Okay, let's go. I really need the bathroom now."

The officer put them in the back of the patrol car and shortly they were at the restaurant. The uniformed officer followed them inside. He took up guard while they went inside the ladies room, and stood, ready to escort them back to his car when they were done. It was really creepy. The back seat stunk, all noise had ceased when they arrived and everyone stared at them. Finally, it was driving Jill nuts so she made an announcement just as she reached the exit to the restaurant.

"We're the witnesses, not the shooter," and the door closed behind them.

CHAPTER 3

"*N*ow that was an interesting experience," mused Jo always willing to look at the positive side of any comment. "I felt like we had a very bad odor. I would have liked to stay behind as a fly on the wall to hear the conversation after your parting comment."

"Me too," agreed Jill. "I would rather walk back than ride in the police vehicle. It really smelled. Even though it was the back seat you would have thought the smell would bother the officers in the front. I suppose that he may have finished taking Marie and Angela's statements and we don't want to delay the investigation."

"For a woman who has spent a fair amount of time around stinky corpses and perhaps formaldehyde, you are really fussy about scents," Jo remarked. "You must be making up for lost time."

"I think my problem is that I would love to contribute to this investigation - get in the middle and direct it, but the police seem quite competent. For all the investigations we have participated in over the years I think this is the physically closest point we have ever been to a murder that came out of the blue. Certainly, in other investigations, murders have happened during the course of the case, but generally they were strangers and we knew why they were dead. This time Angela personally knows the victim and we haven't a clue why he is dead. There is also a 'hit man' feel to this shooting which is an exotic premise for this city."

"Oh well, we have not worked as a team together for nearly six months. I think each of us has only provided a few hours of consulting on the five or so cases you have had since our last big case in Colorado last year," Jo related. "If Angela gains the wife's permission for us to work on this case, it will be a first for us as this is home ground for Angela, Marie, and I. We may be evaluating or investigating people we know in this town as opposed to our usual process of investigating complete strangers."

They arrived back at the second green. Angela had finished being interviewed and was sitting by herself on a bench with her eyes closed while Marie was up in the other tee box telling her story.

"Hey, are you doing okay?" asked Jill softly.

Angela opened her eyes and looked blankly at them for a moment then heaved a big sigh and said, "I was just saying a prayer for Doug, Michelle, and the kids. He wasn't a close friend, but he was someone I expected not to be touched by such violence. I saw him and his family in church every couple of months. I wasn't aware of any risky behavior. Certainly, I can't imagine anyone hating him enough to kill him like this. On a completely different subject, I was trying to think of the words to use with Michelle and even to get past her family today and get her permission for us to initiate a separate investigation. The one thing I have learned participating in all of these investigations is that, as a team, we are really good at solving crimes and peeling back the layers so that we catch all of the criminals. I would go so far as to say we solve some of our cases faster than Interpol or the FBI or the local police. How do I tell an acquaintance, someone who isn't a close friend that she really needs to hire us, even if it is at no cost, to solve her husband's murder?"

"It is very gratifying to hear you say you feel like we make a difference. The sole reason I began doing these autopsies was to make a difference to a very vulnerable group of people and to make sure the right criminals are caught. For you to feel that way about this part time job is really a credit to our team. This used to be my occupation, but it was never yours and I expect you to tolerate it, but instead it sounds like at the end of these cases you feel the satisfaction that I do. Thank you," said Jill and she leaned in to hug Angela. "I have some thoughts on how to approach Michelle but when the police are done here, we'll have a quick huddle and decide."

Jo returned to them with the detective. Her interview had been the shortest. Jill wondered if it was because Jo was likely the fourth person to say the same thing or if it was Jo's naturally unobservant personality that had shortened the conversation.

"Ladies, thank you for your time. I may have additional questions so don't be surprised if I call you. Dr. Quint, I would offer you the professional courtesy of observing the autopsy, but as you told me while I took your statement, it really is quite obvious what killed him and that it was homicide, not suicide or an accident."

"Has your team located the shell casing in the woods?"

"I don't know. Let me check," replied VanBruggin as he left the four of them alone for the first time in an hour.

"So, Jill, what do you think so far of the investigation?" asked Marie with the slightest tinge of hometown pride in her voice.

"It's pretty early in the investigation, but from what I saw today, I can't complain. I wish they would have run into the woods to see if the shooter was still there, but I guess if you're only one officer, than it is not your priority."

"So what do you think the next steps are here today?" asked Jo.

"I think the officers are done with us," replied Jill. "It seems like our next steps are to help Angela craft a message for Michelle that will get her to agree to accept your help. The other thing is it would be really helpful to go into that woods and find where the shooter was standing. I wonder if the Green Bay Police Department is big enough to have a ballistics expert on the force. Let me ask the detective those two questions."

Jill walked over to where the detective was standing talking with both uniformed officers and crime scene staff judging by their respective clothing. The three teammates of the victim were making their way back toward the clubhouse. By now, Michelle should've been notified by the police of her husband's murder.

"Detective Van Bruggin, I have a couple questions for you. Do you have a minute?"

The detective left his group and followed Jill to neutral ground between their two teams.

"Are we free to go? Do you have a ballistics expert in the department? Would you allow us to go into the woods to look for evidence of the shooter? I presume you have not found any shell casings."

"Yes, Dr. Quint, you and your friends are free to go. We do not have a ballistics expert in our department. As far as searching the woods, we consider that as part of the crime scene so I don't think we want you trampling around in there. And what was your last question? Oh yeah, did we find shell casing - no we did not."

"In the interest of full disclosure, I should tell you that it is the desire of my friends and I to gain permission from the victim's wife for us to separately investigate this murder. So it would be helpful if we could examine the woods now."

The detective had an angry look about his face as he asked, "Are you planning on charging the widow for your services?"

"No, we will be asking her to sign a no cost contract. We do need a contract and I have separate authorization forms so that we may speak on her behalf to investigate her husband's death."

"Okay," said the detective with a long pause as he was thinking. "I have never worked alongside a private detective this early in the investigation. What will you do if the widow does not want you looking into her husband's death?"

"We will respect her wishes. It would be very hard to investigate this murder without her cooperation. I am sure she has faith in your department, but my team and I have solved a variety of complex murders where there are multiple and hidden motives. A physician being murdered could be simple or complex."

"Stand here a minute and let me talk to a few associates," requested the detective as he walked off.

Jill just stood there, a few feet from her friends, a few feet from the detectives, all alone looking at where the victim still lay on the green. She wondered how the golf course would clean up the blood and brain mess to have a playable surface. From there, she stared into the woods speculating where the killer might have been. Would he or she have been standing on the ground or sitting on a tree branch? The woods were thick so the shooter couldn't have been very far into the woods. She looked at where the body laid on the green and angles of potential bullets. How would the shooter get away after firing the rifle? Did he or she run back through the woods to a parked car?"

She was so deep in thought that when the detective approached her and put a hand on her arm, she jumped and uttered, "Crap, you scared the wits of out me. My fault, I was thinking about this investigation."

The detective had immediately lifted his hands and stepped back, "Sorry, didn't mean to startle you. It is easy to be edgy at a crime scene."

Jill pulled her sunglasses down and gave the detective a look that said, 'I've seen a hundred crime scenes and I have seen worse than this.' She stayed silent and waited for him to say something.

"We're going to allow you to examine the woods," remarked the detective.

"Great, thank you. Do you have four sets of gloves we can use?

We'll want to keep our fingerprints off of stuff and if we find any evidence, we will leave it where it is found."

Jill wanted to get to the store and print out her contract for Angela's conversation with Michelle, but they were fortunate to get this opportunity to examine the woods. She handed latex gloves to her friends and they put them on as they approached the edge of the woods.

"I am guessing that this is the angle that a bullet would've taken to hit the victim the way it did," said Jill while she was lining up her arm with the path in which the body had fallen. "Let's make it quick as I doubt that we'll find any evidence here but it never hurts to be thorough. If you see something, don't pick it up – leave it where you found it and call out to me or the detective."

"Jill, um, what are we looking for?" asked Jo. "I mean are we looking for clothing, are we looking for a shell casing, or are we looking for evidence that someone was in this area as evidenced by flattened plants?"

"You're correct, Jo, we're looking for all of the things you mentioned. As for flattened plants, some plants will be flattened from the earlier walk-through by the people at the scene. The plants that we're looking for will have had someone standing on them for at least twenty minutes. Make sure you track the angle of the body to your location. We don't want to go too wide or too deep in our examination of the woods. Angela, if you could snap a picture through the trees at the green, that would be useful."

The four friends began their search. They had spread out and were carrying their putters to move stuff out of the way on the ground. Then Marie had come up with a good suggestion.

"I'm just not seeing anything. While we were standing here waiting to be interviewed, I looked this course up on Google Earth. The woods are thick here," gestured Marie. "It curves to the right and eventually there is a house. If you go straight through, it looks to be about a quarter-mile before it ends in farming land.

Should we try walking through here to see if we can figure out what the shooter's path was out of the woods?"

"Great idea!"

They were soon trying to walk through the woods. When they would hit an obstruction in the form of thick foliage and/or trees, they walked backwards and tried another path. They eventually deduced that the shooter had to exit the woods to the right toward that lone house as it was really too thick to get through anyplace else. Throughout their search, they had come upon one piece of evidence only – a candy bar wrapper that had likely been dropped that day. Its appearance was fresh and as there had been rain overnight, the wrapper would not have had that crisp look if it had been rained on. They shared their finding and observations about it with the detective. Then they got in their golf carts and headed toward the clubhouse.

It was about two hours after the shooting. The parking lot at the clubhouse was still two thirds full and now there were media vans parked there as well. The ladies headed straight for their cars. They unloaded the golf clubs and changed their shoes. A reporter came to the parking lot toward them and the four friends looked momentarily like deer in the headlights.

Then Angela said, "I'll take this if you don't mind," and her three friends nodded agreement. They had no time to rehearse what any of them would say and they knew they could trust her to say the right words representing all of them.

The reporter, with cameraman in tow, held out the microphone to Angela as he quickly asked, "Excuse me, ladies, but were you witnesses to the shooting on the golf course?"

Angela gave the reporter a very sincere smile, looked into the camera and said, "We have no comment other than to say that our thoughts and prayers are with the family during this tragic time."

They each climbed into their respective vehicles and the reporter and his cameraman had to get out of the way of their cars backing up. As they were driving away, Jill had the thought that a smart reporter would copy down their license plates and go after them again for comment. When the full story came out, this would be sensational news in Green Bay, Wisconsin. It would be news because so few murders happened in the city, the victim was a physician, and the method of murder was relatively gruesome. Furthermore, at this point, it was unlikely that the police had any suspects.

CHAPTER 4

A few minutes later, they were at Office Max printing up the necessary forms. While Jill was taking care of the paperwork, Marie, Jo, and Angela were outside in one of their cars, strategizing on the script that Angela would use when speaking to Michelle. Of the four friends, Jill generally had the least tact so she just stayed out of the conversation. They decided that this was a very private time so only Angela would go to Michelle's. The other three friends would have a glass of wine at Marie's house, awaiting Angela's return.

They didn't have long to wait. Angela entered Marie's house about thirty minutes after they parted at the store. Jill thought that was a bad sign; she must have been unable to talk to Michelle or get her agreement.

"How did it go? How is Michelle doing?" asked Marie.

Angela held out the contract for Jill and said "She hired us. She wants to meet with all of us tomorrow evening at eight, but she'll reconfirm before that time. The house is busy and she has lots of people around her. She thought her husband was upset about something and was quite relieved to see me with contract in hand. When I told her it was a no-cost contract, she broke down and cried over our generosity. She had me crying at that point. She wants to talk with all of us to hear about what happened at the golf course and she felt comforted to know that you were there, Jill."

"Me? Why would you be pleased to have a forensic pathologist on the scene?"

"I'm guessing that someone told her that as a doctor you were quickly on the scene and still her husband couldn't be saved. It feels better than thinking your loved one laid there in agonizing pain slowly dying and that medical care could have saved him but didn't get there fast enough."

"Okay, I'll run with that explanation. I was worried that I would be viewed as the grim reaper trying to collect a body early."

"That is a terrible visualization," shuddered Marie. "Anyone that knows you would know you would do whatever you could to save a life."

"Thanks, appreciate the vote of support," smiled Jill. "Let's talk about next steps today. I can't think of anything additional that we can get from the crime scene. I thought about trying to determine the angle of impact, but law enforcement should do that as well as the caliber of the gun. What do you guys think?"

We're not experts in how crime scene information is collected, so we leave that totally in your hands," Jo said. "I don't remember the local police being criticized for poor crime scene investigation, does anyone else? We got a good look earlier and I would guess that whatever they collect at the scene will not substantially add to solving this crime. Let's work on a motive."

"I agree with Jo. My untrained eyes did not see much evidence to be collected at the crime scene. The fact that none of us could determine how he or she exited the woods sort of points to a lack of evidence at the scene," Marie speculated.

"I think we are best at motive - how do people fit together in a victim's life such that someone is mad or crazy enough to kill someone else," Angela reasoned.

"That is a good summary of our skills," agreed Jill. "I was debating setting up a website about the company. I have not done so as I have been getting enough referrals without a website and I am afraid it will bring out the crazies - you know 'will you exhume Aunt Eloise who died eighty years ago'. So I continued to stay off of the internet to keep some people away. The folks that really need our team have a way of finding us."

"I have to agree with your strategy, Jill," affirmed Jo. "I think there could be a lot of crazy people in this business. I don't think I could give you any more hours than I am doing now, so if you got busier, you would have to employ someone else with a finance background to help you. The current workload keeps my skills sharp and my vacation account padded, so I am working as hard as I want to."

"Ditto for me," nodded Marie.

"My work is much more seasonal as a photographer than your work," observed Angela. "The holidays are especially wicked for me as that is when families want portraits and the summer for weddings and engagements. I could handle more work in the winter months, but that work should be in warmer locations."

"Good to know," thanked Jill. "It really helps to have your unsolicited feedback on how we are doing as a team. I am a little conflicted between taking on additional work and truly wanting to help some loved ones. My vineyard is getting larger in acres and for that reason alone, I may have to hire some help. I want to grow that business and while the grapes grow at their own pace, I really like to experiment with varietals and that is what I can't get to while we work on these cases. If I am in the middle of one of my experiments and a client calls and I have to leave town, then I have to usually start over when I return which is a pain."

"Okay, let's move ahead with helping Michelle," nudged Marie. "Perhaps Angela could start by telling us everything you know about Doug and his family and his job. Jill, I have some freezer paper that I could put on the wall to set up a 'murder board' for you in my dining room. Ugh, hopefully this will be the last time I decorate a dining room with a murder board."

Marie handed Jill the box of freezer paper and she began laying out her murder board as Angela began her story.

"Doug's full name is Douglas Easley. I don't know his middle initial or middle name. He and Michelle have been married for at least fifteen years and he was probably between forty and forty-five years old. They have twin girls who will be about fourteen now. Michelle owns an interior design firm that she has operated for at least a decade. I don't know if they are native to this area as Doug's parents live in Florida and Michelle's are in Arizona for part of the year. I haven't met siblings of either. As I said earlier, I have taken photos of the family and I did a photo shoot for Michelle of a house she decorated. She wanted those photos for her portfolio of design work.

"As I mentioned, Doug has been an anesthesiologist at Our Lady. He has been president of the medical staff and may still be, for that matter. He is a partner in his anesthesia group and seems to get along with everyone. He had gone back to school to get a business or management degree around the time I took the family portrait, so he would have had that degree by now. Like I said earlier, I saw the family from a distance every couple of months, but we weren't close."

Jill requested, "Marie, can I borrow your printer? I want to make copies of the pictures that Angela took to put on the murder board."

"Sure, let me turn on the computer and printer in my office," replied Marie. "By the way, I could make dinner or we could go out. Let me know your preference so I can take care of any prep work."

"Once I put Doug's murder picture up on the murder board, your kitchen may be too gruesome to cook or eat in," reminded Jill.

"Having seen the murder, live and at the scene, I'm not sure a photo will bother me," replied Jo. "I may have nightmares about the real thing, but the photo, not-so-much."

"I would rather get take-out," noted Jill. "Marie, you're a fabulous cook but I would rather you work on building Doug's profile than have you slaving in the kitchen. I could fetch Thai food from my favorite Thai restaurant. I don't even need to look at the menu - I'll order volcano chicken."

"That sounds like a plan," asserted Angela. "I'm not hungry yet, in fact I'm not sure I'll ever be hungry again. Just give me a glass of wine and I'll start on research about Our Lady hospital."

"I think Angela has made a fine suggestion," agreed Jo.

Jill asked, "Jo, any thoughts about how to approach the money picture here? This is a little different from many of our cases."

"In a perfect world where I could retrieve the data, I would want to know about Doug's finances, his anesthesia partnership, his wife's interior design business, and Our Lady. I suspect that since all of these are privately held accounts and businesses, that I won't find much information except for the hospital. Marie, as the guru of social media, do you have any thoughts on how to approach this lack of accessible financial data?"

"Perhaps we can go about building a picture of assets. How about if you do a property search to see what properties they own? Look them up on legal registries to see if there have been any lawsuits, divorces, foreclosures, or other issues. Check them out for political and other charitable contributions."

"Thanks, Marie, those are some good suggestions," Jo said leaning back in her breakfast bar stool to write down Marie's suggestions and add some of her own.

Jill suggested, "Angela, I think you should be our liaison with law enforcement in addition to interviewing Michelle, her daughters - if mom will allow it, his partners, and the medical staff office at the hospital. Do you know anyone that works at Our Lady? Is there anyone we could get gossip from at the hospital?

"What kind of gossip?"

"We're looking for our motive here. So was anyone unhappy with him? Were there any disagreements between Doug and other hospital staff or physicians? Was his work respected? Did he seem worried about anything? Did people know that he was going to be at this golf tournament? What did people think of his leadership when he was the medical staff president?"

"Wow, that is quite a list. I'll give it some thought to see if there are any additional questions then I'll start working on making connections. I have a few friends who might have close friends that work at that hospital and I'll check my Facebook friends to see if any of them list working at Our Lady."

"What are you working on, Jill?" asked Marie.

"After I set up the murder board, I want to follow the track into the woods. I wonder if I can get satellite records at the time of shooting to see who walks out of the woods. There is a private company in Colorado that has satellites up in orbit. They sell pictures of what the satellite views as long as I can prove that they are for a non-military purchase. I thought I would explore getting satellite pictures over a half-hour period of when the shooter had to have left those woods. I don't know if I can ask for past photos."

"Yikes, that sounds cool and creepy. Cool because it would be great to get those photos, creepy because I hate the thought of being watched by satellite at all times," said Jo with a shudder.

"Well it sounds like we all have avenues to explore that will make this a very interesting case in addition to helping your friend, Michelle," Marie commented. "Does anyone need me to print the Thai menu so we know what we are ordering?"

Jo replied, "Unlike Jill, I don't always order the same meal, so yes I would like to see a menu. Jill, can you stay longer if we don't solve this crime in your remaining four days in Green Bay?"

"That will be a first; usually I am trying to negotiate with you three for extra amounts of your time. I can probably stay an additional two days, and then I'll have to go home. My vines bloomed last month and next month is peak growing season and I have a lot of work to do around the vineyard. I individually look at all my plants each week to be sure that the grape clusters are well supported on the vine, pest free, and evenly growing. Things change quickly this time of year with the vintage. I'm sure Nathan won't mind taking care of Trixie an extra day or so. I need to call him and tell him about this case. This is the closest we have been to danger while not being the target of the violence.

Moments later Marie returned with pictures for the murder board and the menu for the Thai restaurant. After making their choices, they decided to get food early as they hadn't eaten much on the golf course and it might be less disruptive to the flow of their work if they ate now. Before heading out to pick-up the food, Jill called Nathan.

"Hey, how was your golf tournament? Were the jello shots as good as you remembered?" asked Nathan, upon seeing who was calling.

"We didn't get to the hole with the jello shots."

"Why? Did you get rained out? I didn't think there was any rain in your area."

"No, jello shots were on the tenth hole, and a man was murdered on the second green as we were teeing off on the third hole."

"What! What happened? Were you hurt? Are you someone's target?"

"No one was hurt in our foursome. We were not the target. It was the foursome behind us. Let me start from the beginning of this story."

"Yeah, please do, but I am happy you're safe."

"You can look this up on Google Earth - Mystery Hills Golf Course in DePere, Wisconsin," began Jill as she recounted the crazy events of the day. She ended her narrative with, "He was a distant acquaintance of Angela's so we are conducting a free investigation for the widow."

"What an amazingly strange story and you sure have bad luck

being in the wrong place at the wrong time. Most of all, I am thankful that none of you were hurt. How is Angela doing?"

"She is doing okay. I printed out a no-cost contract and she was able to get the widow to sign it perhaps two hours after her husband was murdered. I may end up staying here longer, but no more than two extra days. Are you okay with dog-sitting Trixie?"

"You know your dog provides my cat and I with endless hours of entertainment, so yes I can keep her for additional days. Tell all your friends that I am glad you're all safe and I wouldn't think you would have problems with this investigation turning violent. It just sort of wrecks whatever you were planning on doing during your vacation."

"Not really, I got the major to-see and to-eat at items done already. We're all doing this as a favor for Angela. It will be a high profile case by the police as there are so few murders in this city and they seem like they're good and competent cops."

"How weird that you had a guy murdered on a ski slope, and now on a golf course - who knew that sports were so dangerous?"

"Yeah, but this is going to be harder to figure out, as the killer could be anyone with marksmanship skills. That is probably half of the adults in this area of the country. All the person needed to be able to do was shoot probably a Winchester .308 and be able to walk through the woods for about a quarter of a mile. The shooter could be male or female, and almost any height as it would have been somewhat easy to bring a stool with you to stand on in the woods. About the only people we can rule out are those with alibis. I'm going to try something new with this case. I am going to see if I can purchase a satellite picture of the golf course at the time of the shooting. Fortunately within a minute, we know when the gun was fired. We know the sniper didn't stick around as the police searched the woods shortly after they arrived. So I have at most a fifteen minute window to catch the sniper walking out of the woods. When he entered the woods is another question, he could have chosen to wait there for hours. We had been on the course for about an hour and an half when we reached that hole. The case would be so much clearer if I could find that picture and extremely hard to solve if I can't. We're going to work on the motive, but this case is going to be difficult."

"It sounds difficult, but then I think at the start of all of your cases finding the killer always seems difficult. Even in your last case where you needed someone with the specific skill set of being an advanced skier, you didn't have an answer for a couple of days. You'll figure this out. In fact I can't recall a single case since we have been together that you couldn't solve. Besides, this is home ground for you and the team, which should make it easier. You know where to go and who to trust. Also, for the first time you don't have to worry about your friends flying home before you have solved your case. They simply can't go anywhere."

"Yeah that's true. It will be interesting to conduct an investigation on very familiar ground. Oh well, what is going with you?"

"Well besides being entertained by Arthur and Trixie? I think I told you that I had a client in Napa Valley that was contemplating trying a wineglass design as an extension of his brand?"

"Yeah you did. He was what I would call a sort of a small to medium sized vintner geographically stuck at the end of a long line of eleven wineries in St Helena and all of them operated by appointment only. He wanted to have a wine tasting room that was open to the public, but with all the other wineries being by appointment only, he couldn't generate any traffic to his tasting room. Is this the vintner you are speaking about?"

"Yes, Andrew has been scratching his head on this one and we tossed around a few ideas. He wants to try a combined discussion of wine and wine glasses in his tasting room to see if that will be enough of a unique idea to pull traffic in. Both the design and the marketing materials are exciting to me and I'm enjoying this fresh challenge."

"Have you done any research into glassware to help with your glass design? I mean I think we all know the basic concept of a wider goblet for red varietals to allow more breathing to occur by the wine, but what else is there?"

"Ah, I can feel your eyes rolling two-thousand miles away. Let me ask you a question. Why don't we serve wine in a beer stein?"

"Okay I get your point. Wine is not served in a beer stein because it's generally not drunk like beer as far as volume, it's sipped and savored. Besides beer is carbonated and exposure to air generally makes it taste worse rather than better. Then there are the subtleties like it can be nice to sip a single glass of wine over an hour, by which time a beer would be warm and flat; or you like to give wine as a gift, but you give it as a present to be shared with others not a single glass for yourself. You're brilliant enough to figure out how to sell just about any idea in the wine industry. More importantly, I like the fact that you're trying your idea with a "David" in likely an area of Goliath wineries. Perhaps you'll change the industry with this move."

"Maybe and equally likely the idea could flop. If it turns out to work, I'll do designs for you next, even though you don't have a tasting room yet. I might run out of originality in glassware design, so it will be best to get me early."

"Ha ha! You're a creative genius so I am sure you have years in front of you to exploit this idea."

"Actually I think you hit it on the nose. I am enjoying helping Andrew see if he can get cars to drive by the eleven by-appointment-only wineries to reach his tasting room. I think you can put money into finding new customers by selling to wine stores everywhere or by getting foot traffic to your tasting room. In this case we're trying the second strategy."

"I have to go pick up Thai food, so I will talk with you later. All this talk about wineries has made me thirsty for a few glasses and I need food in my stomach before I do that. Good luck with your design project. Cheers!" and Jill ended their call.

"How is Nathan doing?" Jo asked as she returned to Marie's kitchen.

"He's doing well. He has a marketing challenge for a winery in Napa Valley and that has his creative juices going. He is also thrilled that we aren't in danger for this case and he thought it would go faster since we are on home ground. Did you make your dinner choices?"

"Yeah, here are our choices," said Marie handing the list to Jill. "We already called the meals in including your volcano chicken. You'll need to leave in about five minutes to pick up orders."

"Then I'll leave now. I would really like to indulge in a glass of wine while we brainstorm possible motives for this murder. So the sooner I pick up dinner, the sooner I'll get back here to indulge," said Jill as she grabbed her purse and headed out the door.

"Who else should we invite into this mystery? Since we are on home ground I think we should invite anyone we know might help," Angela suggested. "We can check with Jill when she returns, but her usual theory is the more heads on the topic, the sooner we are likely to solve it. I think we should invite my friend, Ann, and maybe her mom since they are so well connected to everyone in this city."

"I'll add my sister whose kids attend the same school as our victim's kids," Marie added to the list.

"I'll add my boyfriend, Jack, since he can be good to bounce ideas off of and he can keep us supplied with junk food and wine if Marie runs out," Jo observed. "That might be a tragedy for my brain power. Marie, do you know if we have all of the pictures up there on Jill's murder board?"

"Let's see, we have the victim, the three players on his foursome, his wife and kids, and a picture of Our Lady, so yes, I think that is all of the pictures," replied Marie. "Can you think of anything to add?"

"Can you print out a picture of the murder weapon which I think is a Winchester .308 and maybe some data about that model of gun? Perhaps something on the scope as we think the sharpshooter accuracy might reduce our pool of potential killer suspects."

"After Jill gets back, we can start making calls to see if people are available," remarked Angela. "Marie, do you have enough wine and chips for four additional people?"

"I do for tonight but if we gather every night, I'll have to stock up on supplies. Okay, we have that settled, what else do we need to do?"

"Let's put additional names on the side of the murder board of everyone we think is involved so far and their role in this case. Police officers, foursome partners, family, work associates, the organizer of today's golf outing, and any other names we can think of related to the case."

"That's a great idea, Angela. You're keeping us well organized in Jill's absence. For now, let's use sticky notes to write these names down as we don't know how Jill wants them organized on the board," Marie said as she handed out little sticky note squares to Angela and Jo. "If you don't know their name, write their role down and we'll go back later and add names."

Silence reigned in the room as the three of them thought of people that been involved in the case that day as well as anyone they could think of on the periphery of the case. They were still writing when Jill returned, bag in hand, great aromas in her wake.

She looked over at the murder board since they were all staring at it in silence and asked, "What are the little notes for?"

"While you were getting our dinner, we thought of two things to do with this case," Angela answered gesturing at the board. "We are putting the names or at least the roles of people that may be involved in this case to the side not knowing where you wanted that information on your murder board."

"Great idea!" exclaimed Jill. "What was the second idea?"

"We thought we should invite additional people here after we eat dinner. Marie has wine and popcorn in plentiful supply. We thought my friend, Ann, and her mom since they know everyone in town, Marie was adding her sister who has kids at Doug's school. Jo was going to add Jack so we can bounce ideas off of him and have him available for a wine run if we run out. Oh, and we added a picture of the rifle you mentioned."

"Wow, you guys were very productive while I was gone," Jill approved. " As far as adding additional people, I think that is a good idea, but in an effort to protect the victim and his family, I think we all need to take an oath on a Bible swearing that we will not discuss the facts of the case outside of this room. We owe that to Doug and Michelle and the kids. Gossip could be very harmful to them"

There was a chorus of agreement from the three friends on the oath. "Okay let's dig into this wonderful dinner and then you can make calls to your friends and family and bring them in on the case. I really am going to have everyone swear on a Bible, so perhaps after dinner, Marie, if you can find one, we'll plan on having a swear-in ceremony with each new arrival. Will anyone be unable to handle the picture of Doug dead?"

"I don't think so, but we'll check their feelings at the door and turn the picture over if we have to," Angela replied. "When I first started working on these cases with you, the pictures really disturbed me, but then I came to realize that they help us focus on helping the victim and his or her family and I think that will be the feeling of everyone that we have invited here."

"Okay sounds like a plan," Jill noted. "I have one more set of pictures I would like to add to our murder board. Let me get a picture of the third green and the fourth tee box, and the woods we believe the killer departed through."

"Why don't I print those out for you as well as the golf course guide so we can trace our steps from when Angela shook hands with Doug, until he lay dead on the green."

"That is a great suggestion Marie! By the way my volcano chicken is fabulous. How is everyone else's meal?"

When Jill got approving nods from her friends, she continued,

"You guys know I don't like spicy foods, so it must seem odd that I crave this recipe whenever I come to town."

Jo grinned, "We live in hope that you will learn to like spicy food due to repeated exposure to volcano chicken. So eat away!"

Jill grinned back, "I hate to tell you but it is not working. My English heritage craves bland food. Besides my heritage, I told you that I have more taste buds per millimeter on my tongue; so a little black pepper comes across as a jalapeño pepper. That's my story and I'm sticking to it!"

CHAPTER 5

Soon they were all cleaning up their mess, storing the excess in the refrigerator and opening a bottle of wine. The doorbell rang and it was Marie's sister. Marie had outlined the case when she called Samantha, but before she went in to the kitchen, Jill had her swear to keep the conversation about the story of the murder limited to her sister's house. Jill could tell that Samantha was vacillating between feeling foolish and aggrieved that she had to go so far as to swear on a Bible. Jack arrived just as they completed Samantha's swearing-in ceremony and the whole ritual was repeated with him. They were then checked as to their tolerance for the gruesome murder pictures and both had no qualms. They had just settled in the kitchen and Jill was about to walk them through the murder board, when Angela's friend Ann and her mother Mary arrived. They were not pleased with the Bible swearing ceremony, either but forgot their affront once they were handed a glass of wine and viewed the murder board.

Jill took the lead with the explanation, "As you all know, the four of us assist with murder investigations on a part-time basis. Angela, Jo, and Marie put their collective heads together and thought each of you would bring something to the table to help us solve this murder. The police are also working on it, but we can sometimes solve it faster than they do due to the unique skills in this room. Today, we had the misfortune to be on the tee box next to where a murder took place on a green. The victim's wife, Michelle, hired us at no charge to work on her husband's case. Sorry that we made you go through the bible swearing oath, but we really need to not talk about this case outside of this kitchen."

Jill paused and looked for nods which she got.

"Let me take you through the murder board and the events that have transpired thus far." Just as Jill finished recounting the events of the day, she heard her email alert and glanced at her phone. Recognizing the message was from the satellite company in Colorado, she excused herself from the group, saying "just a moment, I've been waiting for this message and need to respond immediately." Half the group nodded understanding and the other half looked at her in puzzlement.

Jill was pleased with their response and sent off a reply.

Looking up she added "that was good news, the satellite company can get me pictures of the woods. They are going to do it for free as long as I commit to share the photos with the police. They see this as a marketing opportunity. Why wouldn't we share the photos with the police?"

"What are the satellite pictures for?" asked Ann looking puzzled.

"Sorry, I didn't explain that avenue of investigation. In recent years, there have been private companies launching satellites into earth's orbit for a wide variety of reasons - weather, communications, or spying. I had heard that private citizens, for non-military reasons could purchase satellite images. I did an internet search and found a company in Colorado that seemed to fit the bill. So I sent them an email asking if they would have the images for a fifteen minute period of time for the woods adjacent to Mystery Hills golf course. They have the images and will share them with us. I have no idea how sharp they are, but they might provide us with information about the suspect's identity."

"Are you also getting them for when the killer entered the woods?" Jack asked.

"I had thought about asking for that, but I decided against it for a couple of reasons. I would have to get several hours of photos since we have no idea when he entered the woods. Did the killer know what foursome that Doug was in? That certainly would have been easy information to get - the shooter could have called the clubhouse, indicated that he or she was running late and need to know what hole he was starting on. Perhaps the shooter stood in the woods and looked through his scope at each foursome looking for Doug. About one-third of the golfers were women, so he could have eliminated them easily, but it seems unorganized to study each man of each foursome for Doug's visage. By the time we arrived at the hole, fifteen foursomes would have played the third hole. If I were the killer, I would have gotten there at the start just in case any last minute foursome changes were made. I would have still casually studied the visages of every man in every foursome, but I would have felt secure that I expected to see Doug when I did."

"So you would like all of us to help solve this murder by trying to get inside the mind of a killer to figure out what they would have done," Jack concluded.

"I don't know if I would wish that on anyone - being inside a killer's head, but I suppose in a way I am asking you to think about what you would do logistically to set up this murder. Actually, we thought that each of you brought different skills to the table. Jack, you're a good listener so we brought you here to bounce off ideas and keep us supplied in wine. Ann and Mary, you know so many people in this community and we thought you could supply us with information about the players involved in this case. Samantha, you know Doug through the connection of your kids and his kids."

"Okay, I understand where you're going," Jack smiled. "I'm going to take my procurement of wine very seriously and start by asking you ladies if you have sufficient wine at the moment?"

The ladies in question held up their wine glasses toasting his question.

Jill's cell phone dinged indicating an e-mail arrival. "I hope these are the pictures from the satellite company."

Taking a moment, she looked at the content of the e-mail and then moved over to the larger screen of the laptop sitting on the kitchen island.

"This is our largest screen to look at the images on; let me pull up the pictures."

"You know, I could bring additional value to you ladies," Jack smirked. "I am a graphic artist and I likely could manipulate the pictures better and faster than you, Jill."

"Jack! How could I have forgotten your skills in this area?" Jill exclaimed. "Okay I have revised our game plan to solve this mystery and I have reassigned the wine procurement to Angela. All joking aside, I'm really sorry that I forgot how valuable you could be with satellite images. Let me forward the e-mail to you and you can load the images on whichever computer makes sense."

They all gathered around Jack as he first pulled up his e-mail account and then a graphics program that Jill had never heard of. There were three files each containing five minute video segments of the satellite's view of Mystery Hills golf course.

"By my recollection, we heard the sound of the gun shot at about 12:13pm," Marie guessed. "Angela, what's the timestamp on your picture?"

"I took a picture of you guys on the green of the third hole at 12:07pm. I took a picture of Doug at 12:17pm. So I think your guess is a good approximation."

Jack turned around and asked Angela, "When you took the

picture of everyone standing on the green, in which direction were you aiming your camera?"

"Jack, you're getting quick in the mode of investigation. That's a very good question," Angela said as she held out her camera viewer screen and pulled up the picture in question for him to view.

"Let me pull out the satellite video and we'll move on to your camera next," said Jack as he opened the first video. Using this software program, he sped through the five minutes determining that no person was seen leaving the woods. Jill had an incredible urge to ask him to slow down the video, but she told herself that he was an expert in looking at images and therefore he knew what he was doing. He loaded the second segment and again they all watched the image in high-speed. This time Jill had to agree there was nothing in the segment. This was the segment that covered 12:13pm, but who knew if their clocks were synchronized. The third segment played out the same way. Again no one was seen exiting the woods.

Jill pondered this lack of evidence and then said aloud, "Do you think we got the time wrong? Do you think the shooter could've stayed longer? I'll have to get a copy of the police report to see what they wrote. It felt like they walked into the woods at about 12:20pm. These videos represent 12:08pm to12:22pm, so they should cover the time period."

"We went into the woods ourselves wondering how the killer departed and we determined that the only way out was towards the house on the right," Marie stated. "What if we are wrong and there is another exit? Were there any tree stands that we missed? Could someone have climbed a tree while the police and the four of us stood below him or her at some point?"

"Now that idea creeps me out," said Jo with a shudder. "I may never go out into the woods again."

"Those are good suggestions, Marie," nodded Jill. "Let's watch the videos again and see if there is any movement at any other exits."

This time they watched the videos at regular speed and each person watching the screen staked out a section of the video to keep watch on. Again they were disappointed as they didn't see any movement.

"We need to go back to the woods tomorrow and search again," Marie proposed. "Could the shooter have been so bold as to step out on the fourth hole in golfer's clothes and casually walk away? Or, did he or she hide up in the trees?"

"Let's study the video again to see if we see movement at the front of the wooded area that wasn't you ladies," Jack suggested. "In fact let's study your movements. We should be able to see you guys drop to the ground if we have the right video feed."

For the third time, they again studied the video segments. Jack was right; they should have been able to see themselves drop to the ground, but there was nothing. Not a single person could be viewed anywhere on the screen.

"Well this is strange. None of us are on the video," puzzled Jill. "I will concede that there are times when no one would be on that golf course, but even after we left, I would have thought the police would have taken another look at the woods, and the golf course maintenance, if they were cleared to do so by the detectives, would have had to clean up the green. Any other theories as to what happened in the woods?"

"I think you need to contact the satellite service and asked them to confirm that the tape you are looking at is today's date in the central time zone," suggested Jack. "Let's eliminate the technical problems that could have occurred with the satellite feed first. I don't believe there is technology yet that could be used to block an orbiting satellite from collecting routine pictures. There are thousands of satellites within our orbit; so in addition to blocking the satellite, you would first have to figure out which satellite is recording this section of Earth. And it's likely that several satellites are trained on these coordinates."

"Those are great suggestions, Jack!" agreed Jill. "I'll contact them now and see what I can find out."

Jill stepped into the living room to make the call to the satellite company. She explained her problem to the technician. With a little research on his end, he was able to determine that while the date on the video feed was correct, the time was actually about two hours earlier due to an error in the company's part. They would be sending her the video for the correct time within the next ten minutes. Jill returned to the kitchen and the conversation that was going on therein.

"Hey Jill, I was just updating everyone on the current state of Our Lady," said Ann as Jill entered the kitchen. "I don't think Angela told you, but I'm on the board for the hospital. Doug gave a presentation on 'quality measurements in a healthcare setting' during a board member orientation that I attended last month. I was really impressed with his passion about the patients at Our Lady."

"Angela did forget to tell me of your service to the board, and now, I'm happier than ever that you've joined us in this investigation." noted Jill. "The satellite company did indeed make a mistake on the time zone. The feed they sent us was from two hours earlier when all the golfers were in or near the clubhouse waiting for the starter's pistol to go off."

Jill looked down at her phone to see an incoming message from the satellite company which she promptly forwarded to Jack.

"Jack, it's all yours to work your magic with," said Jill as she hit the 'send' key.

Jack brought this latest round of images up on his computer and again went through his fast paced review of each video clip. He saw nothing in the first video to make him slow down. Close to the start of the second video clip, he slowed the video down, then stopped, backed-up and the entire room leaned closer to watch in super slow motion as someone left the woods and walked towards the house as they had theorized. What happened next they had not expected...

"It looks like a man and it looks like he might be carrying a rifle, but that could be wishful thinking on my part," Marie said peering intently and pointing at the screen. "We need to look at more footage, because it looks to me like he is skirting the woods with a plan to re-enter them just north of this house. Jill, this was a brilliant idea to request this footage."

"Jack, can you enlarge or get better resolution to this picture?" asked Angela.

"Why don't you let me play with the images for a few minutes while I can see if I can bring the gun into focus. I don't know that we'll ever get enough resolution to see the person's face as the picture is shot from overhead."

"Good point! Let's glean all we can out of these videos, then I'll give Detective Van Bruggin a call to let him know we have some evidence for him."

In the end, they decided they could agree that this was likely the killer, that the killer knew the area based on how he or she walked along the edge of the woods, and that indeed the person on screen was carrying a rifle in his or her hands. The satellite company would have additional footage by email in another ten minutes. It was taking longer this time as they were verifying that it picked up where the other video clip left off. Having embarrassed themselves with the wrong time zone, they didn't want to repeat the error.

Jill pulled the detective's business card out of her purse and dialed his number.

"Detective Van Bruggin," sounded the detective's voice over Jill's mobile phone speaker.

"Hi detective, this is Jill Quint. I was at the crime scene this afternoon."

"Yes, of course, I know who you are," was the brusque reply.

"Yes, well we contacted a satellite company in Colorado to see if they had footage of the golf course at the time of the shooting."

"Who is the 'we', and why would you think a satellite company would have footage let alone share it with you?"

"Actually, detective, they did share it on condition that I notify you that we have it. Which is what I am doing with this phone call. If you would like to see it with the aid of an expert video technician available to manipulate it, I can give you the address of where we are. If you would just like me to email it in its raw form, give me your email address and we'll consider ourselves to have met the company's request."

There was a long pause.

"Detective?" asked Jill not sure what to make of the silence.

"Yeah, well I was just thinking," with a sigh he added, "give me your address."

Jill motioned to Marie to give her address, and the detective said "I'll be there in about ten minutes," as he abruptly ended the call.

Jill looked at the others that had been listening to the call and said, "ok, not sure what to make of that. I guess we'll find out when he arrives."

"Marie, do you want to add your assumptions to the murder board? We still don't know if it was a man or woman who was the killer. I wonder if there was any DNA on the candy wrapper. Trouble is that someone made, packed, stocked, and then sold that candy bar. Any of them could have left DNA and fingerprints on the wrapper that might be confused with the killer's DNA. I wonder if the detective will share that information."

As Marie was adding her findings to the murder board, Jill heard a ping to her email which she hoped represented another email from the satellite company. She was in luck when she viewed her in-box. She quickly forwarded the email to Jack.

They were all standing around Jack's screen viewing the

footage, when Marie's doorbell rang. She went to the door and opened it.

"Ah, Detective Van Bruggin, please come in," Marie invited. "Can I get you something to drink? Coffee, tea, water, soda, wine?"

"I'm fine; I don't need anything," being a detective, he noted everyone gathered around a gentleman and his laptop. He stepped over to see what was on the screen. As he approached, Jill spoke up.

"Hello Detective. I'll perform introductions later. This is Jack," she gestured at him. "He is a graphics expert and he is playing with the video feed to see if we can sharpen the picture of the suspect or of his weapon. We just got this additional feed as it appears that he steps into the clearing near the house toward the south, but then re-enters the woods to go somewhere else. We'll go back and show you the beginning after we see where he walks on this footage."

There was silence in the room as they watched the figure on the screen walk around the clearing and re-enter the woods. They continued to watch the video, but even after another twenty minutes of footage, they never saw the figure leave the woods.

"That was weird," expressed Angela. "I wonder if he was in the woods while we were searching. He would have been deeper in there - at a point that we were unable to reach. Why not just walk out and go home? Could he still be there now?"

Looking outside, Jill offered, "I would have thought that the killer would leave immediately. To hang about in the woods in an area in which you would be unable to hear any conversation going on from the police or anyone else, just doesn't make sense. Now that we are heading toward dusk, it would be pretty dark inside the woods." Peering over at Detective Van Bruggin she added, "If you can spare the manpower, it wouldn't hurt to send some officers just to check out the area."

The detective had barely said a word since he arrived. At first he was afraid of unhelpful interference from all these women - bored housewives or some group like that. However after viewing the murder board and the satellite video clips, he had to come to terms that this team could be of real use to his team. They were ahead of him on the satellite video. He had never used anything like that but had quickly seen its value. Coming to that conclusion, he decided to use this group of people as best he could.

"I'll deploy a group of officers to that scene now," and stepped away from the group to make his call.

Stepping back he requested, "Would you forward the video clips to me? I'd like my team to have some science behind what they are doing as they search those woods."

Jill forwarded the emails to the detective and then returned to the conversation.

"I suppose I could call the satellite company and ask them to send us more footage but it could be several hours to review. The killer could have waited until it was dark and we would not see that. Also since it is an overhead shot, unless the killer looks up at the sky we won't get any better picture than we have so far. What we may see, is how the shooter left the area."

"Dr. Quint, if you don't ask for the footage, I will," cut-in the detective. "Is your contact at the company on your email? I do want to see how the suspect left the area. It will tell us something about him. If it is not in the video feed, even that tells us something. I'm also bringing my partner over here. I think with Jack's help we can obtain the most information in the shortest period of time."

"Please call me, Jill. How about sharing some information with us?"

CHAPTER 6

"*D*epends on what you want."

"I have my own requests, but everyone should feel free to ask the detective for information to help us fill in our murder board," Jill said to everyone standing in Marie's kitchen.

The detective looked pained at her response, and frowning took out his notebook.

"I'd like to see the autopsy results," said Jill starting off the list. "I'd also like a copy of any crime scene evidence that you have collected. Lastly, I would like to drop into your division and view your murder board."

The detective was still frowning as he took notes, but he did not provide any commentary.

"I'd like a copy of your suspect list," Marie requested. "I will be doing background searches on anyone connected to this case.

The others in the room passed on asking the detective for any information. They doubted he had any information on the subjects they were interested in and in some cases they thought it was too early in the case for him to have the information they needed.

"I can't think of anything to ask the detective for at this time, but I might in a few days," noted Jo.

"I hope we have the case solved in a few days as Jill has to leave in four days to return to California."

The detective looked over at Jill optimistically, "You have to leave in four days!"

"Yes, in my experience we have about eighty percent of our cases are completed in that time. If not, someone will manage the case from Green Bay and I'll stay in contact and do my work from there. It doesn't mean we'll drop the case." Jill's words deflated the detective.

They all heard the doorbell ring and Marie walked over to answer it.

Detective Van Bruggin's partner entered. He looked familiar from the murder scene that afternoon, but Marie couldn't remember his name.

"Hello ma'am, I am Detective Haro, I believe my partner is at this residence."

"Yes, he is. Come inside and I'll introduce you to everyone."

They realized at that point that they had not provided introductions for Detective Van Bruggin earlier. So Marie went around the circle and introduced each person and their role in solving the mystery.

Detective Haro looked a little puzzled as to how his partner had got involved with this group of amateur sleuths. Then his partner motioned him over to Jack's computer.

"Jack, would you show Detective Haro our suspect on the tape?"

Detective Haro was always quick to take in a situation and change his behavior accordingly. He was reserving comments while dealing with Jill, her team, and their friends. He never liked having civilians involved in an investigation, but it was undeniable that they had information that the police did not and he wasn't sure, if he was honest with himself, that they would have thought to ask for it. Like his partner, he viewed the video footage and agreed that this was likely the killer.

Detective Van Bruggin had been checking his email regularly and noted the arrival of an email from Jill's satellite company. He hoped this was the final footage.

This time the detective forwarded the email to Jack, who worked his usual magic with the video feed.

"I don't see any exit from the woods through the end of the video," noted Jack.

"Are you sure?" asked Detective Haro. "You went through that video feed at a pretty fast pace."

"Yes I'm sure. I'll slow it down to half speed and you can sit here and watch it." Jack dismissed the detective's concerns stating his intention of not being bothered to watch it a second time.

"Angela, Jill, and everyone else, we're going to take off home," said Ann. "We understand this terrible murder of Doug and what we need to do to collect information on him and the hospital. We'll keep you posted as we hear stuff."

"We really appreciate you coming over and let me know whatever you hear," noted Angela. "The smallest off-hand remark can lead to something big, so don't hold back anything; just pass it on."

"Will do and goodnight and good luck to everyone," answered Ann and her mom with a wave.

Jill looked over at the two detectives, "Detective Van Bruggin, we gave you a list of information we wanted on the case. Can you provide any of that now?"

The two detectives looked up from the computer monitor at her. One with a pained expression, the other with eyes widened with alarm.

When she got no immediate answer, she added to her request with "look, you two have very telling faces. I hope you don't play poker. Why don't you both step outside and have a brief discussion on what your level of interaction is going to be with us. Then we can all move on."

They decided to do just that.

Marie took a break from her research to refill everyone's drink glass and pull out snickerdoodle cookies for everyone to munch on.

The detectives stepped back in the room. Detective Van Bruggin, demonstrating a new air of cooperation, said, "Jill, I emailed you the preliminary autopsy report and our own report. We are going to return to the station now, so if you would like to see our murder board, you can do so immediately."

"Thanks for your help and I see the emails from you. I am ready to follow you to the station to view your murder board," thanked Jill and she added, "Does anyone else want to come?"

She got affirmatives from Marie and Angela. Jo and Samantha decided to stay behind, both engaged in searching for information. So the room emptied as the detectives left in their respective cars and the woman all piled into Angela's car to drive to the police station.

"So what do you think they chatted about outside?" asked Angela.

"I would say the overall topic was our usefulness to them on the case," Jill observed." Certainly we provided them with a feather in their cap that they have a suspect caught on video. From a public relations point-of-view for the community, they can feel safer if the police can announce that they have a suspect in mind. I'm sure they are giving us this information as they think it will amicably end our relationship with them and with the reports we had a legal right to them thanks to the documentation that Michelle signed. They are doing us a favor with the murder board, but they think we won't bother them after this. If we have the same information as they do at this moment in time, I will bet that we will solve the case faster than they will due to the skills of this team. While I think they are highly trained, they don't have our specific skills."

"Jill, I have to agree with your assessment," Marie concurred.

"You have made me suspicious about these murders after these past couple of cases. I'm trying to see what could be the entire iceberg of this case? It seems pretty open and shut. Like there is a single shooter that was mad enough about Doug that he needed to kill him. I mean this is Green Bay! There aren't any Albania terrorists here, female serial killers, or drug psychos."

"Yes, it is Green Bay!" added Angela, jumping on her friend's bandwagon. "We have only one murder a year in this town and this was it. And those murders are due to robbery gone bad, dumb criminals with drugs, or domestic violence - none of which seem appropriate for this murder."

"Well, let's walk into the police station and see what suspects they have on their murder board. We can see what the 'experts' think of the case," advised Jill.

After presenting themselves to front desk at police headquarters, they were escorted back to the Investigations Division where they found Detectives Haro and Van Bruggin. Marie looked around wide eyed as she had never been inside a U.S. police station. Angela had a tour of the station with one of her numerous social clubs. Jill had spent nearly fifteen years around law enforcement offices. This looked like many other spaces she had been in.

The detectives were standing on each side of their murder board awaiting their arrival.

"Hello ladies, glad you found your way back here. Why don't you have a seat and we'll go through it with you?"

The women quickly took their seats. They were all looking for differences between Jill's board and this board. Other than a side column labeled 'suspects', there was nothing on their board that wasn't on Jill's board. Jill stayed quiet about that for two reasons. The detectives had seen her murder board so they knew the ladies wouldn't find any new information on their board, and she was interested in seeing if verbally they mentioned a facet of the case that wasn't on the board.

"In this department, this is how we organize our investigation.

While we are the only two detectives that will work this case, sometimes it is helpful for our crime technicians to know where we are or what we are looking for in case it triggers something in their investigation. During the active phase of the case, each time we update our files, an email gets pushed out to the entire division and the Chief so that everyone is up to speed."

"How many homicides have you closed?" asked Marie.

"Twelve cases," replied Detective Van Bruggin. "I have been in this detective role for over a decade, but as you know there aren't many murders in Green Bay, so we average one murder case a year. We have agreements with surrounding cities to do their detective work as well, so we have picked up the odd homicide case there.

"We have had a couple of cases that were pretty open and shut. We got the killer at the murder scene with the gun or knife in hand. Those didn't require much work by the division to arrest and provide enough evidence to convict our suspect.

"We also have the responsibility for major crimes. In those cases, we have a major crime board that looks similar to this board except there is no dead body on it."

"Do you have any unsolved murders?" questioned Angela.

"None from the past two decades. There are unsolved murders from the 1940s, 1950s and 1960s. However, police forensics made a huge leap forward in the 1970s and that use of scientific evidence has greatly increased our solve rate."

"Did either of you work on the Monfils case?" asked Angela, referring to a notorious murder wherein a paper industry employee was tossed into a vat of acid.

"No, we didn't work on that case. I had just graduated from the academy and Haro was still in high school at the time," replied Van Bruggin, looking at Haro for confirmation.

"Yes, I was in high school at the time of that case," noted Haro. "In fact, it was that case that made me want to join the force. I can remember being horrified at being thrown into a vat of acid, and I was so grateful and impressed with the job the police did to find the killer."

Jill was anxious to move on to the facts of the case. Enough chit chat, and so she asked, "Detectives, what can you tell me about your suspect list?"

Her question was like a record being scratched. It ended the jovial exchange between the two detectives and Angela and Marie.

"Ah yes, the suspect list," Detective Van Bruggin mused. "We start with the usual suspects as we don't have real suspects yet. So that includes the victim's wife and daughters as they are all capable of being or hiring the markswoman. Sadly, we look to the family first for suspects. We have also added additional close family members - parents, siblings. We also added some co-workers. There really are a lot of potential suspects. Once we figure out the motive we'll be able to reduce and focus our suspect list."

"What are your thoughts on a motive?" asked Angela, now in her interview mode. She would have any secrets out of the two detectives in minutes; Marie and Jill just sat back and let her do what she did best.

"It's too early in the investigation to identify a motive. We would start with the usual - money or a personal relationship. Maybe he isn't liked at work; maybe he has a gambling or drug habit; maybe he was having an affair. Like I said nothing has surfaced at the crime scene or during our initial interview of his wife; so really at this point it could be any motive."

"What are you investigating next?" Angela continued.

"Well, thanks to your satellite feed, we'll be examining it for all the possible evidence. We'll be searching the woods at daylight tomorrow. We didn't want to trample on any potential evidence tonight."

"Did your officers see or hear anything when they visited perhaps thirty minutes ago?"

"Again it was a very dark area. They listened for any movement and shone their flashlights into the woods, but they were under orders to stay out of the actual woods."

"Aren't you afraid the suspect will get away?"

"Frankly, I don't know why the suspect would stay in the woods for much time after dark. My theory is that he wanted to hide out until dark when he could move without being seen by cameras. I doubt he was aware of the satellite capabilities as that is a new technology. Maybe he was just trying to stay out of view of any golf course or neighborhood security cameras."

"Did you canvass any of the houses in the area of the woods to see who owns them?"

"That is on our list for tomorrow in addition to searching the woods."

"How about his work? Have you visited his office at Our Lady, or spoken with any co-workers?"

"Not yet," replied Detective Haro. "We spent most of the day collecting witness statements and making sure our crime scene technicians could collect all necessary information. Besides his three foursome mates and you four, there was a foursome behind him. We also spoke with the beverage cart drivers and other golf course employees. No sooner had we finished those interviews and began to construct our murder board then we got the call from you ladies. It's been a busy afternoon and evening."

"Do you have any early insights or hunches regarding this case?"

"No."

"What surprised you at the crime scene?"

"I think the psychology of shooting someone on a golf course. It's unexpected, exotic, well-planned, and hideous for the spectators that were close by. The second weird surprise was frankly, finding you, Dr. Quint, as a witness to the crime. It was nearly as good as having a cop as a witness."

"Okay, I think that answers all of my questions. Jill and Marie, can you think of anything I left out?"

They both shook their heads 'no'.

"I think we are done here," announced Jill. "We'll take off and leave you folks to get on with your investigation."

The women arose and Detective Haro escorted them out of the building.

"So Jill, what do you think of the officers?" asked Angela as they walked to the car.

"Actually, I think they are good. They are doing all the right things, but I didn't see anything extraordinary. Their lack of experience with homicide is not their fault rather it's a reflection on the community. As detectives they have a wide range of experience in major crimes including drugs, burglary, and assault. I think the motives are different for homicide. Overall the city is in good hands. What did you guys think of the officers? You have been on enough cases now that you have experience with talented, corrupt, and uncaring officers."

"I liked them, but I guess when you walk us through your rating scale, I have to agree with you," said Angela.

"Ditto," Marie added.

After a short drive they arrived back at Marie's house to find the progress that Jo, Jack, and Samantha were making. Jo had examined all the public records of Our Lady of Guadalupe Medical Center and concluded the hospital turned a reasonable profit; and the quality and other ratings of the hospital pointed to no problems. Samantha had the passwords of her children's Facebook pages and she used those to see what Doug's children had written. Both areas were dead-ends. There was nothing seemingly distressing in the lives of Doug's children until their father's death.

They decided to call it a night and get back together early the next day to see where they were. In addition, everyone would bring sturdy shoes as they planned to trample around the woods.

CHAPTER 7

$\mathcal{J}$ ill and her team and Jack gathered at Marie's house the next morning. They discussed the murder scene over coffee, muffins, and bagels with cream cheese. Jill decided to go back to the murder scene with Angela. Marie would perform internet searches on the suspect list from the police, the family, and the other three members of Doug's foursome. Jo was at loose ends and took a cup of tea outside to sit on Marie's patio. She had no legal means to demand financial statements of Doug's company, the hospital, or Michelle's business, so she had no documents to analyze. Jack was using some special enhancement techniques to see if there was anything else to be gleaned from the video feed of the forest activity.

As they climbed into the car, Angela wondered, "Do you think the golf course will have cleaned up the mess yet?"

"I think that depends on whether the police have released the scene. If I were the golf course, I would put some soil or sand over the stain and water it. Then I would move the cup as far as I could to the other end of the green. Eventually, I would try to move the green so that the bloodstain becomes a part of the fairway or the rough. I'm sure it will creep out many golfers for years to come to know that they are playing the green of a notorious murder."

Angela shuddered and agreed, "I bet that this golf outing sets up some kind of memorial to Doug - maybe serve his favorite drink, or have some kind of contest that contributes dollars to his favorite charity. He was loved and respected by too many people for his presence not to be noted at this event."

"That's a sad thought, but respectful. Hey, before we turn into the golf course, let's check out that side road to examine where the shooter exited the woods last night."

"Sounds like a plan," replied Angela as she made the turns onto the street. She drove straight ahead and now they could see where the shooter had come out of the woods and skirted the trees only to re-enter at a different point. Unless someone had been standing on the front lawn watching, it would have been easy for someone to transverse the distance and not be noticed. She took a few pictures to supplement the pictures they had printed from Google Earth. Jack had also been able to print a few frames of the shooter walking, but those were overhead shots. Jill then noticed the for-sale sign in the front yard.

"I wonder if the house is occupied?" pondered Jill. "Let's go knock on the front door and see if anyone is home. We could say that we're interested in the property - especially the exterior and would the occupant mind if we had a look a look around."

"Good story," agreed Angela as they approached the door.

Jill pressed the doorbell twice with no sound or activity to be heard beyond the door chimes. They walked around a little and could see the house was completely empty with no furniture inside.

"Well, that's good news," noted Jill. "We can walk around at leisure here; in fact we should be able to visit the green from here. I wonder if the killer knew this house was empty and therefore he wouldn't be under observation when he left."

They spent the next hour exploring paths through the woods looking for evidence and came to the conclusion that either the police had been here before them and collected all relevant information, or the killer had left nothing at the scene.

"Let's go over to the green. I hope the course is closed so that I can place people in their proper positions. We really need a third person. Let's see if Jo is available to join us."

"What we really need are people who are the same height as the players yesterday," Angela pointed-out. "Do you know how tall Doug was and what is your guess as to the height of the shooter? Did the killer shoot straight across or did the bullet go on an upwards trajectory suggesting a shorter height? You may want her to bring a short ladder, milk crate, or stepping stool if we need to get the shooter's height right."

"Those are excellent points, Angela. As I recall from the police report, I believe it stated that he was five feet eleven inches tall, and the bullet traveled in essentially a straight line. So that would lead me to think that either the killer was tall or was standing on something. Let's see if she can bring two milk crates. She can stand on one on the green, I'll stand where I was standing when we heard the sound of the gun firing, and you can be in the woods checking out the angles."

"That will work, I'll give Jo a call now and we'll see what we can arrange," replied Angela.

About fifteen minutes later, Jo arrived on the scene with crates in hand. She also had a toy telescope that Marie's nephews had left at her house that would be useful in sighting the kill view. While waiting for Jo to arrive, Angela and Jill had viewed the hole and it appeared that the golf course was closed for the day as they saw no one playing on any of the fairways.

Soon, they were all in place according to their memories of the previous day and after perhaps twenty minutes of position adjustments they were able to guess where the killer had stood. If the killer moved much to the right or left they would have hit Jill or the bullet would have hit the side of Doug's face. If the killer stepped forward they would have been seen, if the killer stepped back, tree branches were in the way.

Jill knelt down to examine the foliage and ground. She did not see any crushed leaves or footprints. She looked for tracks away from where they thought the shooter was standing. Certainly there should be a footprint toward the exit from the woods. There had been rain recently and the ground was naturally soft. With the aid of a large flashlight in addition to the bright sun, made the tree-shaded ground as illuminated as possible. Jill lifted up a branch and found a solid footprint underneath. It looked fresh and moldable. She measured another two to three feet and found another footprint. They then followed the path of footprints to the edge of the woods where they were lost to the grass.

"Maybe I'll give the Detectives a call and see if they're interested in these footprints. They might tell us if the shoes were male or female and that might provide us with information," Jill thought aloud.

Pulling out her cell phone, she dialed Detective Van Bruggin and the phone rang then went to voicemail. So, then she dialed Detective Haro's number with better results.

"Detective Haro."

"Hi detective, this is Jill Quint from the murder investigation."

"Yes, what can I do for you?"

"Angela, Jo, and I have been examining the crime scene this morning and we think we found some footprints that might be worth casting."

"Where are you specifically?"

"In the woods, where the killer stood and fired the gun."

She heard a sigh on the end of the phone followed by, "Why are you at the murder scene?"

Jill had to sigh now with the ridiculousness of that question.

"Doing my job; conducting an investigation. There is no police tape here so I am not violating any police procedures. Let me repeat, there are some footprints in the woods that might belong to the killer. Are you interesting in casting them?"

"Yes," came his short answer. "I'll be on the scene with a crime tech within the hour."

"Thank you," Jill responded and she disconnected the call.

Looking over at Angela and Jo, she explained, "He'll be here within an hour so we are at loose ends here for the time being."

The temperature was in the low 60s and, like yesterday, they could see the sun's heat burning away the morning mist. Looking around, they could view displays of tulips decorating the course. There was a light breeze with no discernible scent. Given the many dairy farms in the state, it was a blessing not to have the smell of manure in the air.

"Why don't we have a seat on that bench and give thought to who potentially could be the killers," suggested Angela. "I don't like the thought that Michelle is their top suspect. It seems like they defaulted to her for a lack of anyone else. Could she have done the shooting from a technical view point?"

"Yes and no. She is capable of hauling a crate into the woods," replied Jill. "She may or may not be a good enough shooter. If the footprints and the image of the suspect skirting the woods are correct, I don't see how it could be Michelle. Sure she could have worn extra-large shoes, but let's go to the front and see if we can figure out the height of the shooter based on the landmarks like trees. Michelle would have a hard time having the natural walk we observed on the video clip in shoes too big or being much taller than her five feet four inches. That of course doesn't release her from the suspect list as she simply could have hired out the kill shot."

"That's depressing," declared Angela. "I thought I had reasoned she couldn't be the killer based on the reasons you cited, but I forgot she could hire the kill shot! Crap."

"Who else should be high on our list?" Jo questioned. "I am always keen on the money angle. Whose pot of money would be impacted by some action of Doug that the killer needed to insure did not occur? Again we would look to his family first - perhaps a life insurance policy. Next I would look at any business partners, both partners at work and partners in any private holdings like real estate."

"We need to interview Michelle when we are done here to answer Jo's questions," Angela remarked. "It would be great to slip in a question about gun shooting skills. Jo, you are best at slipping in innocuous questions so that no one notices."

"Ha," Jo grunted.

"Let's lay out our questions for Michelle," Jill suggested. "We could give her a call to arrange an appointment, but I really have no idea how long we'll be involved with the police. Let me find pen and paper in my purse and we will work on our questions."

They had worked on their questions for perhaps twenty minutes when they looked up to see a golf cart coming their way containing Detective Haro and another fellow, perhaps the crime scene technician.

They stood up awaiting their approach. The crime scene tech was introduced as Sam and he was carrying a large toolbox.

Detective Haro asked, "Tell me again, in great detail, what you are doing here this morning."

Jill, never one to back down from an investigation, replied, "Detective Haro, can you point out the crime scene tape that we have violated?"

"Excuse me? I don't understand your question. There is no crime scene tape here," puzzled Detective Haro.

"Exactly my point. You're acting as though we have violated a crime scene. My team and I are group of professionals who are here to get at the truth. We are not here to tamper with evidence."

"Let me apologize for my brusqueness this morning. As you can imagine with so few murders in this city, we are under tremendous pressure to solve this case immediately. Between you and me, I don't think we have any legitimate suspects yet. Our number one suspect, Michelle, has an iron clad alibi for the time of the shooting. The police chief is not happy with us nor is the mayor, and probably Doug's friends and family are not happy with our progress either. Let's start over with a new question. What have you and your team uncovered that will contribute to solving this crime?" asked the detective with a small smile.

Jill understood the position that the detective was in and recognized it was time to move on. "We knew we wanted to visit the green again this morning after viewing the satellite pictures last night. Out of curiosity, we drove over to Money Lane to look at the house and the property where the shooter exited the woods yesterday. The house is for sale and is unoccupied. We left Angela's car there and followed the woods around to the green here. As the golf course appears to be closed, we have had unfettered access to try and understand the crime scene.

"Jo stood on the green where Doug was shot. I stood on the tee box where I had been standing yesterday when we heard the gun go off. Based on the preliminary autopsy results, the position of the gun's muzzle was level with Doug's forehead. Using that milk crate," pointed Jill, "we determined the height of the gun and location in the woods. It wasn't hard as there are few options given the positions of the trees that would block the movement of a bullet. After we determined the location of the shooter, I put on my micro goggles to examine the soil between where we believe the shooter stood and where he or she walked to exit the woods. By lifting up some broken branches, we found three footprints that are recent and could be casted to be used for shoe identification. I know this is a long shot, but I'm hoping that it might help us identify whether the shooter is male or female, and potentially their height and weight."

"Ladies, that is excellent detective work. We ordered the golf course closed today because we wanted to come back and look at the crime scene some more. We removed the tape because we believed we had collected every clue available on the green yesterday. That also gave the golf course manager the ability to clean up the green. You appear to have done our work for us on identifying the position of the shooter. Thank you. Let's hear your results."

Forty-five minutes later, Sam, the crime scene tech, had collected three shoe imprint plasters. Those impressions would be photographed and sent to the state crime lab for matching.

Sam indicated, "It will take about two days to receive a response from the state crime lab. They generally like to match a specific shoe to an impression; it was much more difficult to match an impression to as yet non-identified shoe."

The five of them spent an additional twenty minutes on the front side of the woods looking for evidence before they turned their attention to the backside of the woods. Jill had a picture on her phone from Jack. The picture pinpointed where the suspected shooter reentered the woods. No one had explored this area yet in the investigation. They had good sunlight streaming through the trees providing perhaps the best light of the day to look for evidence. They found matching footprints to the front area of the woods. In fact, by measuring the length of the stride they could approximate the height of the killer. Using trees as markers from the satellite pictures and the killers stride, they estimated his or her height at five feet eleven inches.

Better still there was a second candy bar wrapper located and it was the same type of candy as was found the previous day. It had not rained overnight and thus the candy bar wrapper was in good shape.

"Detective Haro, have you received a fingerprint analysis of the first candy wrapper that we found yesterday?" asked Jill.

"Sam, I haven't heard back from the lab as to a fingerprint match. What happened with the candy bar wrapper?"

Sam replied, "We dusted the wrapper and found probably ten different prints on the wrapper. Of those ten, we only have two on file. The other eight fingerprints come from people that do not have their fingerprints on file in any law enforcement agency which is not unusual."

"Who are the two people?" asked Jill. "What is their reason for having touched the candy bar?"

"One person works as a clerk at a convenience store. The other is a local high school student and we haven't figured out his connection to the wrapper. We are contacting him this morning to clarify that."

"A high school student?" mused Jill. "Why would he have his fingerprints on file? Did he have a juvenile record?"

"No juvenile record. He has worked several kid camps and all of those employees get fingerprinted - minor or not."

"Do you know how tall the minor is?" questioned Jill. "That might rule him out."

"I know the kid because he attends the same school as my son and plays with him on the basketball team. He is six feet two inches tall."

"Then I would say that rules the minor out as he is likely too tall to be the person walking around the edge of the woods," Jill concluded.

"Like I say I know the kid and I can't imagine him being Dr. Easley's killer. I also agree that he's too tall and lanky to be our suspect from the satellite images."

Jill sighed, "So we are nearly back to square one with no legitimate suspects for this shooting."

The detective agreed, "So it would seem, unless there is some magical clue on the second candy bar wrapper."

"Sam, when will you have those results back?" Jill queried.

"Later this afternoon. With the detective's permission, I'll e-mail you the results of the fingerprint analysis."

With another pained look, the detective nodded his approval.

"Let's head back to Marie's house and put our heads together on what we should do next," Jo nudged Jill and Angela. In her mind, there were no more clues to be found at the scene, so they may as well move on. They had been at the golf course for nearly two hours and she was itching to move on.

CHAPTER 8

*T*hey arrived back at Marie's house just in time for lunch. It was shaping up to be a beautiful day and they sat around Marie's table in the comfortable sunny conditions. They knew that their enjoyment of sandwiches, friendships, and the weather was in deep contrast to Michelle's day as she was likely planning her husband's funeral.

"This case has been really interesting for me," Angela commented. "I have never been at the scene of a crime let alone at the beginning of one of your investigations, Jill. I know we were at the scene of the crime in Belgium when Laura Peeters suffered from anaphylactic shock as a result of her nut allergy, but we weren't there when someone sneaked into the hospital to murder her. This is different. This time we were on the scene as the bullet was fired that killed Doug. It was so quick. I think for the first time, I have the same information that everyone else has on this team and it doesn't take medical knowledge to understand what happened to Doug. This was so straightforward and yet we have not a single suspect. I am mystified that we don't have a single suspect when it was an acquaintance that was murdered in my hometown where I feel like I know everyone and understand the world at large through the lens of Green Bay, Wisconsin. Does that make any sense?"

"I think that what you are feeling is the essence of why I set up my consulting business," Jill disclosed. "I enjoy the intellectual exercise of searching for a killer, but I'm also very angered that someone has the conceit to think they could get away with killing someone in such a cold blooded manner. While it seems like we don't have a single suspect and therefore we don't have a path to follow and gain information, we do have some snippets to tug on and see if they take us anywhere. I often chase these snippets into a dead end, but eventually they lead us to a killer. Because you guys don't join me at the beginning of these cases and because I am the point of contact, you have not had the opportunity to watch me analyze a crime scene and determine how you can help me solve the crime. That delay in joining me, hides from your view all of the dead ends I have chased to no avail. With this case you are seeing all of my false starts from the beginning."

"I am even more impressed with your detective skills now that I see how little you may have to work with to find a killer," Jo declared. "The only next step I can think of is to investigate the private finances of Doug and Michelle Easley."

Jill agreed, "We definitely want to do that, Jo. I am bothered by the candy bar wrapper. As a clue, the bright yellow and black of the wrapper is screaming at me to do further investigation. I think we can figure out who the teenager is whose prints are on that wrapper by doing a news search of local basketball teams. I want to investigate the teen and his family."

"Really, a teenager?" Angela challenged.

"The wrapper is a loose end and you know how I hate loose ends. Due to the rain the night before we know those wrappers were dropped between whenever the rain completely stopped as there weren't any drops of rain falling off leaves and landing on the wrapper, and when Doug was murdered. So on a school day, why was a teenager running around in those woods dropping candy bar wrappers?"

"That's an interesting question," commented Jo.

"Let's look at who the basketball players are in the Green Bay Press Gazette sports section. We are looking for team that has a player whose last name is Haro and a second player who is six feet two inches tall. Our problem may be multiple players of that height, but let's see what we can find," suggested Jill.

Marie went to work searching the local newspaper for prep basketball information. The game was played over the winter and into early spring so she was searching the archive. In a few minutes she had the high school identified and they were all looking at the team players. One of Jill's questions was concerning the height of the teenager. He might have been six feet two inches during the start of fall basketball season, but he could have had a growth spurt and ended up at a different height; or likewise he could have entered this season at six feet and hit a growth spurt that would have added a few inches to his frame. So the real question was did the school record the players' height at the start of the season or do they update the height as the player grew during the season?

In the end they had eight players that were either the exact height or might have had a growth spurt that affected their height. Each of the women took two players to research. Specifically they were looking for connections to Doug or his family. Doug's kids did not attend the high school in question so it appeared unlikely that the connection was at the student level.

"I need a little more direction here, Jill," asked Marie.

"I think we can read each kids' Facebook or Instagram sites or whatever else they have going and find out about the kid's family. I don't think it is a kid to kid connection. I think if there is a connection - and remember this is a loose end we are chasing - it will be in the parents. So perhaps look for mention of socialization with the Easleys. Another angle is hiring or working with Doug and Michelle.

"The other thing we could do is skip the kids entirely and just focus on the parents of the eight kids. In fact why don't we do that? It is kind of creepy to spy on the kids and based on the shot accuracy, planning, and video of the suspect, I don't believe we have a teenage killer."

"That sounds like a plan," replied Marie. "Give me a few minutes and I'll have the parent names. Of course we are now up to sixteen people whose backgrounds we need to look through."

Within ten minutes, Marie had located all eight sets of parent names. This was complicated by stepparents with two of the kids, so this added an additional four names to their research list. With five adults each, they all knuckled down and began their search. Marie had trained them in her process of doing background searches and while they weren't as good or fast as her, it was a reasonable way to split the twenty names that needed research.

Soon silence reigned in the kitchen with the occasional clacking of keys. Two hours later they hadn't found many connections to Doug and Michelle. Of the original twenty, fifteen had no connection that they could find. Marie went to work on the final five.

Jill worked with Angela and Jo to go back to the murder board and discuss where else they could go next.

"Let's ask the reverse question - who couldn't be the shooter?" suggested Jill.

"Well, it couldn't be the four of us or the three golfers that were Doug's partners," Angela offered.

With a smile Jo added, "Or the foursome in front of us and behind Doug's group. Didn't Michelle have an alibi? Her children don't have the shooter skills to have fired the gun. After that, except people with alibis, shooter suspects comprise a pretty large pool. How do we narrow it down?"

"I think we should focus on the usual suspects - the seven

deadly sins. In particular I want to focus on greed, wrath, and lust. I think sloth, pride, envy and gluttony take a back seat in this case. I can't tell you why, it just feels that way.

"Let's talk about greed first. Who benefits financially from Doug's death? I would assume Michelle and the children benefit. I would think that would be temporary. Doug is more valuable alive and earning an income, then dead with a life insurance policy. Another question worth following is who does Doug have influence on financially. For example, as a physician he is in a private group and I would think he would influence the income of his fellow physicians in his group through scheduling among other things. Let's find out what positions he holds to understand where he might have influence on other people's incomes."

"I'll take those two questions," Jo declared. "I deal with those questions in my day job, so let me see what I can find out."

"Thanks Jo. Maybe Angela and I can take on the second question with a little help from Ann and Mary. Was he or Michelle having an affair? Did he make decisions at work or somewhere else in his life that angered people? Let's see if we can get Ann and her mother over here this morning."

"I'll give them a call and see if they're available," Angela offered.

While Angela made the call, Jill walked over to Marie to see if she had found any interesting connections yet for the teenager's parents. She had one more adult to research but the only connection so far had been an uncle of one teen who had also worked at Our Lady of Guadalupe hospital. Jill had to agree that it was a long shot. In a community geographically close to the hospital there was bound to be family members with ties to the hospital as it was one of the largest employers in town. Jill and Marie decided to ignore that connection for now, and Marie focused her attention on the research the final adult.

Jill returned to the search for lust or wrath angles just as Ann and Mary arrived.

"Good morning, ladies," said Jill with a smile as they walked into Marie's kitchen. "Did you find out anything through your connections?

"Good morning back to you all," responded Ann with a smile. "You look like you have been hard at work on this mystery for a while."

"Yes, we returned to the scene of the murder this morning to see if we could pick up any additional clues," replied Angela. "Jo pretended to be Doug, while Jill was herself at the third hole tee box and I walked around the woods to determine where the shooter would have stood. Once we figured out the position of the shooter we called Detective Haro to come out and plaster some footprints we found in the woods. And remember that house located close to where the killer exited the woods the first time from last night? Well, it turns out that house is empty and for sale. We then searched the backside of the woods where we think the killer hid for most of the afternoon and found another candy bar wrapper that the police are fingerprinting. Also based on the height of the trees in the clearing, we figured the shooter to be about five feet eleven inches tall. Michelle is off the suspect list as she has an iron clad alibi according to the police."

Jill picked up the story and continued, "So now we are working on the motive for this killing as a means to identify who the shooter was. We are focused on three of the seven deadly sins – greed, wrath, lust. Sometimes when the evidence leads you nowhere, you have to look to motive for new clues. Jo is trying to run down the greed angle; looking for who financially benefited from Doug's death. Angela and I were about to embark on the lust and wrath angles and figured you two would be very helpful. Have you heard of any affairs by Doug or Michelle? Have you heard of anyone that Doug blew up at or who is mad at Doug?"

Ann and Mary took a moment to think back to what they had learned in the previous twenty-four hours about Doug or the hospital.

"Doug seems to be a saint. I don't say that lightly," Ann noted. "I couldn't find a single person that had something bad to say about him. It wasn't about not wanting to speak ill of the dead, he truly was a smart and caring individual. Based on what you told me about your visit to Michelle, I would almost say that many of the hospital folks are more devastated by his death then she was. People are just wearing their emotions on their sleeve about Doug at the moment.

"As for anger, again I didn't hear of a single episode of where Doug blew his cool and got mad at someone. To be fair, I didn't directly ask the question of 'had you seen Doug mad at anyone?' but no one brought it up in their conversation. Mom, did you hear anything from your sources?"

"Like you, dear, I heard no even mildly disparaging comments about Doug," replied Mary. "Nor did I hear any rumors of an affair."

"How about his fellow physicians?" asked Jill. "Was he well respected? Were there any arguments? Were there any rumblings from his practice about his management of the anesthesia group? Were there any comments about an unfair distribution of income in the group?"

"Again none that I heard," Ann stated. "Frankly there were comments about how hard he worked both as a leader and as a physician. I couldn't find anyone who was angry with him or something he did."

"And Michelle, any gossip from the interior design angle? Was someone mad at her? Was she having an affair?"

"I'm not as well connected to her side of this family. I have never been to her studio nor do I know anyone who has used her. That doesn't mean that she is not successful - it's just that she is on the east side of town and I and most of my friends are on the west side of town."

"Ok, we'll leave Michelle alone for now," observed Jill. "So Doug never raised his voice to anyone nor was he observed to be in a shouting match with anyone recently. It appears that this likely has nothing to do with his personal life. I just don't sense that there is any woman out there, Michelle included, who lusted for or with Doug enough to generate the passion required for murder. This was no impulsive shooting; it took too much planning to leave us with so little evidence. So I guess we're back to greed as the motive for Doug's murder."

Angela advised, "Perhaps we should tell Ann and Mary about the candy bar angle and then get an update from Jo on the finances."

"Good idea, Angela." Looking over at Ann and Mary, Jill gestured at Angela and added, "As she mentioned earlier, we found two candy bar wrappers: one in the front of the woods close to where the shooter stood and another in the back of the woods where we think the shooter reentered that cluster of trees. We knew that both wrappers had to have been dropped on the day of the murder because there was no rain damage to the wrappers whatsoever. The police fingerprinted the first wrapper. Even as I explain this, it seems like a long shot," noted Jill chagrined. "The first wrapper had prints leading to ten different people. As you can imagine during manufacturing and distribution, a candy bar might be touched by many different people before it ends up in the hands of the person that buys it. Of the ten people found on this wrapper, only two were in the fingerprint system so we don't even know who the other eight sets of fingerprints belong to. Of the two that we were able to match, one is a clerk at a convenience store that likely touched it as he stocked the items in an aisle, or he touched it at the time he ran up the purchase. The second print belonged to a teenager that plays on a basketball team with the detective's son and the police have not released his name to us. We do not think we have a teenage killer behind the murder of Doug. It seems implausible given the accuracy required to fire the weapon that a teenager could fire the gun. The figure walking around the clearing doesn't look like a teenager - all lanky and awkward."

Angela suggested, "Jill, should we check a national weapons accuracy website to see if there are any Green Bay, DePere, Ashwaubenon, or other cities' shooters from this region of the state?"

"Great idea and then we can rule out the kid. We all have a bad taste in our mouths for even considering the kid," replied Jill. "Why don't you check that out - there must be a database with the National Rifle Association or maybe connected to the Olympics. Shooting is a medal sport for the Summer Olympics so there must be some kind of Junior Olympics that feeds the US team. Marie, did you find anything on that final adult?"

Marie looked up from her computer screen and replied, "No, the final adult checks out clean."

"Thanks, Marie," noted Jill. "Jo, you have been looking at the financial impact of Doug's leadership at the hospital and in his private practice for the past half hour. Have you come across anything of significance?"

Jo looked over at Jill and gave her a one eyed squint, "yeah I've had a whole half an hour and guess what? I have no new information and don't bother asking again for another half an hour."

"I guess that's your way of telling me to be patient. You know that's not my skill set!"

Jo heaved a sigh and went back to her search on Doug's financial impact on other people's lives.

Jill looked over at Ann and Mary and said "you have both been very involved with Our Lady of Guadalupe. I'd like to understand more about the hospital. Can you tell me how it's organized? How many years has Doug been in a leadership role there? Have you ever heard of the hospital struggling with anyone? What do their finances look like? Tell me about any quality issues or patient satisfaction concerns that you've heard about. Finally, Ann, you presently serve on the board; what other roles have you and Mary served at the hospital? Sorry about all the questions, they are just spilling out of my brain."

"You asked me so many questions I'm likely to forget them all. So if I don't give you the information you want just ask me again," Ann imparted. "Let's see, where to begin? Mom, why don't you start by describing your role and any role that dad had at the hospital?"

"Your father and I go way back with the hospital. I think one of the two of us have been on the board, served on committees, or been a volunteer with the hospital for nearly forty-five years. Your father served the board for perhaps thirty years. I did it for five – it's not my cup of tea. No one has fun at these board meetings listening to reports about serious things. I couldn't wait to transfer the family's role on this board to you. I still do about two volunteer shifts a month; much less time than at my peak of volunteering where I probably served four days each week. I don't remember Doug's name coming up during my tenure at the hospital. Nor do I remember even a discussion about the anesthesia group or quality, but it has been probably at least five years since I was in a major meeting at the hospital. As all the contact I have now is my few volunteer shifts, I can't think of any information I have that will add to this case."

Ann reached over to give her mother a hug as she remarked, "I have served on hospital committees for about nine years and have only recently joined the hospital's board of directors. I met Doug for the first time during my orientation. The hospital set up a four-hour orientation and had various managers explain hospital reports and sort of the regulatory role of board oversight of the hospital. It was a lot of information to absorb in the four hours. I'm trying to think back to whether Doug's presentation stood out in my mind and I can't say that it did. I had never before thought about quality in the hospital and may be for the first half of his presentation I kept thinking 'doesn't the hospital do everything perfectly?' And then I would tune back in to what he was saying. I don't remember any of the presentations alluding to a problem area in the hospital; there were no temper tantrums mentioned nor inappropriate behavior between anyone associated with Our Lady."

"Have you attended any board meetings or has it just been the orientation so far?" queried Jill.

"I have attended two board meetings and the orientation was between my first and second board meeting. I would be the first to admit that I had a hard time understanding the language – acronyms used by people during the first meeting. I felt slightly more comfortable at the second meeting due to the orientation I had although I still didn't know many of the acronyms."

"Do you have the materials from the board meetings or the orientation sessions? As a not-for-profit business, some of Our Lady of Guadalupe hospital's board proceedings are confidential," Jill observed. "Any malpractice discussions, any physician perfor-mance discussions, or any business affiliations discussions would be considered confidential under peer review statutes or competi-tive business rules. Ann, would you be willing to share the mate-rials that you received for those board and orientation sessions? I can assure you that they will remain confidential. My sole purpose in reading them is to look for Doug's killer."

"Jill, you put me in a difficult position. I have responsibility as a board member to protect and strengthen the hospital. I also have a duty as a human being to do what I can to help find Doug's killer. I know I would not want you to share anything you saw in those materials with the police, and I don't know how you could not share something with the detectives if it was material to finding Doug's killer."

The conversation was getting hairy and Angela broke in with her view of Jill's request.

"Ann, you know I've worked with Jill on her cases over the past five years. We have had confidential information pass through our hands in the past and we have not immediately picked up the phone to call law enforcement. I think that those documents might help us by directing us to a motive for this murder. If for example it said in the medical staff meeting minutes that a fight was broken up between Doug and Dr. B, we wouldn't turn around and share that with anyone outside of this room. Instead we would do a lot of research on Dr. B trying to ferret out a potential motive for the homicide. You could choose to share the information with just Jill as she knows no one at the hospital. Marie, Jo, and I would excuse ourselves from reading any of the documentation and we would simply follow Jill's direction into researching whether certain people might deserve to join our suspect list. Will that meet your confidentiality standard?"

Ann seemed to be ruminating on Angela's remarks and then she said, "I'm going to return to my house to gather up the documentation. I'll make my mind up as I drive home and think about what you said as to whether I will share the documents with Jill. If by the time I get home I decide not share, I'll give you a call and let you know. I'd still like to help with the case if I can even if I make the decision not to share documentation with Jill."

Angela gave her friend a hug and added, "You know you can trust us, and we will love you even if you decide not to share. There'll be no hard feelings as I know we have put you in a difficult position."

Ann nodded and she and her mother left Marie's house.

Jill looked at Angela and asked, "Do you think she will bring the documentation back here?"

"I really don't know. We have put her as in a very awkward position."

Jill sighed and looked over at Jo who was maniacally tapping away at her computer. She seemed to be in the zone and despite her curiosity as to what Jo was typing so enthusiastically she knew she had to leave her alone. Looking over at Marie and Angela, she was stumped. Her mind blanked out as to which direction they should take next.

"You know, guys, I am fresh out of inspiration as to where this investigation should do next. Angela, did you complete that search on shooting skill competitions containing contestants from this area?"

"Not yet. Let's do that search now and see if the three of us can find any Olympic sharpshooters calling Green Bay or the surrounding cities, home."

CHAPTER 9

A short while later after an extensive internet search, they were unable to find any sharpshooters that listed the Green Bay area as home. Sighing in disappointment and with a lack of forensic evidence to explore, Jill was again dumbfounded as to where to go next. Fortunately, they got a call from Ann indicating that she would share the documents that she possessed concerning Our Lady of Guadalupe. She was going to put her trust in Jill and the team that her documents would stay confidential. She wanted to do her part to help find Doug's murderer.

Jill looked over at Jo and commented, "Okay I've had the patience of a saint; what has so engrossed you that it required all of that high-speed tapping on the keyboard? Have you found the vaguest link to a possible motive for murder?"

Jo looked up quickly, and then her eyes returned to the screen as she questioned, "Huh? Did you ask me a question?"

"Yes I did. What have you found that has you so entranced?"

"I have been trying to understand where Doug had influence on other people's salaries. I have found multiple angles for us to investigate. Let me explain how the medical staff is organized at the hospital. There are a series of medical staff departments like

Surgery, Medicine, Pediatrics, OB/GYN, Anesthesia, Emergency Medicine, and Radiology. As you can imagine there are many more departments that operate to provide care to patients or service for patients. The laboratory consists of pathologists and those physicians are part of the Department of Surgery. Likewise there are Intensivists which are critical care physicians and they are in the Department of Medicine. So every physician has a hospital department that makes decisions about policy and procedure and has a plan in place to monitor quality."

"Yes I'm aware of the usual medical staff department structure in the hospital," noted Jill. "While I have never worked for a hospital, many of my medical school friends do and they talk about it from time to time."

"So normally you would find Doug chairing the department of Anesthesiology. However, there has been turnover in the medical staff leadership ranks at Our Lady. In between elections for new department chairpersons, Doug has also served as the chairman of Surgery and Medicine, although not recently for medicine – that was more than five years ago."

"How is this related to money or murder?" Jill asked Jo.

"I'm getting to that point, have patience. Doug has served as interim chair of surgery for the past nine months. During that time and perhaps because of his knowledge in the operating room, he has implemented a couple of policies that might anger some of the surgeons. One policy in particular might affect the income of different surgeons."

"What's the policy? I have never heard any of my friends complain about a hospital policy that affects their income."

"From the information I can see online, I can't tell for sure if the policy disadvantaged any surgeons. I can only see that the hospital board approved that policy and I can guess that the implementation would have at least at some point affected some surgeons." Jo was in the zone of understanding something complex but she was unable to articulate to everyone else in the room what that complexity meant in terms of murder.

"What is the policy?" asked Jill for a second time.

Jo startled and looked confused for a moment before she said, "the policy? Oh what policy am I talking about? It's the operating room policy."

"Which operating room policy?" asked Jill knowing that given the complexity of an operating room there would be many policies for its performance.

"The board minutes that are publicly available are couched in vague terms using words at a ten thousand foot level. So, about a year ago the minutes mentioned a problem with the operating rooms starting at their scheduled time. A policy was created by the hospital and approved by the board that restricts a surgeon's access to the operating room if they have a problem starting on time. As a surgeon, you earn income by doing surgeries and caring for patients in the hospital. You also earn income from seeing patients in your office but it's generally a much smaller amount. If you see patients in your office but then can't get their surgery scheduled at the hospital, then that hurts the surgeon's income and causes dissatisfaction for the patient."

"What do you mean by the operating room starting at its scheduled time? I guess I never thought about how operating rooms schedule surgeries. I sort of thought that everybody showed up in the morning and you went to the operating room whenever someone got around to it. Do you mean to say that there is an actual schedule? I can't ever recall for me or my family members, being told to show up at any time other than early in the morning," said Angela, her voice dripping with sarcasm.

"Actually the operating room is a very complex beast to organize with very expensive resources in order to get to the endgame of the completed surgery. Each surgeon does specific surgeries in a specific area of the body. For example, neurosurgeons operate on the brain and spinal cord and may need a million-dollar microscope for their surgery. If the microscope costs a million dollars and you have five neurosurgeons that operate at your hospital, then you would likely want to arrange the schedule so that each neurosurgeon doing a surgery that requires the microscope occurs on different days. You want to keep your million-dollar microscope in use five days a week and you don't want your expensive and talented neurosurgeon standing around waiting to use the microscope. Thus the operating room schedule has to consider certain expensive equipment, instruments that are needed for specific surgeries, specially trained staff that operate lasers, special rooms that are outfitted for different types of surgery, and then the surgeon themselves."

"Okay you make this sound like a ballet," declared Angela. "I can imagine that much like a ballet when the dancers are not in perfect synchronicity, terrible chaos would result in the operating theater if one of the major resources did not perform according to schedule. If the patient showed up late, or the doctor showed up late, or you needed the gigantic room and you only had the medium-sized operating room, or I needed a robot and it was in use elsewhere that not only would that be bad for that scheduled case; but much like dominoes, things would fall apart around."

"That's an awesome analogy, Angela. Amazingly, it's a fairly common problem across the country. The dancers get out of sync and the ballet looks terrible to the audience," agreed Jo. "Our Lady was having problems with their ballet. They brought in a consultant to look at the operating room and discovered many bad dancers. The previous department of surgery physician leader was committed to fixing the problem. I don't know why he left and I'm hopeful that when Ann arrives, she'll have documentation that will describe how bad the problem was in greater detail. I'm curious as to whether that is why the previous chairperson stepped down or left the organization. Marie, perhaps you could do a search on a Dr. Randall Phillips to see where he is now."

The all heard the knock on Marie's door and hoped it was

Ann. Listening intently, they heard Marie and Ann exchange pleasantries; Jo was relieved to hear Ann's voice. Ann soon entered the kitchen, carrying a large canvas bag containing binders and other paper materials.

"I feel like I'm making the right decision by sharing these reports with you. They have confidential written all over them, but I want Doug's killer found."

"We are really very ethical people. Even if I found something in your documentation that would give me a competitive advantage as a healthcare leader, I would ignore it. I am narrowly focused on finding a link to Doug's killer in that documentation. Besides in all truth, if we didn't have the highest ethical behavior, Angela would have dumped us as friends long ago," Jo declared.

"That's true," Ann agreed. "I've known her for twenty years and she has the highest standards for integrity. I brought with me many months' worth of board meeting materials as well as the orientation packet given to me as a new board member."

"Ann, do you know a Dr. Randall Phillips? He was the prior Department of Surgery Chairman before Doug, but he seems to have left the hospital. Do you know why?"

"Actually I do know and it's really very sad. He died and the announcement was made at my first board meeting. I didn't know the man, but based on what they said of him at the board meeting, I would expect the Pope to begin the process of elevating him to sainthood."

Ann's response was not what Jo expected and so she probed, "did they say why he died?"

"I believe it was an accident; let me think back to what was said in the meeting. They announced his death from," and Ann stopped in her tracks thinking about the meeting, "A snowmobile crash. He was up north with another surgeon and they each had their own snowmobiles and were riding through the woods. Dr. Phillips was found by the other surgeon after he had an apparent heart attack and crashed the snowmobile as he was clutching his chest. It was all very dramatic and very strange for me as I had not known Dr. Phillips."

Jill gave Marie a look that said 'something isn't right here, please research it.' To which Marie nodded.

Jill said to Ann, "thanks for coming over with this documentation and thanks for giving us insight into the conversation concerning Dr. Phillips's death.

Minutes later after Ann's departure, they were sorting through her materials. Jo left the financials alone. She was confident she had found sufficient financial information online to prove the hospital had not influenced Doug's decision-making or downstream revenues. Their revenues were robust and could be attributed to good insurance contracts and strong patient volumes.

"Guys, I'm really interested in any information or orientation materials relating to quality and medical staff meeting minutes," noted Jill.

In the end, they had reviewed all of the materials since Ann had joined the board relating to medical staff information. The quality reports presented to the board were the standard accreditation reports and there was no new information contained within.

Marie called Jill over to her screen to read the police report and obituary notice for Dr. Phillips. It stated he was on a snowmobile trip with a Dr. Lewis. They were riding their snowmobiles in the Northwoods, a good two and a half hour drive from Green Bay. Drs. Lewis and Phillips had been enjoying a nice ride through the trees when all of a sudden Dr. Phillips hit a tree. When rescuers reached him he was found off the snowmobile lying in the snow clutching his chest. Because of the remote location, it took the rescue squad twenty minutes to reach Dr. Phillips and he was quite dead by the time they did.

"Let's look at the police report to see if it indicates if anyone did an autopsy?" suggested Jill.

Marie continued to peruse the police report looking for a comment on the autopsy. They were staying in a cabin near a town called Glidden in Ashland County, which is small and rural. The coroner was not a physician. After rescue workers declared Dr. Phillips dead, and Dr. Lewis suggested that he had a massive heart attack, the coroner did not complete a full autopsy but rather ruled the cause of death as a heart attack.

"Hmmm, that is a little too convenient for me," Jill mused. "Too bad we don't have autopsy results. Where is this Dr. Lewis now, is he still working at Our Lady? What type of physician is Dr. Lewis? Can you find out where Dr. Phillips is buried? We may want to exhume his body to do a full autopsy."

"You can do an autopsy on a body that has been decaying for nine months?" Marie asked. "Can I just say how creepy that sounds; to have to touch something that has been dead for a while?"

"Actually I have had older corpses than that. Not everyone is found immediately after they have died or have been murdered. Sadly, I have had several corpses that were in the open air for two to three years. All I have to work with is often bones and clothing. We don't know if Dr. Phillips was cremated or buried. If he was cremated, then there is not much I can do. If he has been buried in a moisture locked coffin, then I can do a fair amount of diagnostic tests. The embalming fluid interferes with some analysis, but there is still a lot of information that I can retrieve from Dr. Phillips's body."

"Dr. Phillips's obituary says he was survived by his parents, a wife, three children, two brothers and a sister. There doesn't sound like there is a history of heart disease. It says he was laid to rest at Resurrection Cemetery so it sounds like you have a body to exhume if you get to needing that."

"Let's go back to Dr. Lewis," directed Jill. "Who is he and what kind of physician is he?"

Marie finished a quick search on Dr. Lewis and announced,

"He is a general surgeon. He has been in town a long time as I think I remember him operating on one of my aunts. 'A nice guy with good bedside manner' according to many online reviews of the doctor. He has been at Our Lady for over twenty years. He is on marriage number two with grown children from his first marriage and a second family with his second wife."

"Did any of the teenagers we investigated this morning have a last name of Lewis? I don't recall that name," Jill remarked.

"No, Lewis was not one of the last names of the kids we investigated this morning."

"I'm going to call Ann, and see if she remembers hearing anything about Dr. Lewis? Any good or bad comments at the hospital or among her friends?" said Angela.

A minute later, she had Ann on her cell phone. She put the phone on speakerphone so the others could listen or ask questions.

Ann replied to Angela's query with, "His name sounds familiar but I can't place where I heard it. I had one friend who was operated on by a Dr. Lewis. Unfortunately my friend had complications and an expected one-day stay in the hospital became a three-week stay with some time spent in the ICU. My friend just seemed to have really bad luck but I know she liked Dr. Lewis."

"Thanks, Ann, that's good feedback," Jill noted. "Do you remember what kind of surgery she had?"

"I think she had gallstones. She went to the hospital in severe pain and she was randomly assigned to Dr. Lewis for surgery. After the surgery, she got a really bad infection and that was what took so long – the reason for her hospitalization."

"When did she have the surgery, and how she doing now?"

"It seems like it was a year ago and she's doing fine now, but I remember at the time that they had to take her back to surgery because her stomach or gut was dirty. I don't know what it means for your stomach to be dirty but I do know she developed an infection."

Anne continued, "If I understand the implications of the most recent conversation you guys had, you may suspect Dr. Lewis of killing Dr. Phillips last year while they were snowmobiling. Did I understand you correctly?"

"We do have suspicious minds and consider every possibility," Jill pointed out. "One of those possibilities is that Dr. Lewis has killed two physicians with whom he worked at Our Lady. This theory may sound like it is coming from left field, but you would be amazed at the unexpected killers we have found through our numerous investigations. Basically, until we can rule this theory out, Dr. Lewis gets added to the murder board as a suspect. I know this is a shocking theory and I would ask that you keep it confidential. Imagine the horror your friend would feel to know who the surgeon that operated on her last year is a killer."

"OMG! Of course I'll keep this theory confidential. I wouldn't want to slander a good surgeon nor do I want a killer coming after me if he hears that I am part of the team investigating his actions. Will you share this with the police?"

"We will if anything pans out here. At the moment, this is a just a far-fetched theory. If we can add a little meat to this theory, then I'll bring the police in. Certainly if we get around to exhuming the body, the police would have to be involved. I can't imagine the family agreeing to my request to re-autopsy their loved one," Jill remarked after she ended the call with Ann.

"So what are your next steps to put 'meat on the bones' of this story?" asked Marie.

"Let's start with getting a picture of Dr. Lewis to see if he could possibly be the shooter from yesterday. I'd also like to pull his state hunting license records to see if he hunts, as well as his driver's license to know his height and weight. I'd like to know the schedule from General Surgery to see if he was in the operating room or at his clinic seeing patients during the murder time. We know the killer spent several hours in the woods. Finally, I'd love to know if he has any quality concerns recorded in Our Lady medical staff services office."

"That sounds great, Jill, but how do we get some of those pieces of information?" Marie interjected. "It's not like it is public knowledge. We need a computer hacker to get some of that data."

"Angela, do you think this is something that Nick might be able to hack into?" asked Jill.

Nick Brouwer lived in Amsterdam and had assisted them with two previous cases. Jill's client in one of those cases, David Gomez, had been able to assist Jill and the FBI with some serious hacking abilities. He was so good that the FBI had offered him a job. David and Nick had stayed in touch after they returned to their respective cities with David teaching Nick enough of his substantial computer hacking skills so that Nick could help with future investigations. Nick did not know how to hack into a bank or into anybody's checking account, but he could go to other sites and hack his way through. Given what they were about to ask him to do, Jill was glad that he was in Amsterdam and out of reach of American authorities. Furthermore, if Nick couldn't get them the information they needed yet another good friend Henrik might be able to assist.

"Let me give him a call and see if he can help," Angela replied. She was soon using a contact to dial Nick and enlist his help.

CHAPTER 10

"Hey Nick, it's Angela."
"How is my favorite American friend doing today?"

"I'm doing well, how about you?"

"Doing well also, and if you're calling me this late at night, I'm guessing it's because you want help with the case. I thought you said you were going to be on vacation with Jill, Marie, and Jo. So why are you calling me?"

Angela loved how his mind worked and how quick he was to sense what she was calling for.

"You're right, we are on vacation, and we do want your help. We were playing in our most favorite golf tournament yesterday, when a man was shot and killed on the green behind us."

"You guys have some serious bad karma when you get together as a group to vacation. I thought you were extolling the virtues of the low crime rate in Green Bay. If I recall, you said that you have one murder a year in your town. Was this that one murder and you just happened to be close by?"

"Yep this was our one murder and it was quite gruesome. He was shot between the eyes and so the golf green has blood and brain material on it. It was so bad that Jill knew it was pointless to do CPR."

"That sounds like an exotic shooting for an industrial city. Do you have a suspect?"

"Jill was brilliant and asked a satellite company in Colorado to provide us with video feed of satellites aimed at this part of the world at the time of the shooting. We can see the shooter on video, but we haven't identified him yet. There is hardly any forensic evidence."

"How can I help? I assume you want my assistance with something."

"Actually we were hoping you would do a little hacking for us especially since you're in Amsterdam rather than America. If I recall, David Gomez taught you a few things after that case in Colorado."

"He did teach me some basic skills and I practiced on a server he set up, and I won't mention where else I have practiced. What do you need?"

"We need you to hack into a few websites. None of them are financial sites. We were hoping you could hack into the Wisconsin Department of Motor Vehicles, the Wisconsin Department of Natural Resources which grants hunting licenses, and Our Lady of Guadalupe Hospital Medical Staff Services and on-call roster."

"Those sound like a challenge. The last website you mentioned might present the biggest difficulty as I can only hope that what you're looking for is actually posted on-line. If the data is on someone's hard drive and not on their network, it will be hard to find. Am I looking for a specific name in any of these databases?"

Angela could see that Jill wanted to take over the conversation, so she handed the phone to her, "Hey Nick! It's Jill. Glad to hear you're awake at this time of the night I know it's late in the Netherlands."

"Hello, Jill, I haven't talked to you for nearly six months and I can see that crime seems to follow you around. As I understand it, you're visiting Angela, Marie, and Jo and a murder occurs not fifty feet from where you're standing on a golf course of all places. You can be a deadly person to hang out with."

"Ha ha, hey the four of us made it off the course in good health. We didn't ask to play next to this foursome. We were happily gulping margaritas. Back to the case, we really appreciate your help. We have sort of hit a roadblock on where to go next and then we thought of you. Angela just sent you an e-mail with the pertinent information. I would not call Dr. Lewis a suspect; rather we're just trying to gather a little more data on him. Really the only people eliminated as suspects in this case have been the victim's wife and the foursomes out on the golf course. Pretty much anyone else in town with shooting ability could have killed Doug Easley or I suppose that really everyone is a suspect as they could have hired someone with sharpshooter skills to take him out."

"Why the focus on Dr. Lewis?" asked Nick

"The man who was killed was an anesthesiologist, and Dr. Lewis is a surgeon at the same hospital. Doug Easley was the temporary chair of the department of surgery, because the previous physician died during a snowmobile accident. However, I do not like the coincidences of the snowmobile accident. He was up in the Northwoods as we call that region of Wisconsin with his friend Dr. Lewis snowmobiling. Because he died in a city with a population of less than five thousand that was in a county with a population of just more than sixteen thousand residents, they have a coroner who's not a physician. As near as I can tell, he was declared to have died from a heart attack without a pathological finding to lead one to that conclusion. I just find it odd that both chairs of the department of surgery are dead within a few months of assuming the role. That is statistically very unlikely. Since we don't have a lot of leads or evidence to chase with this case, I'm ending up chasing far-fetched coincidences. I have nothing more than that description to explain why we are investigating Dr. Lewis. If we were in law enforcement, a judge would likely say that we do not have probable cause."

"What other leads are you pursuing on the case?" asked Nick, intrigued.

"We have the satellite video wherein we can see the suspected killer walking, but it's so poor that you really can't confirm whether the killer is a man or woman, or guess their age. You can tell that the shooter was Caucasian but so is something like eighty-five percent of the town. The only other clue is two candy bar wrappers left in the woods that we have had dusted for fingerprints. We know they were dropped on the day of the murder as it rained the previous night and that would have damaged the wrappers. Trouble is that there are ten sets of finger-prints and only two of the ten are in databases so that is as big a long shot as chasing Dr. Lewis is."

"Wow that is a lack of evidence given that the murder occurred in so public a place. Give me about an hour and I'll see what I can find for you. Thanks for the opportunity to practice the hacking skills that David taught me; I have been itching to look for something, anything illegally, but I didn't want to go to prison for hacking into something I shouldn't, just for practice."

"It's not often I get thanked for asking someone to do some-thing illegal. Thanks for your help Nick, talk to you soon," promised Jill as they ended the call.

"This is a frustrating case," Marie commented. "For all the cases we have completed with you, I have never seen such a lack of clues for us to follow. Maybe the clues we have are really strong leads and we just haven't realized it yet."

"So you think we have a candy bar eating teenager as our killer?" probed an alarmed Angela.

"Jill, maybe we should take a leaf out of your book on assump-tions," Jo suggested. "I heard you say that at the start of an autopsy you like to assume the case is a homicide and so you gather evidence as though it is a murder. In this case, we would assume that the candy bar wrapper is related somehow to the person that committed the murder. Further we would assume that Dr. Lewis murdered Dr. Phillips, and covered it up to look like an accident; and he had some deadline that he was facing so he couldn't wait for the perfect opportunity to kill Doug Easley and make that also look like an accident. Therefore, he did it as soon as he could find the perfect place in the woods. So if these clues are absolutely related to the killer, I suggest we go about finding the evidence to support Dr. Lewis as the murderer."

"Since I'm lacking ideas on where to go next, there is a fair amount of merit to what you've suggested, Jo. I think I'll try your path after I call Detective Van Bruggin to see if they've come up with any additional suspects," agreed Jill. "I'm not ready to tell him about our crazy suspect theories at the moment."

Just then, Nick called back. He was amazingly quick to find information given that he was relatively new to the idea of hacking computer systems for evidence.

"Hello Nick. That was quick. What did you find?"

"The first two databases were easy to get into. Your Dr. Lewis has a hunting license - both bow and gun, as well as a snowmobile license. Information from his driver's license I'm sending you via email. You may want to do a facial recognition match between the person in the clearing and this driver's license picture."

Jill heard the ding signaling the arrival of new mail as she replied "I would have done that earlier if we had enough of a face to match, but we don't. The satellite is overhead and the shooter has a hat on so there are no eyes or cheekbones. We have a little bit of a jawline, but that's not enough to do any recognition with."

"I'll go to work on the hospital information you requested now. You also might check with any amateur shooting accuracy organizations. Your shooter sounds like he or she has excellent aim and someone with that kind of aim practices a lot and enters contests."

"That's good advice Nick and thanks for the quick response. I look forward to your next call," and they ended the call.

Jill pulled up the e-mail from Nick to see a copy of Dr. Lewis's driver's license and application. In one part of her brain she found it a little scary how easy it was for him to look at that database, but she wouldn't worry about it now. As she looked at Dr. Lewis's picture, she wondered if she was looking into the eyes of the killer and in fact perhaps a double murderer.

"According to his driver's license, he has the physical requirements to be our shooter. He's the right height and the right weight. Granted everybody lies on their driver's license but if you had asked me what our shooter's weight would be based on the satellite pictures I would've given this weight. All this tells us so far is that we can't rule Dr. Lewis out based on his physical characteristics. Let's hope that Nick can get into the hospital databases."

Jill probed, "Jo, since we now have a Social Security number from the license application, can you look up his tax returns or get any personal financial data on him?"

"I don't know. Let me see what I can find," and after receiving the number from Jill, she was soon clacking away at the keys.

"So how do we admit to the police that we have certain information when it would be clear that we could only have obtained it through illegal means?" Marie questioned.

"I don't have an answer for that yet. It would be helpful if we could find any contests or awards that Dr. Lewis has won in shooting tournaments. There's another gun organization called the United States Practical Shooting Association. Let's look at local tournaments to see if our Dr. Lewis has won any of them. Perhaps the Olympic level was too elite for our purposes. Angela, would you do the search for that while I call the detective to see if they have any new clues," noted Jill.

"Detective Van Bruggin."

"Hi this is Jill Quint. I have two questions for you. Have you added anyone to your suspect list and did you get fingerprint results back on the second candy bar wrapper?"

"As yet we have not added any new suspects to our list. As for the candy bar wrapper, we had nearly the exact same sets of fingerprints as on the first wrapper."

"So how are the fingerprints different? You did say that you had nearly the exact same set so how are these different?"

"We had the same teenager's fingerprints on this wrapper and another eight sets that we could not identify as they were not on file. So that piece of evidence appears to be dead end as we know the kid was in school at the time of the shooting."

"So what piece of evidence are you focusing on now?"

"Dr. Quint, I have answered your questions about the candy bar wrappers since you located those pieces of evidence. Now if you have no further questions relating to the wrappers or the video feed, I need to get back to work."

Jill blinked rapidly quickly searching her mind for any additional questions and coming up with none, "no I don't have any further questions," and they ended the call.

"The two detectives must be under pressure to come up with clues for this murder. I feel better about the investigation knowing the cops are frustrated with their lack of results as well."

"So, Nick was right about checking the shooting organization. I found that over the course of several years, Dr. Lewis has entered about three contests a year testing his shooting ability. As I understand these results, he's quite talented with a rifle," Angela had tallied the various competitions.

"Is there any relationship between the teenager and Dr. Lewis? We know Dr. Lewis has the technical skill to be our murderer," Jill commented. "I'm also convinced that whoever dropped the candy bar wrappers was our murderer. I hope Nick can break into the medical staff office - that will likely give us some answers."

"Ladies, other than the work that Jo is doing we seem to be a standstill in this investigation," Angela observed. "How about if we drive to the Pearly Gates bar for a drink, some appetizers, or dessert? Marie, I am sure you have drinks and food here, but maybe the change of venue will stir our creative juices and develop new leads."

"Great suggestion, Angela!" agreed Marie. "I have not been to that bar in years, but I remember trying their deep fried cheesecake. It was delicious and a heart attack on a plate. Jo, are you at a convenient place in your research to take a break?"

"I'm always at a convenient place for break! Especially a break that contains beer and deep-fried cheesecake. Let's go!"

They all piled into one car to drive to the bar. It was nearly close enough to walk, but there was rain in the forecast and they opted to stay dry by taking a car. Pretty soon they were entering the Pearly Gates and stepping up to order their drinks at the bar. It was mid-afternoon and they all took a turn ordering their favorite beer. Angela liked Stella, Jo liked Corona with lime, Jill liked Guinness, and Marie had a Bud light.

The Pearly Gates bar had been open for more than a hundred years. Before the diocese closed Holy Martyrs of Gorcum Catholic church for lack of priests, the bar was a favorite of churchgoers in the neighborhood yet it also had a large biker following. The bar survived the church's closing as more houses were built close to its location. It was the perfect change of setting to clear their minds and give them a fresh perspective about the murder when they returned to Marie's house.

They soon moved on to a discussion of the upcoming NFL draft. The Packers had made it to the playoffs the previous winter but they hadn't gone deep into the post season. Jo and Angela had the best football minds and it was good to listen to what holes they thought the Green Bay Packers should plug through the draft. The Packers were primarily a drafting team. They did not like to spend big dollars on free agents. In the end they agreed that they wanted the defense bulked up as well as one or two players on the offensive line so the quarterback was better protected.

Several beers and snacks later, they were ready to return and re-focus on the murder. The only thing that had Jill feeling slightly better about this investigation was it seemed the cops were as stuck as their team was in figuring out who was the killer. This was all the more amazing because they had the killer on video.

CHAPTER 11

*L*ooking out the window, they watched an ambulance roll by the bar. Our Lady of Guadalupe was one of four hospitals in town. This ambulance would be stopping at a different hospital located closer to the bar as Our Lady was across town. The ambulance was speeding with sirens loud and light flashing. Jill hoped that whoever was inside made it alive to the hospital. The ambulance had a squad car leading it. Jill reasoned it was just trying to clear the way for the ambulance and not because there was a victim or suspect inside the ambulance. They paid their bill and were getting ready to return home, when they saw two more squad cars head up the road in the direction from which the ambulance had come.

"Hmmm, I wonder what is going on up the road. It is unusual to see an ambulance running toward the hospital and squad cars heading in the other direction. We could head that way on our way home; go be lookieloos at an accident or crime scene," suggested Jill.

"Haven't you had enough gross crime scenes with the brain matter on the green yesterday?" asked Marie. "Oh wait, I forgot -

you were with the crime lab, Jill. No wonder you want to go see - you're like a tow truck that can't pass a car accident."

"Hey, you can take the girl out of the crime lab but you can't take the crime scene investigator out of the girl. Let's go be spectators and maybe it will jiggle loose another lead for our current case."

The group of friends just smiled with tolerance at their friend's desire to view a crime scene, so they piled in the car to see if they could locate where the police cars had gone. At first there was no sight of them anywhere and Jill was about to suggest they just return to Marie's house. It had been a pleasant diversion, but now it was time to go back, and then they saw the squad cars. Then Angela noticed the two detectives from Doug's case.

"That's strange," Jill commented. "You would think that the two detectives would be working full time on just Doug's murder. That is unless there has been another murder, but there shouldn't be another murder in this town for another twelve months. We saw an ambulance roll by us but maybe there is another victim here."

Angela, eyeing the two detectives commented, "I think they said they did major crimes so maybe there is an assault here or a burglary."

Just then Detective Haro caught their eye and he turned and said something to Detective Van Bruggin.

"Rats! We've been caught acting like lookieloos," said Jill as she sunk lower in the seat and motioned Angela to just drive on by. Then the detective waved them over so they pulled to the curb and lowered the windows.

"What are you ladies doing at this crime scene?" queried Detective Haro as he gave them the squint eye.

"We were down the street at the Pearly Gates when we saw an ambulance head toward the hospital and police cars head this way so we thought we would drive by this scene on the way back to Marie's house." Jill knew she was rambling but it was the first time she had ever been caught doing something so juvenile as stopping at a random crime scene. "What happened at this location?" Jill had already stepped into a cow pie, so she may as well smash it as long as she was standing on it.

"The detective and I wondered what you were doing here. Your explanation makes sense as I suppose I would have a hard time avoiding a crime scene in another jurisdiction. Actually though, if you have time we could use your help inside." Eyeing the other women in the car he added, "Just you Dr. Quint. We'll get you a ride home when you're done here."

Jill shrugged at the detective request and said "Sure I'll help. Guys, I'll meet you back at Marie's house," and she got out of the car to follow the detective..

Jill started to walk toward the house with the detective and predicted "You must have a forensic pathologist's question, do you have booties and gloves I can change into?"

"Yes, just outside the door here," replied the detective, motioning to a corner of the front porch.

After putting protective gear on so she wouldn't contaminate the scene, she said to the detective, "Tell me what happened here."

"We were called to the scene by the victim's employer when she failed to show for work this morning. Normally, you would wait twenty-four hours to file a missing person's report, but her supervisor was most insistent and said that we may as well send a patrol unit over to the house and if he had to he was going to break-in to check on his employee and so we reluctantly dispatched an officer. He had been her supervisor for twenty years and she had never failed to show up for work as scheduled so he was convinced that something was wrong. The supervisor arrived a few minutes before the squad car did and he had just broken into her house. He found her unconscious with a faint heartbeat on the living room floor. He called 911 and started doing mouth to mouth. Our officer ran out to the patrol car to get a tank and mask and kept her alive until paramedics arrived to take her to the hospital."

"So far, other than the broken window, I'm not sensing a crime was committed here. Rather if only we could all have such a conscientious supervisor."

"At first, those were our thoughts as well. We took a second look at her just before she was loaded into the ambulance. Her skin had pinked up a bit with the extra oxygen. It appeared that she had ligature marks on her wrists and a bruise inside her elbow where someone took blood or injected her. She has not regained consciousness yet. We have sent our crime scene tech to the hospital to get blood and evidence from her. Her employer is Our Lady of Guadalupe hospital by the way."

With that last sentence, Jill's head whipped around to look at the detective, "That hospital is becoming an extremely dangerous place to work."

"Exactly our thoughts and since you happened to be driving by, we figured your expert eyes might see something here. We haven't called our own coroner to the scene as there isn't a death yet."

"Do you have pictures of the victim?"

He did and held out his cell phone for her to view. She looked at the pictures and zoomed in to get a closer look at the ligature and elbow bruise.

"I would suggest your crime scene tech swab the skin injection site and request the hospital run toxicology tests. Did she ever wake up? Was she completely limp? Was she lying as though she had fallen? Any other injuries? Is the supervisor here to ask questions of?"

"Yes the supervisor is here. Which toxicology tests?"

"I would run tests for prescription drugs that depress the respiratory system like Valium, Propofol, and alcohol. This doesn't look like a drug overdose, but rather very suspicious circumstances because of the ligature marks. For all of the weird and kinky overdoses I have seen over the years, none included a ritual where hands were tied together then later untied as the person started to get drowsy. I would like to speak with the supervisor after I ask you a few more questions."

"We have him in the kitchen so as to keep his explanation untarnished by our conversation."

"Can you describe where you found her on the floor in this room? Did she appear to be wearing pajamas or street clothes? Does anyone else live in this house?"

"She appeared to be wearing street clothes like she had dressed for work and he said he found her with her head there," said the detective point toward a coffee table, "and her feet there," moving his hand back and forth suggesting how she was stretched out on the carpet.

"No blood, or vomit or anything lying near her body. Her purse was sitting on that sofa like she was ready to go to work and there is cash in the wallet so this wasn't a robbery. All the doors were locked. No TV or anything on. No pets here and no one else in the house. The supervisor says she lives alone with her grown children occasionally visiting her and staying here, but they live several hours away. They have been notified as next of kin and are on their way here."

"Okay let's go speak with the supervisor. Why don't you introduce me as Dr. Quint, a consultant that your department occasionally uses."

"That's not far off the mark at this point," he said as they walked into the kitchen.

"Mr. Swanson, hi I'm Detective Van Bruggin, this is Detective Haro, and this is Dr. Quint who is a private consultant. I know we introduced ourselves earlier, but in the chaos I wasn't sure you would remember."

"Hello detectives and Dr. Quint. Do you have any word on Helen? Is she doing better now that she is at the hospital? I knew something was wrong when she didn't show up to work. She has never done that in over twenty years. I am glad that I came over here and smashed the window to get into her house," John Swanson knew he was rambling on, but he couldn't help it - he was deeply worried about Helen.

"We have no news from the hospital other than she has not recovered consciousness yet for us to interview," replied Detective Haro. "Can you take us through what happened today? Start when you first noticed that Helen did not arrive at work."

"Helen and I have worked together for nearly twenty years. In all that time she has never been late and maybe she had to call in sick to work perhaps once or twice during that time. Her shift was supposed to start at ten. I was out of my office, but returned perhaps at eleven and she wasn't there. I spent the next two hours calling her home phone, calling her cell phone, and even calling one of her kids that is listed as an emergency contact. I was trying not to alarm them, but I just knew something was wrong."

"Helen is lucky to have you as both a supervisor and a friend," murmured Haro. "You knew her well enough to sense when she was in trouble."

"I am sorry sir but that was what I told the dispatcher that they may as well send you guys as I would be breaking into her house. I knew she couldn't wait twenty-four hours for me to file the missing persons report, and it turns out I was right. So I got to this house and I could see no movement in the rooms that had the curtains open. I tried all the doors and windows, but none of them were unlocked. So I decided the best window to break was the side glass panel by the front door. It would allow me to reach inside and unlock the front door. I thought it would also be the cheapest to repair and so I broke the window pane closest to the doorknob."

Jill thought the guy was very logical and precise. He made a good witness and friend to Helen.

"Once I opened the front door I called out for Helen as I moved from room to room. I quickly found her on the living room floor. I called 911 for an ambulance, felt for a pulse, then started doing respirations since she looked a little blue and her chest didn't seem to be moving much. An officer appeared perhaps a minute after I started giving her mouth to mouth, then went to his car for oxygen and a mask. He stayed with me, using the mask to get air into her and a few minutes later the paramedics arrived. They took over, quickly got her on a stretcher and drove off to the hospital. I think the officer followed the ambulance and then you two detectives arrived I think about the same time as the ambulance departed."

"Mr. Swanson, can you tell me how Helen was lying on the carpet?" asked Jill. "Did her position look natural to you?"

"What do you mean natural?"

"Were her legs or arms at any odd angles? Or did she look like she might have fainted and dropped to that position on the ground?"

"She looked like she had laid down on the carpet to take a nap. She was curled on her side. I hesitated, calling out her name when I first saw her because I thought I might be interrupting her sleep."

Jill continued with her questions, "What made you run to her if she looked like she was sleeping?"

"It was her lack of movement and the quietness of the house. I am the father of five children and no one sleeps that quietly or with so little motion."

"Was she curled tight and was she curled on her right or left side? Do you remember the position of her lower arms?" asked Jill.

"She wasn't curled tight, but she had her weight on her left hip. It wasn't that she was lying on her back looking to the side rather her hips were turned to the side. And her arms, let me think about that… umm they were folded in front of her almost in a prayer," and he imitated the arm position.

"Can you remember anything about her clothing? Was any of

it out of place, do you remember if she was wearing work clothes?" asked Haro.

"She was definitely in her work clothes. The sweater she had on was a gift from her co-workers and I remember her opening the gift at a birthday party. So it looked to me as though she was nearly ready to go to work and then for some reason she fell asleep on the carpet. But it wasn't sleep because her color wasn't very good and I couldn't wake her up so she must have had a medical emergency."

Jill couldn't resist asking the one question that no one wanted to ask of Mr. Swanson, "What was her state of mind recently? Was she depressed or worried about anything? Had she ever mentioned that she was having problems?"

"No she was not suicidal if that is what you're asking. She was a very content and happy person, proud of her children, hoping for some grandchildren soon."

Van Bruggin finally asked a question, "What did Helen do at Our Lady? You said you're her supervisor; what was her role and what is your role at the hospital?"

"Helen is our Director of Quality and I'm a Vice President at the hospital. As Director of Quality she handles a variety of services like Accreditation, Regulations, Risk Analysis, Patient Satisfaction, and Quality Improvement."

Jill had her last question, "Is Helen a nurse by training?"

"Yes, she is a registered nurse."

Jill looked at the detectives and nodded that she had asked all of her questions. She soon heard Haro and Van Bruggin usher Mr. Swanson out checking to see if he was safe to drive and making sure they had all of his contact information and admonishing him to not talk with anyone.

Haro re-entered the kitchen and said, "That was probably a waste of air - asking him to keep his mouth shut. So what do you think? Is this an attempted murder or a botched suicide?"

Van Bruggin responded, "I don't like the coincidence of our

murder victim also working at Our Lady. One murder and one attempted murder among one group of employees within a week is a very rare event in this town."

"Three."

Detectives Haro and Van Bruggin looked at Jill puzzled by her word 'three', Jill could almost read their minds as they were asking themselves if they had heard 'free' or another word.

Jill repeated herself, "Three murders or really two murders and so far one attempted murder."

Both detectives turned to stare at her, questioning looks on their faces.

"My team did some research on the hospital specifically looking at the leadership roles that Dr. Doug Easley occupied. What you are probably not aware of is that he was the interim chair of the Department of Surgery." Jill paused then added, "I can see the skeptical looks on your faces wondering where I am going with that remark."

Both detectives hated being so easy to read.

"So the reason he is the interim chair is because the previous chair died in a snowmobile accident six months ago. He was on a vacation with another physician from Our Lady who stated that Dr. Phillips had a heart attack while snowmobiling. As the event was witnessed by a physician there was no reason to do an autopsy. The Chair was in his forties with no family or personal history of heart disease. I would like to exhume his body and do an autopsy. He is buried at Resurrection Cemetery, so it's possible," Jill's far-fetched lead was getting stronger by the moment.

"There are a lot of things to say about your statement, Dr. Quint, and I'll start in no particular order of importance," begin Detective Van Bruggin attempting with all speed to match Jill's understanding of the potential scope of victims in this case. "I have never requested a body be exhumed for examination and I'll have to refresh myself with the regulations. You're not licensed in this State so you can't do the examination and I would guess we would want to send the body to the forensic lab in Madison. Since I have never tried to exhume a body, I don't know what kind of justification we need but I bet that what we have now is insufficient."

"Detective, I don't know your rules in the State of Wisconsin either. There are two routes we can follow. The one is to put evidence before a judge and order an exhumation. I agree with you that no matter the standard in Wisconsin, we likely lack the evidence to meet that standard. The second route would be to approach his widow and gain her permission for the exhumation. Again you could send the body to Madison, or I could assist your local coroner in the gathering of evidence. As you said I can't sign any legal documents, but I could advise your coroner of what signs to look for and tests to run."

"Can you definitively determine the cause of death in a body that has been buried for six months and is filled with embalming solution?" asked Haro, his voice full of skepticism.

"You would be amazed at the forensic evidence in a body. Just last year a Chilean poet's body was exhumed thirty years after his death. He is a famous poet and he won the Nobel Prize in Literature. His family claimed he was murdered by poison from an assassin. His bones underwent toxicology testing and it was determined that the only chemicals in his system were the chemotherapy agents used to treat his prostate cancer."

"Wow, thirty years after his death," Haro was awed by the science of forensics.

"Let's go back to the suspicions about Dr. Phillips's death," redirected Van Bruggin. "The only reason we are doubting the heart attack is because of the connection to Our Lady?"

"Yes and just as importantly is the lack of personal or family connection to heart disease. I have never seen someone go from being perfectly healthy to death from heart disease in their forties without history or symptoms. Even with electrical malfunctions, there are symptoms. So there are two good reasons."

"What is the doctor's name that accompanied Dr. Phillips on that fateful snowmobile trip?" asked Van Bruggin.

"It's Dr. Bradley Lewis. He is a surgeon. Oh and he has won several state United States Practical Shooting Association tournaments."

With this last statement, the two detectives let out a whistle.

"Dr. Lewis has won awards for accurate rifle shooting?" asked Haro.

"Exactly, there are some really interesting loose ends with this case." Jill pointed out.

"Obviously, you and your team have done more research on Dr. Lewis," declared Van Bruggin. "Care to tell us more? At what point in this investigation were you going to discuss the circumstances surrounding Dr. Lewis?"

"Without the attempted murder of Helen, you would've thought I was a crank investigator. Heck at this stage we don't even know if Dr. Phillips was murdered; we just have a lot of suspicious circumstances at the moment."

With a huge sigh Haro asked, "Is there anything else about this case that we should know? Your team seems to be steps ahead of us. Speaking of your team, what are they currently researching? Because I'm sure they're up to something based on how fast you have arrived at some solid conclusions about Dr. Phillips."

Jill ignored his question and asked a few of her own, "Are you done here? Are you waiting for the crime scene technicians to arrive? Are you even going to treat this house as a crime scene when there is no clear-cut evidence yet that an attempted murder was committed here? The hospital will likely get toxicology tests results in about another hour from now and you may have some answers then, or in the best of all worlds, Helen will wake up."

"Dr. Quint, would you agree that we need to rule this house as a crime scene?" Van Bruggin questioned. "Certainly if we found Dr. Lewis's fingerprints in this house, we would have to bring him in for questioning. However, if he is behind the murder of Doug

Easley and Randall Phillips, then he's a very smart killer and I can't imagine he would be so dumb as to leave evidence around this house. Frankly if certain surfaces are wiped clean of finger-prints; that in itself, is an answer to whether someone attempted to murder Helen. Are we done here? Yes. Will the crime scene technician come here when she is done with Helen at the hospital? Yes."

"Good, I believe this is a crime scene and you're correct that my team is continuing to do more research on Dr. Lewis. One of our favorite areas of investigation, because it is so often the source of murder, is looking at the finances. That was how we were alerted to Dr. Lewis to begin with. We were looking at the angle of greed, what could Doug Easley do or decide that might affect someone's income? In order to figure out the answer to that question we needed to know the full range of decision-making positions he occupied at the time of his death. That was when we discovered that he was interim chair of surgery. We also know that Dr. Lewis's height and weight on his driver's license likely matches the height and weight of the shooter that we caught on video feed. When you're done here, you're welcome to return to Marie's house and see what we're up to in terms of the investigation. I can also help you move forward with requesting the exhuming of Dr. Phillips's body."

"How did you get it the data off of Dr. Lewis's driver's license?" asked Haro.

"Let's just say, you don't want to know my source. I invite you to look up his driver's license yourself and verify what I've said."

"You just want to cover your own unauthorized entry into the State's driver's license database," accused Haro.

Jill just looked at the two detectives blank faced and unblink-ing. She had got farther in the investigation then they had, they knew they needed to ignore her acquisition of certain pieces of data and so they would, for now.

Jill just thought of another problem, "Do you have an officer guarding Helen at the hospital? She may be in great danger. We know that Dr. Lewis only practices at Our Lady and I don't believe Helen's ambulance took her there. However, if he is our killer, it would be easy for him to sneak in and harm Helen while she lays unconscious."

"We did have an officer who accompanied her to the hospital. I'll assign an officer to her until we have some resolution—she wakes up, we confirm this was an overdose, or we issue an arrest warrant for someone in this case."

Jill relaxed. "Thank you. Perhaps we have a serial killer on our hands and just the thought of that gives me a few more angles to research. If you detectives are ready to leave, I need a ride to Marie's house. If you're not, let me know and I'll get a friend to come get me."

"We need to speak with the crime scene technician and then stop in at the hospital. I would advise that you have a friend come get you."

Jill was glad to see them concentrating on the murder and she was perfectly fine calling her friends for a ride. She was sure they were dying to know what had happened at this house and how it might change the direction they were going with their investigation. She waited less than ten minutes before Angela appeared. She hopped in and they were off.

"Okay, we're all dying to know. What was inside that house? Since an ambulance took off, we're thinking that it wasn't a dead body."

"Her condition is not good, she is unconscious. Her employer is Our Lady and the police don't like the coincidence. I'll explain it all at once when we reach Marie's kitchen. I'm curious to hear what you guys found as well. I haven't looked at my email to see if Nick sent us anything. Have you guys heard from him?"

"Yeah, he sent you an email with a question in it and when he didn't get an immediate response, he called me to get his question answered and find out what was going on."

"What was his question?"

"He was able to break into the hospital's administrative system, but he doesn't really know where to look, so he was hoping to get some specifics from you. When he called us to ask the question we didn't know enough about what you were looking for to assist his search. He's gone to sleep as it is past midnight in Amsterdam but he said to send him what you need and he'll get up and work on it."

"It's really nice of Nick to give up sleep to help us. I'll have to sketch out what he should be looking for. It's hard to explain but I'll give him an explanation of what data looks like if he ends up in the right spot in their administrative system."

"Also, we have an appointment with Michelle later this evening. She wants to get out of her house, so she is meeting us at Captain's Walk Winery in the upstairs parlor so we can question her. We thought of interviewing her at Marie's house, but then we would have to hide the murder board and any other stuff and really that parlor is a very soothing room with good wine. She sounded very exhausted on the phone. It's going to be painful interviewing her."

Angela and Jill entered Marie's kitchen. Marie and Jo looked up from where they were each seated in front of a computer obviously searching for information about their victim and the mysterious Dr. Lewis.

CHAPTER 12

"Jill, tell us what happened at the house," Marie requested. "Our imaginations have been working overtime conjuring up all kinds of crime scenes inside that house. So what really happened?"

Jill had to smile and said, "Marie, you sound like a narrator of a made for television drama with your questions! So I will add a little drama to my answers just for the fun of it. Guess where the occupant of that house works?"

Marie and Jo looked blankly at Jill. They were not expecting that question. Jill could see that they were trying to reboot their heads to the question that she had asked. After a few more seconds, Jo blurted out, "Our Lady of Guadalupe. Oh my, I can see that your far-fetched, in the next galaxy, murder suspect in Dr. Lewis, might be looking like a solid lead."

"Bingo, jackpot goes to Jo! At this time, in that house, police are investigating an attempted murder of an employee of our favorite hospital. The employee has not recovered consciousness to tell police what happened. She works for a wonderful supervisor who freaked out when, for the first time in over twenty years, she failed to show up for work. He called the police to report the situation and they told him he had to wait twenty-four hours to file a missing persons report. He said 'thank you very much but I'm going over to her house and break-in; you may as well send an officer to charge me with burglary'. It was a good thing he was such a passionate supervisor as he found her with a poor respiratory effort and began mouth-to-mouth until rescuers arrived to take over. It's too early to tell if she'll ever regain consciousness but our friends, Detectives Van Bruggin and Haro, invited me inside the house as they did not like the coincidence of two tragedies striking two employees of Our Lady within a few days of each other. Like most members of law enforcement, they don't like coincidences."

With a sly smile, Marie asked, "And what did they say when you told them there were three employees from Our Lady involved in terrible tragedies?"

"Is it a personality defect that has me gaining pleasure when we can out-think law enforcement? I guess I have a small mind, but it was so satisfying to utter the word 'three' when they kept saying 'two' employees of Our Lady. But I have my small pleasures and I'm ready to move on and try to be helpful. They're coming over to talk to us after they finish directing the crime scene folks.

"Let me back up and tell you one more thing about the employee found in that house—she was the director of quality. Her death would have been made to look like a suicide but whoever staged it did a poor job. She was dressed as though ready to go to work, with her purse on the sofa seemingly just waiting for her to walk out the door. That's just not the behavior of a suicidal person. They're doing toxicology screens to see what kind of drug is in her system, but if Dr. Lewis is related to this event, then more than likely, it's an anesthesia drug he might have access to either in his private practice or in the operating room. I spoke to the detectives about exhuming Dr. Phillips's body. I think in a strange way they are grateful that we're working on this case because we're cooperative and we understand the medical world more than they do."

"Green Bay is feeling like a creepy little town if this Dr. Lewis has done all the crime we potentially think he might have done." Angela was mourning over the loss of innocence for her town.

"Wait till you hear about what we have found on Dr. Lewis on the internet," Jo imparted. "It will add more weight to the theory that Lewis plays some kind of a role in this murder."

"I want to hear what you guys found. Then I need to send an e-mail to Nick about what kind of information we're looking for in the administrative files at Our Lady. I need to do that outside of the presence of the two detectives so let's be quick about this. If we don't finish before they arrive, you may see me spend longer than usual in the bathroom while I compose an e-mail to Nick. I slipped up while I was talking with him earlier, and said that Dr. Lewis's height and weight likely matched the gentleman we could see in the video feed at the time of the shooting. They asked me where I got the information and I just stared him down refusing to answer. It's a minor concern of theirs in light of one murder, one attempted murder, and potentially a second murder from several months ago in another county."

"Let's focus on Dr. Lewis then," Marie prompted. "Dr. Lewis was born in St. Louis, Missouri. His mother was young and hooked on drugs so he was given up for adoption almost immediately. His mother was found dead perhaps a year or two after she gave birth to him. Lewis is his adopted parents' surname. He seemed to have a normal childhood with four younger siblings birthed by his adopted parents. He went to public schools and then on to St. Louis University for pre-med and then medical school at the University of Wisconsin. He met his first wife while he was in medical school and they married shortly after graduation. He had two children through that marriage which lasted about ten years when she died unexpectedly.

"I look through obituary records and newspaper articles but

couldn't figure out what she died from. He married his second wife two years after the first wife's death. He's had three children from that marriage which has lasted close to twenty years."

Marie continued after Jo gave the basics on his background. "If you look him up online, he has very favorable patient comments. He accepts all the major insurance companies and he makes the occasional trip to Haiti to volunteer and do surgery for Haitians."

Jill inserted, "He sounds like a regular Boy Scout."

"On the surface, he looks like your average American doctor. Seems like he's been a good father to his children and he is well respected in the community. He has had some interesting legal problems. He has been picked up for two driving-under-the-influence incidences. He's gone to court for both cases and got them tossed out of court. Even though he could not pass tests such as walking a straight line or touching his fingers to his nose, his blood-alcohol level was zero and he didn't test positive for any illicit drugs. As the District Attorney could not prove what he was driving under the influence of, she lost the cases."

"He must be using prescription drugs that don't fall under testing protocols for illicit drugs," Jill theorized. "I hope he doesn't go into the operating room under the influence. It would be criminal if that was tolerated by the operating room staff or the anesthesiologist."

"He's had additional legal problems in the financial area. He has lost two properties to the state for failure to pay taxes. Apparently, his first wife was wealthy. She created a will after the second child was born. She had some real legal eagles that set up a trust for the two children. All of the personal wealth that she brought into the marriage, upon her death, was directly deposited into a trust for the children. Her husband did not get a dime of her inherited wealth. She set up a separate executor and trustee to manage the children's trust. He tried to fight her will in court and lost."

"How about the current wife? Was she independently wealthy, as well, at the time of their marriage?" asked Angela.

"It looks that way to me. He was sued in small claims court about the time of his marriage for failure to make the installment payments on a diamond engagement ring."

"He must be blowing through large sums of money because he certainly makes enough as a surgeon to be able to afford an engagement ring for his wife," Jo proffered the explanation. "So what's he spending his money on? Can you tell if he's a gambler? It seems that he doesn't have an illicit drug problem, but even if he's got a prescription drug problem, where is he getting the drugs from?"

"Those are interesting questions, Jo, and I have not found the answer to them yet," agreed Marie. "It would be helpful to have law enforcement's assistance to gain some information about Dr. Lewis. Does he have frequent trips to Vegas, perhaps indicating a gambling addiction? These financial troubles seem like they were many years ago. We need to find out what's going on now with his bank accounts. There have been no recent suits in the last decade against him."

"All of these troubles seem like they might play out in his care of patients," Jill remarked. "Either he might try to increase his income by rushing patients through his office or by rushing them through the operating room. Many insurance companies pay based on an episode of care. So you can't take out someone's gall bladder and then see them a bunch of times in your office and get reimbursed for that. Typically, you get one post-operative visit. Any additional visits are out of the physician's own pocket. There are really no public rating systems of surgeon skills and few hospitals have developed a methodology to rank physician skill within a hospital department. There is a real lack of data, public or private."

"So how would a hospital or a patient know if their surgeon is performing well?" puzzled Marie. "It seems archaic that they don't have measurement systems"

Jill observed, "It's not as easy a thing to measure as you would think. It's often the patients themselves that make it difficult to measure. Let's take two forty-five year old males having gall bladder surgery. One of them is normal body weight, gets regular exercise and takes no medication other than a multi-vitamin and an allergy pill. The other is morbidly obese weighing in at 375 pounds, is an insulin dependent diabetic, has poor mobility because of bad circulation in his feet. He has high blood pressure from the weight, diet, and lack of exercise. Which patient do you think is more likely to have complications? Will the surgery take longer because there are more layers of tissue to go through to find the gall bladder? Since the second patient had poor circulation to start with, he develops a blood clot after surgery and a surgery site infection again because of his diabetes and skin quality. Someone has to decide which part of these complications are attributable to the surgeon and what part is attributable to patient characteristics. Then let's talk about support systems around the patient at home. Let's say the first patient goes home to a ranch home surrounded by his family and cared for by his wife who is, oh by the way, a nurse. The second patient goes home to low income housing. He is still not moving around much because of pain from the incision and because he hasn't been moving around much for the past three years. He is seen once a day by a visiting nurse who changes his surgical dressing and does blood sugar testing which finds him high in sugar which is bad for wound healing. The point is that some patients can have social and medical conditions that affect their outcomes regardless of the hospital or surgeon. Statistically calculating those nuances is what can take so long to figure out if you have a quality problem. Sorry about that long-winded explanation, but I think it helps to understand why it may be hard to spot a bad physician."

"Jill, that was a good explanation and we can see why it is hard to quantify poor individual quality. Where does that leave us? What do you tell Nick to look for if he does hack into the quality records?"

"Frankly, I think we ask him to look for any document that has Dr. Lewis's name on it. Without sorting through it myself, I can't begin to direct Nick as to what's important and what is not."

"That could be very time-consuming and what are we going to do with the information that we illegally obtained?" asked Jo.

"What I'm hoping to do with any information that Nick finds and regarding Dr. Lewis is to verify that he should continue to be on the top of our list for suspects. I would hate to be so focused on him that we ignored another clue we should've been following. The second thing I'm hoping is that with the information revealed, if we see a problem we'll know which way to direct someone to obtain it legally. The legal path will be very difficult because physician performance data is protected under special laws called physician privilege. I think this is an instance of we'll decide what to do with the information once we see what it contains."

"That's a fair assessment of where we stand with this case," noted Marie, her face wearing the disappointment. "We have a lot of coincidences, but we're no closer to solving the case then when we heard the sound of the gun ring out in the air on the golf course. I really thought it was going to be much easier than this seems to be."

Jill acknowledged the statement with a nod of her head and began typing on her laptop "I'm going to drop a quick note to Nick and ask him to look for anything with Dr. Lewis's name on it - e-mail, data, event reporting. Then I suspect the detectives will arrive soon and so I think we should agree to avoid the entire surgeon quality discussion with them. I'd like to concentrate on how the employee is doing at the hospital and whether they've got any toxicology tests back on her. In addition we should plan on gathering more information on Dr. Phillips's death. Unfortunately we can't admit to our suspicions of Dr. Lewis to Dr. Phillips's widow so we'll have to be very cautious if they ask her permission to exhume the body."

Angela added another angle, "I think Nick has Dr. Lewis's social security number from the driver's license application so Jo may be able to get some personal financial information."

"Having his social security number gives me considerable ability to look into his financials," agreed Jo. "It's not legal for me to do that but I have to run with the idea that this guy may be our killer and we're looking for evidence and links. When the Detectives Van Bruggin and Haro arrive I would like to question them about what data they have access to through their law enforcement systems. If we can direct them to get some of this data legitimately through their system that allows us to stay clear of prosecution - especially if we are wrong about Dr. Lewis."

They heard the doorbell ring. Jill took a look at the murder board and everything they had up on their screens or lying around. She saw none of their research gained by unauthorized methods in view of anyone casually looking around the room. She signaled to Marie that it was safe to let in the detectives.

Van Bruggin and Haro were looking frayed around the edges. Their clothes were wrinkled, Haro was working on a five o'clock shadow and Van Bruggin had very pale skin reflecting the lack of sun on the skin in the deep winter of Wisconsin rather than the pleasant sixty degree plus days of May. This time, when Marie offered them a drink and cookies, they acquiesced, gulping down diet coke and managing to chew and swallow three cookies so quickly that Jill had to look twice to verify the speed with which they had devoured Marie's cookies.

"How's Helen doing?" asked Jill.

"The hospital has her stabilized," Haro announced. "She has not regained consciousness and they will be putting her through a series of tests over the next twelve hours to determine her brain function. Given that she was blue and breathing poorly when her supervisor arrived, her doctor says she may have sustained some brain damage from the event. She's in the ICU with a police officer guarding her around the clock."

"I think we have to presume that word of her condition has reached Dr. Lewis by now," Angela suggested. "This is a small town and word of a cop guarding a patient for her own protection at a local hospital will have the gossip lines buzzing. If he has done all that we suspect him of, I wonder what his next steps will be."

"That is indeed an interesting question," agreed Haro.

"Do you have him under surveillance?" asked Jill.

"After our conversation at Helen's house, we placed him under light surveillance," noted Van Bruggin. "He has the resources to easily be a flight risk, but I am very uneasy about keeping him under surveillance. We are doing drive-byes of his residence and work locations. We're also monitoring if he tries to depart airports. We can't afford to have him, or really anyone else, discover our surveillance. If he is innocent, we would harm his reputation. On the other hand, if he goes into the hospital, he is impossible to track as he has access to places our officer doesn't and there are too many exit doors. I have asked to be alerted if he goes through airport security or crosses into Canada, so hopefully these actions will stop any flight risk."

Angela repeated her question, "What do you think Dr. Lewis's next actions will be? Personally, my vote would be to try to harm Helen, and beyond that to take care of anyone else at Our Lady who knows something that they shouldn't about Dr. Lewis."

"What do you mean knows something that they shouldn't?" probed Van Bruggin. "What would a random collection of hospital employees know about Dr. Lewis that is a threat to him? Was he having an affair? Is that what he was afraid would get out?"

"Perhaps it is an affair that he wants to keep hidden from his family. Who knows? We don't even know if he is our killer," Jill reminded the two detectives. "All we have is extreme coincidences. We did a legal proceedings search on Dr. Lewis and we found financial distress about twenty years ago as well as some driving under the influence charges in the past five years that were dropped. We're wondering what you can find in your systems regarding his activities. Both wife number one and wife number two seem to come into his marriage with financial assets. Wife number one died about ten years into the marriage. We found no explanation for her death. That is not to say there isn't a good explanation; rather we haven't found any reason in any newspaper articles about her death."

"Before we came over here, I made a call to the office and I have an analyst pulling data on Dr. Lewis. Since you dropped his name on us an hour ago, we're behind compared to you." noted Van Bruggin. "If he is indeed our killer, if he is Dr. Phillips's murderer, and should we prove that he killed his first wife, we'll need to call in additional resources as this case has become huge. These are all "ifs" because we have not proven a single theory yet. This could all be a wild goose chase blinding us from the real killer."

"Yeah, we were worried about the distraction from the real killer as well," Marie agreed. "We talked about that just before you arrived. We noticed a string of financial difficulties about two decades ago. Do your computer systems have more information on legal proceedings? I would have thought that in any financial distress lawsuits that Dr. Lewis would've had to provide some financial information about himself at that time. He's gone through a lot of money and we're wondering why. Is he a gambler? Does he have a drug habit? Does he have an offshore account that he's storing spare money in?"

"Great questions - and I'm not sure we have the answers, yet. I'd like to connect you folks to my team back at the station. We don't have a medical expert connected to the force and there seems to be some connection to medicine that we can neither see nor understand," Haro commented. "We're heading back to the station now; are you available to meet us there in say, an hour?"

The four women looked over at the clock and then at each other. The two detectives watched as the women seemed to be able to read each other's minds. Finally, Marie spoke.

"We are meeting Michelle Easley at the upstairs parlor of Captain's Walk Winery later for wine, and conversation. We haven't had an opportunity to interview her yet. As she is our client, it's been a hole in our investigation. I think she finally got beyond funeral plans and the immediate changes to her life so she can take a moment to sit down and tell her story. We can give you about two hours at your station and then we'll have to leave."

"We interviewed her yesterday and she couldn't point us in any direction to find the killer. Mostly, she must've told us ten times, what a wonderful human being her husband Doug was and how could this happen to him. I hope for the sake of this investigation that you get more out of her. However, if Dr. Lewis is the source of the problem with this case, Michelle Easley likely wouldn't have any knowledge of Dr. Lewis.

"Dr. Quint," Haro continued, "we would also like you to talk to our Lieutenant about the typical process for re-examining the cause of death for Dr. Phillips."

"I would be happy to discuss the process with anyone on your staff or in your district attorney's office if it comes to that. We will be at your office in an hour. I assume the meeting is at police headquarters on Adams Street."

"Yes ma'am and thank you."

Soon the two detectives were leaving and there was a slight expulsion of hot air since the women knew they could now return to not so legal means to collect information about the case. Jill was the first to reach her laptop to see if Nick had found any material for them to look at. She was probably expecting too much from Nick as it had only been about half an hour since she had sent him the request for more hacking.

"Hey there's an e-mail from Nick here. He says 'there are several files for Dr. Lewis. It was easier to hack into as it runs on a separate administrative system. Since there is a lot of medical terminology I don't really understand the content. So I have saved the files and sent them to a cloud storage drive. I think it better if I save materials to an encrypted cloud rather than leave an e-mail trail. I've sent Angela a picture via Snapchat of the password to reach the cloud storage. The picture will disappear forever ten seconds after you open it.'"

"Good thing I have a Snapchat account. This is increasing my anxiety about this case since he's going to extra lengths to encode his data."

"Of course you have a Snapchat account – you are a photographer and it's your business to put new and beautiful pictures out in cyberspace. Let me know what the password is so I can dial into this cloud storage thing. I hope he doesn't get more technical than this because I maxed out on my understanding of the internet."

Soon Angela was sharing over the password with Jill who logged in to the cloud storage drive. She began pulling up files and explaining to the others the content of the file.

"This is Dr. Lewis's credentialing file. Every hospital has a file on every physician. These files are critical to a hospital being licensed. They typically include a driver's license picture of the physician. First and foremost, they need to prove that they are who they say they are. Next you usually find copies of their medical degree, their state license, and their specialty board certification. The medical staff and then the hospital board of directors are required to approve each physician who is given privileges to care for patients at a hospital. The medical staff department maintains these files which is no easy feat. Most hospitals have at a minimum three-hundred to five hundred physicians that go through this process every three years. There is also probably a hundred or so other positions like physician assistants, certified nurse anesthetists, midwives, or nurse practitioners that must also be privileged. So you have to stay on top of these files, making sure those licenses and specialty boards are kept current by the physician.

"This next document outlines what exactly the privileges are. For example, if you are an urology surgeon you will have to be granted the privilege to operate a robot in the operating room. Each physician by specialty has core privileges that likely every surgeon has – so again going to the urologist, it's a core privilege to perform removal of the prostate gland. Every surgeon is expected to not only have done this surgery in the residency but to have done a certain quantity of these surgeries in residency. If they want to do this surgery with a robot then that is a separate privilege.

"The next document is about ongoing education. Different specialties and different accreditations require certain amounts of ongoing education. For example, a trauma surgeon may be required to take twenty hours of intensive care education for the critically injured trauma patient training every three years. Then there are routine certifications like advanced cardiac life support.

"At the time of re-credentialing, the hospital typically checks with the state medical board and the national practitioner database to see if their license has been restricted or if they've had malpractice claims settled against them. These can be red flags. Not always, but they can be.

"So, Dr. Lewis took his general surgery boards at a time when that certification was lifelong. So he is grandfathered-in as newer regulations require recertification every five to ten years depending on the specialty. What this file tells us is he is allowed to do the full range of general surgery services. Within general surgery in the past decade, breast cancer surgery and colo-rectal surgery have become subspecialties of general surgery. The hospital has been tracking the number of the different types of surgery that Dr. Lewis has performed. In looking at this document you can see in the past year that he's done fifty removals of the appendix, twenty breast cancer surgeries, sixty hernias, ninety gallbladder surgeries, and fifteen surgeries for colon cancer. The hospital likely has a minimum required number of each of these surgeries for a surgeon to retain the privilege. Certainly, you would worry about the quality of the surgeon who may only do one colon cancer surgery a quarter."

"Okay this is really complicated," Marie declared. "However, I must say I am impressed with the regulations that require this extensive physician training documentation. I feel more protected as a patient. Certainly when my sister had gallbladder surgery last year not one of us thought to ask how many gallbladder surgeries the physician had performed in the last year. Where are the alarm bells for us in this documentation? Is it that national practitioner database with reports of lawsuits?"

Jill had paused to sip some ice water after her lengthy explanation of a physician credentialing file. With a final sip she continued, "The national practitioner database contains settled lawsuits and lawsuits in process. The settlement of a malpractice case often assigns responsibility between different parties that might have caused or cared for the patient. Maybe it's the surgeon, a bedside nurse, a pathologist analyzing the specimen, a radiologist reading an x-ray. Most errors result from more than one person. So even though a person is named in a malpractice case you have to look at the details to know if it's a problem. Typically you have a physician from the same specialty read the details of the settlement and discuss with other medical staff members in a meeting concerning individual blame versus a full range of risk factors. The trouble with medical malpractice cases is that it takes several years to settle. So it's not necessarily a very timely assessment of physician skill. The other trouble with lawsuits is mistakes are made every day in the healthcare setting and not all of them end up in court. It is often just the tip of the iceberg. There are lots of journal articles about how charisma and bedside manner absolutely reduce the filing of lawsuits.

"Dr. Lewis has no reportable events. He has no admonishments from the state medical board. His license and required continuing education are up to date. He appears to be a physician in good standing. There should be more information about his performance in his record. These are reportable complications that a hospital is required to track. Included in this list of complications are: retained foreign objects, antibiotics started and ended on time, and unexpected perforations requiring repair or return to the operating room. We don't have that data yet from Nick."

"What's a retained foreign object?" asked Angela. "That sounds really awful and gross. Like you sewed the person up over some big metal thing like a scalpel or pliers or a saw."

Jill answered, "It's rare that it's something like what you just named. Most often, it is a sponge that is the retained foreign object. Before you imagine the sponge at your kitchen sink being left in your body; it's often something much smaller. The term sponge refers to a two inch by two inch piece of gauze - perhaps the same size as has been placed on your arm after blood has been withdrawn. Sponges are used to soak up blood in the surgical space and because they're covered in blood, they often fit right in with the appearance of tissue. For the past one or two decades hospitals have required sponge counts at the end of surgery to make sure they got them all out. Sometime in the last decade, they've added radiopaque qualities to the sponge so that you can easily see it on x-ray in the operating room. I believe it's still the number one reported complication in the United States."

"So tell us about perforations," Marie requested. "Exactly what gets perforated and why does it matter?"

"Perforations occur for a variety of reasons. You can lose track of where you are inside the body because you're operating in a small bloody space. Some perforations are small and easily repaired and inconsequential. Other perforations cause massive bleeding or they may leak stuff from one organ to another. Since the intestines are so dirty if you puncture them then that dirt or bacteria gets out and causes infection. So bleeding and infection are the primary reasons a hospital tracks perforations."

Angela was really starting to look squeamish, "Has that complication ever killed someone? Like could you accidentally puncture the heart?"

"I've never had someone on my table for an autopsy from a perforation, but it does happen occasionally. Not the heart puncture, but just deadly consequences from a perforation."

Jo pronounced, "You've made us afraid to ever have surgery."

"Sorry about that. While some of these complications sound really bad, they often are not, resulting in no additional treatment whatsoever. You're safe having surgery in a hospital but it wouldn't hurt you to ask the surgeon how many of the type of surgery that you are about to have he or she has done in the past year."

"So we don't have any report on complications from Nick yet," Angela noted. "Are you sure that we'll find that data in these files?"

"No I'm not sure. Every hospital operates differently. I'm just hopeful. Shall we gather up our laptops and head to police headquarters?"

Soon they were all out in the car with Marie driving them to police headquarters.

CHAPTER 13

$\mathcal{J}$ ill had been in more police stations in her role as a consulting forensic pathologist then as someone who worked for the state crime lab. Marie and Angela had joined her here the previous day, but Jo had not been inside before. The Green Bay Police Department, in Jill's experience, reflected more of a small town feeling. In her mind that was a good thing since Angela, Marie, and Jo had known few if any criminals in their life. It reduced the distraction to their murder case if they did not have to walk through a group of handcuffed thugs on the way to a meeting room.

They were soon directed to the Detective Division. Detectives Haro and Van Bruggin were with a group of officers and, they guessed, crime scene investigators. Marie and Jo had their computers with them, but they left them turned off and stored in the shoulder bags. The two detectives had everyone take a seat and introductions were performed.

"I'd like to start with a summary of where we are with this case so that we're all on the same page," Van Bruggin remarked. "From there, I would like Dr. Quint and her team to share what they have researched in regards to this case. I feel as though they are chasing some long-shots here, but given my experience in the role of detective, I sense there is substance to those theories. Let's start with my team first. Please summarize all evidence that we have found both on the golf course and at Helen's house. Be sure to specify whether the results are back, and if they're not, when they're expected back."

One by one, the detective team described their evidence, as well as the theories they were pursuing in regards to the results of that evidence. It was pretty much what Jill expected with a few caveats. They had confirmed the bullet caliber for Doug's death. The door knobs at Helen's house were wiped clean. It was a clue that would connect Helen's unconsciousness to an intruder in the house. A person about to commit suicide does not go around and wipe all the door knobs clean of fingerprints.

There were no findings in the autopsy that presented any surprise to Jill. Dr. Easley died from a bullet shot to the brain and she was pretty certain she would have arrived at the same cause of death. In the case of Helen, the initial toxicology screens were completed and Helen had no illicit drug or alcohol in her blood-stream. She also lacked several prescription drugs rumored on the internet to be great suicide drugs. There were a few drug tests outstanding as well as an analysis of her stomach contents.

The crime scene techs had also collected a lot of evidence from Helen's house. While they had found the door knobs to be wiped clean, there were fingerprints elsewhere in the house that they were analyzing. They had also done swabs of glassware and items in the garbage looking for something that shouldn't have been there. They debated whether to use goggles to examine her skin for puncture wounds, but thanks to the great emergency care that she had received, she was full of puncture wounds for IVs and blood draws. In summary, they seem to have no new clues amongst the physical evidence found at both scenes.

Next they discussed who they had researched as far as suspects. Using a variety of their computer systems sources, they were able to verify Michelle's alibi at the time of the shooting. Those sources also provided data on her interior design firm and there were no red flags there. From there they moved on to Doug's anesthesia firm and again the firm seemed to be financially sound.

Jo took the opportunity to speak up, "Would you mind sharing those documents with me? I'm a CPA and I am usually really quick at analyzing documents like tax returns."

The law enforcement team looked nonplussed. It was simply a question that had never been asked of them before. They looked at each other and then at the two detectives for an answer.

Finally, Van Bruggin spoke, "you can look at the document here but it can't leave the station. Please sign this confidentiality agreement and this is a reminder that all documents that you view are confidential. I would like each member of the Dr. Quint team to verbally affirm that nothing we share with you here will be shared by you outside of the station."

He then made eye contact with Jill, Jo, Marie, Angela and each individually stated they understood the confidentiality and graveness of the information that was about to be shared with them and they promised not to share the contents with anyone outside the station.

Shortly thereafter, Jo was looking at the tax records of Michelle Easley. In about a three minute time span, she scanned the document with its attachments and agreed with the police that everything was in order. She took a little longer with Doug's anesthesia firm's records. Again while nothing looked incorrect or suspect, she was curious to view the range of salaries of the firm's partners. If there was great disparity between the partners and it couldn't be traced to hours worked, then they had a potential motive for murder. When she calculated the hours worked by each partner, the variance was less than five percent.

"Detective Van Bruggin, I agree with your team that there is nothing suspect in Michelle's tax filings. Furthermore, based on the hours that each partner worked, the variation between anesthesiologists is less than five percent or about twenty-five thousand dollars. With these large salaries, I can't imagine that the five percent is cause for murder."

"Moving on to the new suspect, Dr. Bradley Lewis, we see red flags everywhere we look. Let's go through some of the highlights now."

With that introduction, one of the crime scene investigators began a discussion on what their research had yielded in regards to Dr. Lewis. Much of it was a repeat of what Jill and her team had noted earlier.

"Do we know where Dr. Lewis spends his money?" asked Marie. "Given the financial problems he has had to contend with in the legal system, and given that his salary as a general surgeon should be quite adequate to keep one's head above water; we wondered where he was spending money."

"Yeah we noted that in our research," said the investigator, "but we haven't figured out a source yet either. We're checking with the narcotics division to see if he has any reputation in the community and then we are examining his credit card records to see if that throws us any clues."

"Do you have his tax return?" asked Jo.

"We have the most recent return but the State is also giving us his returns going back to the failure to pay for his engagement ring small claims suit. It will take them an additional twenty-four hours to get those returns for us. We also have the court documents filed with the county takeover of property for delinquent taxes and the small claims case around the engagement ring."

With a non-verbal question eliciting a nod from his supervisor, he passed the documents over to Jo. Silence reigned in the room while she quickly skimmed the documents. She held out one piece of paper and said, "this is the detail provided by Dr. Lewis as to why he couldn't pay for the ring. He indicated two-hundred-thousand in medical school student debt. That seems weird. Medical School was much cheaper in the early 1980s when he would have graduated. It's also suspicious because of the trust the first wife set up. I would love to talk to the attorney or the kids to understand why they think the first Mrs. Lewis wrote the trust. Do they live in this area? Were the kids incorporated into the second marriage? Since they were likely no more than ten years old at the time of her death, they should have been a part of the new household."

"Those are excellent questions and we'll see if we can answers by the time you finish your description of what information you found for Dr. Lewis," directed Van Bruggin.

"Thanks for that lead-in," replied Jill. "As I mentioned earlier to the two detectives, we started by looking at the leadership positions that Dr. Easley occupied. Leadership positions can have an impact on either power or money in any setting. Jo looked at his Anesthesia practice, but all the physician partners were compensated equally once you calculated their hours worked. Next we moved on to leadership roles at Our Lady. That was when Marie discovered that he was the interim chair of surgery after the previous chair had died on a snowmobile trip. I think the odds are small that two physicians holding the same title should die so close in time to each other when it's not related to a disease like cancer. It was then that we looked into the details of that snowmobile accident.

"The four of us are not snowmobilers, but living in this part of the world you hear about snowmobile deaths and injuries every winter. I never paid attention as to where those deaths were or how they were handled by the local coroner. Dr. Phillips could have died just as was described in the coroner's report, and it probably made perfect sense to many people at the time it occurred. However, an autopsy should have been done to confirm the findings of a heart attack. You would have seen heart muscle death related to a blockage of the artery. I suspect that likely it would have been done except for some influence by Dr. Lewis. He was a powerful witness and a physician and that might have been all the evidence the local coroner needed to complete the death certificate. Why leave a huge scar on a young man's body if you have confirmation from a physician on the cause of death? I think we need to exhume the body of Dr. Phillips, but I don't know what we could tell his widow is a reason for the request without pointing the finger at Dr. Lewis. If he should be innocent, we will have decimated his reputation for the rest of his life.

"My team agreed that if he murdered both physicians, he had to have had a reason. Both physicians would have had minor impacts on his earnings, unless they were threatening his privileges at the hospital."

"Dr. Quint, what do you mean by threatening his privileges at the hospital?" asked a puzzled Detective Haro. "What are privileges and how do they affect income?"

"Every physician in every hospital in America has been granted privileges to practice medicine by a group of their peers. Generally, a decision to grant privileges is based on education, training, and past experience. So for example, an orthopedic surgeon would never be granted the privilege to deliver babies at a hospital. They simply are not qualified to perform that procedure. It's a way for hospitals to control which physicians do what procedures with the desired outcome of better quality for patients. Likewise, a physician can lose a privilege because they are doing a low-volume of that procedure or because they're experiencing higher than expected complications. So, again as an example, let's say you have a physician delivering less than a baby each month and you have other physicians delivering a baby daily. You would likely pressure that low-volume physician to give up their privilege to deliver babies. Does my explanation make sense?"

"It sounds very complicated, but where is the money or power impact?" asked Van Bruggin.

"The fewer privileges you have, the less opportunity you have to earn income by caring for hospitalized patients. With some physicians a single procedure might be responsible for a quarter of their income. That is the money impact. The power side comes from one group of physicians taking away the privileges of another physician. If they don't voluntarily give up privileges, then the individual physician does not see the problem. If they can't see their own problem, then they likely view the reduction of privileges as a power move."

Van Bruggin agreed, "So how do we find out if Dr. Lewis lost or was scheduled to lose privileges? Who at the hospital do we talk to find out about such actions?"

"The information is protected under the law, and I would guess that we lack evidence for a judge to issue a subpoena to allow you to review the records. There is a database called the National Practitioner Database and hospitals are required to report the removal of privileges to that organization. The data is operated by the federal government so again it will take a court order to gain access to the system."

"So you're telling me the motive for murder may be out there, but because of privacy rules I can't get to the data?"

"Basically, yes. Also, keep in mind that this is a very slow process. It can take months to spot a trend and months more for the peer process to occur and appeals be handled. I am aware that the removal process from start to end can take two years in some cases because attorneys get involved helping the physician fight for their rights. So if this is a recent problem, there won't be much of a paper trail at the hospital.

"As for your second question, who knows at the hospital? Most of the time, these actions are kept as quiet as possible because you don't want to impact a physician's reputation unnecessarily. Just because they lose the privilege to do one procedure does not mean that their entire body of work is bad. A physician may also choose to give up certain privileges and that avoids some reporting. The records are kept in a department called Medical Staff

Services and perhaps their CEO or Chief Medical Officer may be aware."

"So these problems are always handled in such a confidential manner that few people know and there is little to no paper trail for us to follow and examine," Haro summarized. "So how do we go about approaching this angle? I understand your explanation of what occurs in a hospital, but we are no farther ahead as to how to verify if Dr. Lewis had problems and was eliminating the physicians that were trying to take action with him."

"We don't have an answer for how to find evidence of Dr. Lewis's problems yet. We're exploring a few avenues and if anything turns up, we will share with you," Jill noted. "We need to leave soon to get to our meeting with Dr. Easley's widow, Michelle. One of the questions we are discussing with her was anything said in passing by her husband concerning problems at work."

"We already asked her those questions when we initially interviewed her," Haro stated.

"We assumed you did, but you know through your vast years of experience that people remember different things at different times," Angela pointed out. "You spoke with her on the day of her husband's death, hours after she was notified. I think most people in that position don't have their best thinking on. I am hopeful that in the casual setting of a winery and with the aid of a glass of wine that we might learn some new information from Michele. I am really quite good at drawing information out of people. This comes from years of trying to make people comfortable on the other side of the camera lens."

The detectives sighed, but really had no ideas on how to proceed at that point in time. Maybe a few hours away from the case spending time with their families might stimulate an idea on how to move this case forward. The women started packing up their belongings getting ready to leave when Marie paused to ask, "Any word on how Helen is doing?"

"The hospital says that her vital signs are stable, but she was still unconscious."

The women piled into Marie's car and decided to sit there for a moment composing questions for the upcoming interview with Michelle.

"Anyone have any ideas on how to ask Michelle if her husband had any problems with Dr. Lewis without mentioning his name?" asked Marie. "That seems to be the crux of what we need to question her about."

"As usual, I would like to handle the majority of the interview.," Angela said. "However, I think in regards to the question about problems with Dr. Lewis, we would all do well to take a combination tag team and exploratory tone to our questioning. We can do that by having a puzzling inflection in our voices. So I will ask her the question of 'what kind of concerns was your husband having with his coworkers'. That would be a great time for Jo to add 'were any of the physicians concerned about dropping income as it's something I hear occasionally from the physicians I deal with'; and Jill, once Michele answers, you can tag onto changing insurance reimbursements'. Let's play this by ear and see where the strategy gets us. She may really have no knowledge of anyone upset with her husband."

Marie started up the car and they drove the few short blocks to the Captains Walk Winery to meet with Michelle. It was easily a distance they could've walked, but for some reason they didn't want to advertise that they had come from a meeting with the Green Bay police.

CHAPTER 14

*W*alking into the winery, they could see that they had arrived before Michelle. A sign stood at the base of the stairs announcing a private party for the upstairs parlor. They checked in with the tasting room attendant and each selected a glass of wine before venturing upstairs.

The parlor contained a sofa and three wing chairs. Jo and Marie occupied the sofa, while Angela and Jill took the chairs. Angela would do most of the interviewing and would be directly facing Michelle. If she arrived without wine, Jill would obtain some from the attendant. Marie had removed a box of Kleenex from her car and it rested on the coffee table in front of the sofa. The players were in position and the stage was now set, they just needed the tragic widow to arrive for the show to begin.

About five minutes past the agreed upon meeting time they heard Michelle approach. After introductions were made, Jill left to get Michelle a glass of Chardonnay. Soon they had all resumed their seats and the interview got underway. Michelle was anxious to return home to her two daughters who were greatly in need of comfort over their father's death.

"Michelle, we appreciate you taking some time to meet with us here during what has to be a very difficult time for you and your family," murmured Angela as she started off the interview. "As you may know there is not a lot of evidence that would lead law enforcement to your husband's killer. We are equally puzzled, because this seems like almost the perfect murder there is such a lack of clues. Tell me about Doug's mood prior to the golf outing. Was he his usual self? Was he happy and looking forward to the outing? Did he seem secretly worried about something? Describe his state of mind for us, please."

"The police asked me that same question and I had a hard time answering them at the time because I couldn't think much beyond the fact that Doug was dead. However I've had some time to think about the questions that the police asked me and perhaps I have a few more answers. Doug had been looking forward to the charitable golf outing all weekend. I don't play golf, but he loves the game casually. He had three friends that were making up his foursome and he was looking forward to chatting with them about the upcoming NFL draft. I don't pay much attention to football and so I'm not a good conversant about the Packers. So I would say his overall attitude was simply one of anticipation of a good day. Certainly, I saw no worry or thought on his part that it would be the last day of his life."

The last sentence reduced Michelle to tears and after passing the Kleenex box to her, they just waited in comfortable silence until she seemed ready to move on.

"I don't know that much about Doug or you, Michelle. I had a great time taking your portraits two years ago and doing the photography for your portfolio, but our paths just don't cross that much. Can you tell me about Doug and where he spent his time? Obviously the hospital was a priority and your daughters and yourself. Where else did he spend time? Did he have hobbies or was he active in any civic organizations, or perhaps our church,? Tell me about him."

"He worked as an anesthesiologist I would guess about thirty to forty hours a week. By that I mean he was in the operating room caring for patients and essentially unreachable. Beyond those hours, he spent additional time in a variety of administrative duties as far as documentation of what he did for patients and what was going on with the entire anesthesia group. Hospital committees and recruiting would also consume another ten to fifteen hours each week. I would say he spent the bulk of his waking hours doing something related to his patients or for the hospital. He served on a variety of committees that he would tell me about in passing but I couldn't at this time remember the name of any of them. I would listen but at times he would break into speaking in acronyms that I'm sure all healthcare people speak in but I didn't always interrupt him and ask him what a particular term meant.

"He was pretty good at attending activities that the girls were involved in and he even coached their soccer team one year. He was always there for parent-teacher conferences and he was just an ever present dad in their lives.

"He didn't have much spare time after the family and work. Like I said, he liked casual golf, played a little tennis, and had a group of guys that he liked to hang out with to watch or attend Packer games."

"So did he have any worries about his leisure activities? His golf game or his tennis game?"

"No he wasn't the type to worry about his score; he just wanted to enjoy the time spent in those leisure activities."

"Was he worried about your daughters? They have hit the teenage years so were you or Doug worried about any grief your daughters were giving you or perhaps their friends?"

"No worries about our daughters; we've always been blessed with great kids."

"So let's talk about work. When he came home at night, did he talk much about his work?"

"Not really. His operating room cases were, for the most part, steady and routine; occasionally he would mention that he had had a bad case, but it was more of an apology for a certain grave affect to his personality. He would recover in a day or so and be back to his normal happy self. I think it was his way of grieving for patients."

"How about his partners in the anesthesia group? Any concerns with them?"

"The anesthesia group is doing well and they had a really good group of guys that got along well. It wasn't always that way. And probably the first five years that they were together as a group they had turnover as doctors did not fit in with the group. For the past ten years, this group liked and respected each other. And I say 'guys' because that was how Doug referred to them, but there were both male and female anesthesiologists in the group."

"Doug held many leadership positions at Our Lady of Guadalupe. Did he enjoy that work? What did he think of always being tapped for various roles? Did he like everyone that he worked with? Did he come home and tell you any stories about his roles? I know I am throwing a lot of questions at you but it is just to get you thinking about Doug's feelings or impressions from different angles."

"Angela, I appreciate you asking the question several different ways. As you can imagine, my brains are scrambled at the moment from grief and lack of sleep and stress and my mind needs those different angles to help me think back to what Doug may have said."

"Exactly!"

"Back to your questions, I don't recall Doug being mad at a particular person or action - that wasn't his nature. He liked to look at data and discuss anything he was truly concerned about. Sometimes he would drive you nuts because he was so patient and could wear you down with facts concerning something that you were passionate about." With a small smile, Michelle added, "he even drove me nuts when we would have an argument about the kids, our friends, or the color of paint on the wall. He was willing to hang in there and keep a discussion going long after you cared about the answer."

Marie chipped in, "I know exactly what you're talking about; I have a few friends that drove me nuts with those kind of discussions until I learned how to avoid getting in that situation.'."

"Maybe it's a guy thing," Jo proffered the explanation. "I've met several people that behave like that in the workplace and it drives me nuts, but I admire them for the strength of their argument."

Finally! Angela heard her friends chip in as she was beginning to be worn out by all the questions she was trying to think of to keep the interview going.

Jill's friends looked at her obviously expecting her two cents worth about the conversation so she finally spoke up, "don't look at me. I have the love of my life in Nathan," referring to her boyfriend back in California. "He's pretty damn perfect so I don't know what you are talking about!"

Angela looked over at Michelle and said "I do have to admit that Jill's boyfriend, Nathan, is pretty darn perfect. Michelle, do you think that very doggedness in an argument would be enough to make someone homicidal towards Doug? Was it that annoying a trait, that you observed others changing their behavior around Doug in order to avoid the endless discussion?"

"It could be a very annoying trait. I had learned in many years of marriage how to avoid getting in such a discussion with Doug. I often knew his opinion on many issues, so if I knew the issue to be one that we were polar opposites on, I would refuse to discuss it with him. I could be just as stubborn as he was though I am sure he thought I was irrationally stubborn; while he was not stubborn at all and merely pointing out facts to the uninformed. As to whether that put people off, it did sometimes. He had a close circle of friends and I was never sure if they had no arguments because they had adopted my strategy, or if they were close friends because they agreed on everything."

Angela shifted her position and lowered her voice to say, "Pardon us for asking, but we have some personal questions for you as well. How were your finances? Did you have any worries as to how to pay the bills?"

"Oh, we had no worries there. Doug earned a good income, and my interior design business is just icing on the cake. The girls' college accounts are well funded and our mortgage was paid off."

Marie built on Angela's question, "How about your marriage, was it going well? Did you have a sense that Doug was happy as well? Believe me I know that just because you have no financial problems, doesn't mean that your marriage is still solid."

Michelle was looking taken-aback by the questions now. She had also adjusted her position in the chair and her body language was starting to look closed off. She had her arms across her chest and was no longer sitting in a relaxed position.

"Our marriage was great. When you have been married for over fifteen years, you settle in a rhythm that works to keep it together and that was where we were."

Jill thought 'not exactly a golden endorsement for the state of marriage', but she could think of no follow-up questions.

Fortunately Jo had a question, "Michelle, did you and Doug have any big plans for the coming years? Like buy a second home, adopt a child, move to a different city?"

Michelle appeared to need to give the questions some thought. She seemed to be shifting through memories in her head, and then said, "No".

Angela could sense the interview was drawing to a close and therefore, asked her final question."Michelle, can you think of any reason that someone might want to kill Doug?"

"I have been racking my brains since I received notice of his death and I can't think of any reason. I have thought back over conversations and he wasn't worried about any one person and so I can't think of any reason that someone would want him dead."

The last words ended on a sob, and then there were fresh tracks of tears running down her face.

Angela looked at her friends and saw silent agreement that the interview was finished. She then got up and went over to Michelle's chair to place a hand on her shoulder. She looked at her wine glass and noted it was empty and asked, "Michelle, would you like a refill on your glass of wine?"

Michelle shook her head and said, "No thanks I need to get back home to the girls."

She stood and exchanged hugs with Angela, shook hands with Jill, Jo, and Marie and left the parlor.

"I really like this upstairs parlor," Jill declared. "Why don't we get a refill on our wine and sit here and discuss the case for a while?"

There was quick agreement with that idea and they were all soon downstairs selecting their wine and briefly chatting with the tasting room attendant. It was a nice break as it had been an emotional discussion for Angela as a distant friend of Michelle's. The brief discussion with the attendant had served to cleanse their minds momentarily of the cloud of grief that had descended upon them while in Michelle's presence.

CHAPTER 15

They returned to the parlor and settled into the comfortable chairs and sofa.

"What did everyone think of our conversation with Michelle? Were there any new nuggets or leads to follow?" asked Jill.

Jo and Marie were clearly interested in hearing what Angela had to say first. Angela reminded Jill of someone tasting a new wine. She seemed to be thinking about the tastes of the interview much like she would search for tannins, berries, and other fruit flavors in a new wine.

"She answered all of our questions with very appropriate responses. I don't think she was hiding anything or lying in her responses. As to new clues, it seems like we found our first disagreeable personality trait in his refusing to let an argument go and wanting to shower someone with facts until they changed their opinion."

"But? I can hear a *but* in your voice."

"Something was off. Did anyone else have a sense that she was not in love with her husband? She liked and respected him, but she didn't love him. Who knows, maybe I am picking up a totally wrong vibe, or maybe I just don't know her well enough."

Jo went next in her appraisal, "I agree with you, Angela, I got the same sense as you. I don't think she was passionate about her relationship with Doug. As for Doug's personality trait, I've known other people with that same trait and well, it's not enough to make you homicidal. This will sound like a strange comment but it felt to me that the emotion she was feeling towards Doug was much like you might feel toward the loss of a longtime friend, but not the loss of someone you were deeply in love with. As to new clues, I didn't pick any up other than perhaps someone could have had reason to be jealous of their financial security. But frankly, if you feel that way, there will be a lot of people to kill in this town for that motive."

Marie added, "I agree with what Angela and Jo said about Michelle. I can't think of anything else to add. How about you, Jill? What did you hear that might possibly be a new clue?"

"I think the same thing that is concerning the three of you, concerns me. The emotion didn't seem right coming from Michelle, but who am I to judge? I've never had a husband murdered, then again I've never had a husband."

They all smiled at that comment and sat in silence a while longer sipping their wine.

Jill decided to put words to the white elephant in the room.

"Do you think that Michelle had anything to do with Doug's murder?"

There it was, the unspoken question that each of them was asking herself. Again silence reigned while each of them thought about the answer.

"Might be another one of those long-shot clues," said Maria slowly as if exploring the words. "She clearly was not the shooter. She's not tall enough and she has a solid alibi at the time of his murder. So did she conspire with the killer because she wanted him dead, or is there a second person out there that paired up with her to want Doug dead?"

"If we assume she had a role," Jo speculated, "what would we do differently in this investigation? By the way, if she had a role, why did she hire us?"

"Did you notice that although you said there were not many clues in the investigation, she showed no curiosity as to the few clues that we have," Jill noted. "I don't think we told her about the satellite pictures we have of the killer. I wonder if the police told her about the pictures? As to why she hired us if she has a role in this killing? Either she thinks we're lousy detectives or that she is smarter than us and all evidence is covered up; or if she has a partner in this crime, the partner advised her to hire us so he or she could stay close to the investigation.

"As to your question on what we would do differently, I guess we should ask ourselves why would Michelle be interested in having her husband dead? Two common reasons that wives kill husbands are for money, like insurance policies, or in self-defense as a victim of abuse. Neither of those reasons seemed to be the basis for this case. I might suggest another reason - is she having an affair? If that's the case, then we need to ask ourselves, why couldn't she just continue to have the affair; why did she need him completely out of the picture?"

The tasting room attendant walked up the steps into the parlor and announced they would be closing in ten minutes. The announcement caused them to examine the contents in their glasses and increase the speed with which they were imbibing; no one wanted to let a drop of wine go to waste. A short time later they were outside and piling into Marie's car.

"Let's call it a night," Jo suggested. "We can re-group tomorrow at Marie's for breakfast. I'll stop at Not by Bread Alone and grab some breakfast stuff."

"Jo, you know I love breakfast and I know that you're not a morning person," Jill said envisioning her breakfast arriving at lunch. "We're running out of time to solve this mystery. Do you think you could start the day early and be at Marie's house by eight?

Jo swallowed hard, straightened her shoulders then said 'yes'.

Jill still doubted that Jo would be on time but at least she wouldn't wait hours for her breakfast, which was her favorite meal of the day.

They reached Marie's house and Jo went to her car while Jill and Angela headed to Angela's car. Jill often stayed with Angela when she was in-town visiting. Jill was glad she was staying at Angela's house as she wanted to see if they had any new information from Nick. She would really like to understand what if any was the problem with Dr. Lewis medical staff file.

Soon after arriving at Angela's house, they had both changed into their pajamas and were contemplating contacting Nick. Really, it was 3am in Amsterdam and it was outright rude to call Nick without an invitation.

So they didn't. He deserved to sleep since he was hacking illegally on behalf of their case.

CHAPTER 16

The next morning they all met at Marie's house early. There was a sense of urgency to get to the bottom of the case as Jill was scheduled to leave for California late the next day, and Angela, Jo, and Marie were returning to work the following day.

"Let's look at the e-mail from Nick first. It's midday in Amsterdam so if we need more research from him, we've got time to call him," Jill noted. "I'm really curious to see if he found anything. We have a lot of disparate clues, but nothing that connects Dr. Lewis in any way to the actual murder of Doug Easley."

Angela opened the e-mail from Nick chuckled to herself that his message and begin downloading his attachments. He had labeled them simply as attachments one through six so Jill had no clue as to what each attachment contained.

"Oh well we'll start at the beginning with attachment one," Jill observed. "It looks like it's a fairly large file."

Jill took a few moments to examine the contents of the file before determining it was of little use.

"This is a record of routine tests Dr. Lewis has to have done as a member of the medical staff. He's tested negative to tuberculosis for a long time, he's been a regular at getting a flu shot, and he has a positive titer for rubella which means he had measles some time in his life. What this all says is that he's cooperative with hospital regulations and policies. In the medical staff rules and regulations, they called it good citizenship. Let's move on to attachment two.

"This attachment is more interesting. It's a report on the use of antibiotics by his patients."

"Why is that interesting?" Marie asked. "Why the focus on antibiotics?"

"Good questions. So I explained a little earlier how difficult it is to measure quality. Despite it being difficult, there are a few measures that are collected by the federal government and reported on by individual hospitals. One of those measures concerns the use of antibiotics. They are used to prevent infection and there are many professional organizations that recommend the use of antibiotics prior to surgery. That makes sense, doesn't it? Infection is the number one complication that doctors worry about with surgery patients. They discovered through research that in order for antibiotics to do their best to fight infection, they need to be started one hour prior to the first slice of the scalpel. The reason for the hour is they want the antibiotic to reach all the tissue of the body. You could start antibiotics two hours before cut time and that is fine, it's just the patient is sitting there an extra hour in the pre-op area. So what happens if there are problems and for some reason antibiotics are started just as the patient is being wheeled into the operating room – so maybe fifteen minutes before cut time? It's an inexact science. Some patient's tissues will be saturated with antibiotics in fifteen minutes and they're fine. When antibiotics actually get started are rarely under the surgeon's direct control. Part of it has to do with when the patient arrives at the hospital for surgery and sometimes it's about when in the flow of things to be done for the patient, that nurses hang the antibiotics to start the infusion. So the measurement is really a reflection of operating room efficiency not of surgeon skill.

"There's a second measurement in regards to antibiotics and it's again attributed to individual physicians but it can also be about hospital process. You want to stop the use of antibiotics twenty-four hours after surgery because the incision is no longer open and overuse of antibiotics creates antibiotic resistance. The sticky problem is actually the measurement of the twenty-four hours. Pharmacy systems are highly computerized and medications are administered via barcode system so if the last dosage was supposed to be at ten in the morning and it was actually given at 10:15 then that's considered a failure to meet the standard of discontinuing antibiotics at the twenty-four hour mark. But again in the scheme of things, is this poor quality for the patients? No. Again it's not a reflection of the surgeon's activity in the hospital; it's more likely nurses or pharmacists that are responsible for missing the deadline by fifteen minutes.

"Let's return to this report. The good news is that for both measurements of starting and ending antibiotics that the numbers have improved for Dr. Lewis's patients over the past five years. So I would have no concerns with Dr. Lewis on this quality metric."

"If I understand what you said about Dr. Lewis, there is nothing here so far to set him off with murderous intent," Jo remarked.

"Not yet, let's move on to attachment three," Jill agreed.

She opened it and quickly put it aside. "That was his cardio-pulmonary resuscitation training records."

After opening attachment four, and studying it for a moment Jill said, "This might be connected to something else. This is the annual volume of procedures that he does at the hospital which we discussed earlier, but this report has five years of data displayed. If I look back at prior years he was doing almost twice as many colon cancer cases two years ago. I wonder what caused the decline and who got the volume of his cases? Those cancer cases would have been his best reimbursed cases between the surgery itself and the aftercare in the hospital."

"I'll take a look at the information on all the hospitals in town and see if a new colorectal surgeon arrived and snagged his volume," Jo remarked. "If not that, then his own fellow surgeons likely picked up his volume. I would only expect colon cancer cases to increase as more people get tested for detection and people live longer. A century ago, the average lifespan was fifty-two; people didn't live long enough to develop cancer."

"Great, thanks. Okay let's take a look at the next attachment. Hmm… this is information on surgical cases. Looks like a standard format report, not a special report for Dr. Lewis. Let's see what they track here - they compare his number to a group average for other surgeons performing the same surgery. Okay, let's see if he has problems anywhere," Jill noted as she skimmed down the page of statistics.

"This is not an area that I know a lot of about. I did a surgical rotation while in medical school and that might be the extent of my knowledge. None of my medical school friends that I have kept in touch with: specialized in surgery. In skimming down the page, I can see that he's out of alignment with his peers for many of the metrics they measure. Give me a moment to figure out if that is good or bad."

Jill studied the numbers. They tracked his performance for his five most performed surgical procedures. The length of time patients were under anesthesia was on average twenty-five minutes longer than those same surgeries performed by his peers. The list did not say what the expected length of time was for each case type, but an extra twenty-five minutes was way out of alignment. It also exposed the patient to the risks of anesthesia for an extra amount of time.

The next statistic looked at his on-time starts for which he had a first case of the day scheduled. Again he performed unfavorably compared to his peers, being nearly twenty minutes late to start each case. Any inherent delays caused by the operating room staff should have hit all of his peers and Dr. Lewis equally. Jill wondered what the problem was that would cause a twenty minute delay.

A third statistic looked at the costs of the instrument pack that he needed to complete a specific surgery. Physicians typically had preference cards which listed how many instruments like retractors, sutures, trocars, and forceps that a physician needed to complete a surgery. The trays were either labeled as standard appendectomy tray or Dr. Lewis's appendectomy tray. Again the number of instruments that he seemed to need in his kit was larger than that of his peers. Jill understood surgical instrument kits as she had used them in the pathology lab. In her experience the use of additional instruments was usually due to an out-of-date preference card. Occasionally, a surgeon will 'overstock' their tray because at some time in their career they were missing a particular instrument when they needed it. For the rest of their surgical career, they made sure that every kit had two of the particular instruments so that they would never have an unavailable instrument again. In the end, Jill didn't know what to make of the statistic.

A fourth statistic examined complication rates. Included in this number were deaths, infections, and accidental nicks during the surgery itself. Dr. Lewis's numbers were statistically worse in this area.

Jill tuned back into the room and noted her friends were speculating about the charity that had sponsored the golf outing. The tournament had been about a third complete when the murder occurred. The charity had already incurred the expenses of the food and beverages for the event. It also collected all of the green fees to play in the charity golf outing. In the end, they decided that without some of the fundraising that took place on the holes, and at the silent auction following the dinner the charity had lost out on some significant donations.

"I don't pretend to be an operating room expert, but it looks to me like Dr. Lewis has some performance problems. I can't imagine that the report itself was worth killing over, but the question was with the problems spotlighted in this attachment," said Jill pointing to her laptop screen, "What was the hospital doing with the information? Certainly they should have been alarmed with the complication rates."

"I've heard discussions before about physician quality issues and the actions that people take," Jo disclosed. "I can't say that I paid attention to the discussion as it was often times too medically technical for me to understand. Hospital people speaking a lot of acronyms can make it difficult to follow a conversation."

"I think I have one more attachment to open here and perhaps that will have information on actions the hospital was planning to take in regards to Dr. Lewis's performance."

Jill then took a moment to study the final attachment. She had never been credentialed by a hospital so she was somewhat unfamiliar with their process. As a medical resident, her performance was not tracked in the way that this surgeon was tracked. It was comforting to see that the hospital was trying to measure physician performance. Yes, medicine was an art as much as it was a science, but that philosophy shouldn't be a cover for never measuring how well someone was performing.

"It looks like this is a listing of where Dr. Lewis's performance was discussed throughout the hospital. He has spoken with the Surgery chairs - both of them, the medical executive committee, and the credential committee."

"Did he retain an attorney for those discussions?" asked Jo.

"I can't tell since I don't know any of these names. There is a list of people and I can't tell what their credentials are. Something is going on with Dr. Lewis but I can't figure out what the hospital is doing. I think the files are deliberately vague because they may be discoverable under state malpractice laws."

"So what are our next steps?" asked Marie. "I know with some personnel matters that we are vague so as to not leave much of a paper trail. In those cases, you usually have to talk to someone verbally to get the scoop. If the hospital is smart, they will not have left a paper trail. It seems like we need a contact inside the hospital that would be willing to talk. Also, I guess we need to ask ourselves what do we share with the detectives? We certainly can't tell them where we came by the information."

"Good points, Marie," Jo agreed. "I think we need to think strategically on a couple of issues. How do we get insider information from the hospital? What do we share with the detectives? How do we talk Dr. Phillips's widow into exhumation? Where has Dr. Lewis spent his income that would account for the need to file bankruptcy? Are we going completely down the wrong road with Dr. Lewis? Who might he need to kill next to keep this story covered up?"

Jill had been writing down Jo's questions as she spoke. Now all four friends stared at the murder board thinking about all of the right questions and what their next steps would be.

Marie added to the list, "Does Dr. Lewis have an alibi for the time that Doug was shot? If he has a rock solid alibi, then all the other questions go away because the killer is not Dr. Lewis."

"Thanks Marie, for that succinct question. That is a bottom line key question we need answered. Any ideas on how to go about getting that answered?"

Angela replied, "Ah, could the police just ask him?"

"They could ask him, but I don't think they have probable cause at this time to even have him on a suspect list," Jill mused. "He is not a dumb man, and would ask why they were asking the question. Without a good reason I don't think they have a legal right to ask the question. So perhaps we need Nick to do some more hacking for us. What if we got the physician on-call list for the day of the golf event and the surgery schedule? If he is not on either list, then he might still have an alibi if he was in his office seeing patients, which would be a whole other system to gain access to."

Angela put another call into Nick asking for the information with a few hints of where he might find those two lists. Given that he could use a specific day and Dr. Lewis's name, he thought he might have the answer for them in an hour as he had two variables to search with.

While they were waiting for an answer from Nick, Angela suggested they circle back to Michelle.

"Is there anything more we need to research on Michelle? We didn't get a good vibe last night, but what do we do with that feeling, if anything? What research have we already done on Michelle? We looked at her business tax returns, right? Have we done a background search on her?"

"I have not done a background search on Michelle," noted Marie. "Give me a few minutes and let me see what I can find."

"I'll take a second look at her business financials to see if we learn anything," Jo stated. "We are a little further along in this investigation, so maybe something will call out to me in a second review."

"I'm just going stare blindly at our murder board and see if any other ideas come to mind," Jill remarked. "It feels like all of you need about an hour to come up with new information."

Angela announced, "I'm going to go for a walk for inspiration. I have my phone with me to record any brilliant ideas or to hear the arrival of Nick's email ping. Cheers."

Soon, silence reigned in the room, except for the clacking of Jo and Marie's computer keys making a sound. Jill listened to the rhythm of Jo's typing for a while. There would be silence, followed by a flurry of key sounds, and then sounds would trail off to one key every few seconds. Marie, likewise, would have a burst of speed and then longer periods of silence as she was reading something on the screen. She typed in a softer manner than Jo.

CHAPTER 17

$\mathcal{M}$arie had been scanning through the social media sites looking for additional information on Michelle, but that was not where she discovered the most interesting piece of information. She was skimming through Michelle's interior decorating website when she hit the critical connecting thread.

She looked up at her friends and said, "Hey I think I found a link between Michelle and Dr. Lewis."

Jill and Jo looked up and both said simultaneously, "What!"

"Come over here and look at my computer screen and tell me if you see anything unusual."

Marie had Jill looking over one shoulder and Jo the other while they examined the website displayed on Marie's screen. They both looked and initially saw nothing then they saw the significance of the picture that had caught Marie's attention.

"Marie, that is brilliant!" Jo noted. "I had taken a look at the website and I missed this the first time through."

Michelle had pictures of the interior design work that she had done for clients. On the screen were pictures of the living room, dining room, and master bedroom. The pictures referenced that they were from the home of Susan and Bradley Lewis.

"Did we asked Michelle when we interviewed her if she knew Dr. Lewis?" asked Marie. There was silence in the room as they all thought back to the conversation the night before over wine. They would check with Angela when she returned home but so far no one could remember that Michelle mentioned any clients by their name.

Angela chose that moment to return to the house. As she walked into the kitchen she said, "I got an e-mail back from Nick and he was able to verify that Dr. Lewis was not on the call schedule for the hospital during the charity golf outing nor was he scheduled for any surgeries."

Jill added, "That is interesting news. That means he could have been free to be our killer although we still have to check with his office to see if he was seeing patients in the clinic that day. Angela, guess what Marie found on Michelle's website?"

"What did she find?" asked Angela, smiling at the anticipation in Jill's voice.

"Angela, come take a look at this website and tell me if you see anything unusual about it." Angela walked over to the computer where they were all standing and studied the information that was pulled up on the screen. She seemed to read every word of text and then they watched as her eyes flew back to the point that had startled Marie ten minutes previously.

"Oh my gosh, she did an interior design job for Dr. Lewis and his wife."

"Angela, do you remember if Michelle mentioned any of her clients and/or Dr. Lewis when we spoke with her last night?" Marie asked.

Angela stood there a moment longer and then shook her head indicating she didn't remember a conversation about any clients, let alone Dr. Lewis. She added, "This could have been an honest omission and it could be nothing; or it could be our connection between Michelle and Dr. Lewis if the two of them are somehow involved in Doug's murder. So what are our next steps?"

"I think we have two new threads to research. We need to find a way to verify if Dr. Lewis was in the clinic seeing patients at the time of the murder," Jill suggested. "Then we need to do a deep dive on Michelle Easley to see if we have a solid connection or just a random piece of information. In a town this size, it would not be unusual for some physicians and their families to hire Michelle to provide interior design services. Maybe this is a coincidence but you all know how I hate coincidences."

"Any thoughts about how we can check into whether Dr. Lewis was seeing patients in his clinic that day?" Jo asked.

"How about if I called the office and said that I had forgotten to show up for my appointment at one o'clock two days ago and I wanted to reschedule," Marie proposed. "I'll get one of two answers - either I'll be told that Dr. Lewis had not worked that day or they'll transfer me to an appointment desk for rescheduling at which point I end the call. I'll make the call now before I lose my nerve."

Marie was soon punching in the number for Dr. Lewis's office and she began the story just as she had suggested. Soon they could hear on her side of the call that she was apologizing for being mixed up and it must be a different physician that she had her appointment scheduled with and she ended the call. Her friends were soon clapping and congratulating her on a job well done. None of them were good actresses or liars, so this was positively an academy award winning performance on the part of Marie.

"Okay so we know he doesn't have an obvious alibi so far," Jill noted. "Let's look for a link beyond the interior design business. Are they connected through their kids? Do they live geographically close? Do they attend the same church?

"I think we also need more research on the family finances. Is there a life insurance policy that Michelle will receive? Marie, did you find anything else on Michelle other than the huge discovery on the website?"

"The remainder of what I located on Michelle is not worth mentioning. She is just your average wife, mother, and business owner going through life. I'll go back and take a second look for any additional Lewis connections, but I think I would have found them the first time."

"Jo, can you work any new angles on the finances?"

"I think we should take a break for lunch," Jo replied. "How about if we go to lunch at Curly's at Lambeau Field. I would think that football setting would perhaps "cleanse our brains of the trivia involved in this case' and then perhaps we can re-focus and go back at it again in an hour."

Marie who had joined Jill and Angela in laughter, said, "Cleanse our brains in a football setting? Jo that is so Zen of you! Perhaps the ghost of Vince Lombardi will steer us in the right direction."

Jo just smiled, with a serene look on her face.

Soon they were seated at a table in the sports bar at Lambeau Field. They had to agree with Jo that the bar was a 180 degree turn from their discussion about a murder at a golf course. Wherever you looked on the walls, there were sports pictures of times past and present. Televisions played sporting events ranging from baseball and soccer, to basketball and tennis. Newscasters were focused on the upcoming NFL draft. It could be a great people-watching from the viewpoint of some of the high calorie meals served at the restaurant. You had to wonder how someone could eat all that food.

After a relaxing hour, they journeyed back to Marie's house. The clock was ticking down and so far all they had was a series of coincidences surrounding Dr. Lewis but no hard evidence anywhere. After the beer and brats at the restaurant, they might have to fight off a desire for an afternoon nap.

"Jill, what would we do to prove Dr. Lewis is innocent?" Angela asked.

Jill appreciated Angela's prompting her to think like a pathologist and said, "First we would look for an alibi for the time of the murder. We would also look for a lack of a motive – find proof that Dr. Lewis had a good relationship with Dr. Easley. Third, we would find someone else that committed the murder. Fourth, we would prove he lacked the skills to carry out the murder. Can anyone else think of something to add to this list?"

After her friends shook their heads 'no', Jill continued, "So we proved that he has the skills to carry out the murder and on the surface it doesn't look like he has an alibi."

"Let me work on the question of Dr. Lewis's relationship with Dr. Easley and Dr. Phillips. I'm going to look deep to find the link between them all," Marie asserted.

"I, of course, think that money is at the heart of all murders," Jo observed. "I'll take a leaf out of your book Jill and assume that all is right financially for Dr. Lewis. I'll see what documents I can find to prove that point."

Angela added, "I wish I could interview Dr. Lewis. I'm going to do some research to see if I can find a connection to him and by happenstance turn up where he is expected to be in the next couple of hours, as long as that's not the operating room. I'm not a talented enough actress to bluff my way into the surgical suite. I think the game would be up the moment I fainted dead away from seeing blood. Do we need Nick for any additional research?"

Jill thought for a moment and replied, "At the moment, 'no', though we reserve the right to contact him if something comes up. It must be getting close to his bedtime there, just wish him sweet dreams."

It seemed like everyone had an assignment except Jill. She couldn't think of anything to add to the investigation and then inspiration struck. She was soon composing an email to the satellite company in Colorado. She wanted the footage of the Northwoods where Dr. Phillips was killed in the snowmobile accident. Her problem was she didn't have an exact latitude and longitude location for his death. She would have to review the death certificate again to see date, time, and location of his death to see if she could narrow the location down.

She went online to the Cook County Sheriff's website to see what information was accessible. There seemed to be press releases for police related events in the county but she saw no release for the snowmobile accident. She might need Nick to hack into their system. She would see first what she could get from her local detectives.

"Hey guys! I may have a brilliant idea. How about if we view the satellite footage of the Northwoods at the time that Dr. Phillips had his snowmobile accident? We should be able to see whether we have the same figure on video footage as we do for the golf course shooting."

Her friends immediately brightened with renewed excitement.

Angela said, "That is a brilliant idea. If they had that kind of evidence then the police could bring Dr. Lewis in for questioning and we could find out if he has a solid alibi or not."

Jill said, "I thought about calling Nick and asking him to hack into the Cook County Sheriff's site but then I thought about our local detectives. Could they act as a liaison for us and get that report from that sheriff's Department? That way we would have the geographical markers that are required to ask the satellite company for footage."

"Excellent idea!" said Marie. "Let's call them now, and I agree we shouldn't use Nick if we can get the information legally."

Jill dialed Detective Van Bruggin's cell phone. He must recognize the number now as he said in a resigned voice.

"Hello, Dr. Quint"

"I think I have a good idea to move this case forward especially in regards to Dr. Lewis. Will you call the sheriff in Cook County and ask him for the police report of Dr. Phillips's death?

I was thinking it might include the exact location. With that information, I was planning to ask the satellite company to pull video footage that corresponds with the date and time of Dr. Phillips's death. But I'm not exactly sure where he died up north and I need the police report to pin down the geographic coordinates."

"That's a great idea! I'll make a call to the sheriff right now and see what I can find out for you."

"I figured if we could confirm some unsavory behavior on the part of Dr. Lewis in regards to Dr. Phillips's death then not only could you interview him for the snowmobile death, but it would give you grounds to bring him in and chat with him concerning Doug Easley's death."

"That is an excellent idea, Dr. Quint. We have been scratching our heads trying to think of new leads in this murder investigation. If Dr. Lewis is our killer we sure have a lack of evidence to connect him to Doug Easley's death."

Jill silently commiserated with the detectives. Evidence for them was as difficult to locate as it was for her and her team.

"Detective Van Bruggin, one thing that we have somewhat rundown is the call schedule for the hospital, the operating room, and the clinic; it seems that Dr. Lewis was not in or schedule to cover any of those three areas at the time of the murder."

"How did you get that information?" asked the detective.

"Let's just say that one member of my team has some very good acting skills and it's amazing what you can find out if you ask the right questions."

"Good work. Expect a call back from me soon," and the detective ended the call.

Jill looked over at her friends and said, "He is going to call me back as soon as he gets the report from the county up north. Have you guys come across anything yet?"

She got exasperated looks from her friends as they had been searching only a short period of time.

"How about that gun group he belongs to? Are there any pictures of him with that group that might supply clues?"

"I'll add it to my list of websites I'm looking up on Dr. Lewis," sighed Marie.

"Jo, is Jack available to come over later and help us with the footage if we get it from the satellite company? He was so much faster than all of us with viewing largely boring video."

"Let me give him a call and ask. I don't recall him having any pressing appointments that would prevent him from helping. I'll leave him on stand-by for us until we know when the video footage will arrive."

Soon silence reigned in the room again as her friends returned to their searches and she was left staring at the murder board. She kept replaying the story in her head. She shuffled through information seeking another suspect. Had they pursued every avenue open to them, legal or not, to cement the connection of Dr. Lewis to the murder? Was Michelle involved in the case somehow? Until she had some more information from her friends she was really just banging her head for nothing.

She decided to step outside and call Nathan. Marie had a nice patio and she could park herself on a comfortable lounge chair for a relaxing chat with the love of her life. Hopefully he was available as he had such an unpredictable schedule.

"Hey babe, how is the murder investigation going?"

"I'm stuck at the moment and thought that maybe hearing about Trixie and Arthur or wine glass design might steer my mind in a new direction."

"It's rare for you to have so few clues to follow. Your dog is missing you mostly because Arthur is in charge. Clearly Trixie thinks it's wrong for a cat to be lord of all he surveys."

"Sounds like you have the usual comedy troupe with those two. What else is on your schedule for today?"

"No meetings, just time to design all day."

"Wine labels, wine glasses, or marketing materials?"

"So far, none of the above. I've been working late which means I have been getting up late. All I have done today is take Trixie for a run and practice my hapkido skills in the gym. I was just finishing lunch and about to settle down in my studio. It's been a real lazy day."

"You know you need those on occasion. It keeps you fresh."

"So how I can help you with the investigation? You told me the doctor was shot on the green and you were close by and your suspect is some other doctor. Have you got to question the suspect yet?"

"No, we don't have enough evidence to bring him in for questioning yet."

"Is this going to stop you from getting home on time tomorrow?

"I don't think so. I can run the investigation from California. The others have to return to work as well the next day so even if I stuck around I wouldn't have any help."

"Have you thought of doing some surveillance? Watch your suspect for a few hours?"

"That's an interesting suggestion. I don't recall doing surveillance in the past, but I am getting on the nerves of Jo, Marie, and Angela because I essentially have nothing to do at the moment. They would, I am sure, love to see me exit the house. I am waiting for the police to call me back with information on a potential connected case, but once I get that information I could handle the next steps with my iPhone. I guess I'll follow your suggestion. Got to run and go do that. Thanks for the great idea. Love you honey, goodbye," and Jill ended the call.

Fortunately, Nathan was used to her abrupt changes in direction when she was in the middle of an investigation. She would call him again later, if the surveillance proved tedious.

She went back inside the house and asked them if anyone had Dr. Lewis's home address. Shortly thereafter, she was out the door with plans of heading towards the home of her suspect. Twenty minutes later in her rental car, she drove past a two-story Tudor home in the village of Howard. Being new to surveillance, she knew she didn't have a clue as to proper technique. She had actually taken a minute before leaving Marie's house to look up surveillance techniques on the internet.

Dutifully following her newly acquired advice, she parked as far down the road as she could, yet still see the front door and driveway. She had grabbed a pair of binoculars from Marie, and was wearing black clothing, and a black wide brimmed hat. She owned her own set of dark sunglasses to complete her 'disguise". Angela had lent her a camera with a zoom feature in case she wanted to take any pictures. Besides Dr. Lewis, his wife and two children also inhabited this home, but it was late afternoon so they could be any number of places around town.

She watched a Range Rover SUV, with a woman at the wheel and a teenager in the passenger seat turn into the driveway, wait for the garage door to open and then disappear from sight as the big door closed. Well, isn't this exciting, Jill thought. I watched a car pull in to the house and what did that tell me? Pretty much nothing. What to do next?

Jill waited another half hour. During that time she had received an email from the detectives with more specificity on where Dr. Phillips was killed. She sent the email off to the satellite company and they thought they would have an answer within the hour. Jo was arranging for Jack to drive over to Marie's to assist them with the video and the detectives would be joining them as well. Jill had her head down typing away on her cell phone. She jumped when she heard a knock on her window.

She looked up into the eyes of Dr. Lewis. He looked exactly like his picture and his sudden appearance startled her. This would be Jill's last surveillance assignment as she was an utter failure at this thing. She rolled her window down.

Dr. Lewis said, "Why are you parked in this neighborhood? I've seen you from my window for the past thirty minutes, and you seemed to be watching my house. I'll be calling the police if I don't have a satisfactory answer from you and I have written down your license plate."

Jill was the poorest actress at the best of times. Coming face to face with a potential murder suspect was shocking and her brains were slow in responding. She opened her mouth but nothing came out. She closed her jaw and mumbled, "I like the landscaping and paint contrast of your house. I was snapping pictures then looking up the various plants on the internet so I could figure out how to duplicate your design."

Jill heaved a silent sigh of relief at what she thought to be a pretty good lie for her appearance. She had that relief for all of about three seconds as the man was not stupid.

"If you were taking pictures of my landscaping why are so far away from the house. You can't get good pictures from this angle. Let me see your camera. I don't believe you."

Yikes! This was getting hairy. She decided to go on the offense.

"Look my being here is obviously upsetting you. I'll just leave," Jill said as she quickly started the car and put it into drive.

She watched him in her review mirror as she continued down the street. She would have to remind herself to avoid doing surveillance for future cases as she was such an abject failure at the technique. She had not seen him walk up to her car and her heart was still pounding wildly over that encounter. She would bet the only reason he hadn't reached in the car to try and disable it was because she was a woman and she had noticed a neighbor out front watering at another house.

The trip back to Marie's house was a little faster as her heart was still pounding. She soon entered the house and went straight to where the wine and wine glasses were kept. She poured herself a full glass, took a large swig, then turned around to find her three friends had moved into the kitchen and were staring at her.

CHAPTER 18

"Okay, I am failure at surveillance. If I ever say I want to do surveillance again, stop me. Remind me how bad I am at spying on people."

Angela asked, "What's wrong? What are you trying to fix with that very large glass of wine? You seem unhurt so what went wrong?"

"While I was busy composing an email to Jack and the detectives about a time to meet here to look at the video footage, Dr. Lewis came over and knocked on my car window. He scared the bejeezus out of me as I hadn't seen him come over to the car," Jill described the encounter with her hand to chest, still somewhat breathless.

"You're kidding. OMG! I would be sipping a large glass of wine too," replied Marie with a grin. "Why don't we all have a glass and we'll toast the end of your unsuccessful career as a private detective doing surveillance."

"Thanks guys, I need the laugh," smiled Jill. "I have never stared into the eyes of a suspected killer before and it was unnerving. He said I seemed to be watching his house and he was ready to call the police. I then told him I was admiring his landscaping and taking pictures of it and looking up the individual plants, a comment I thought quite brilliant on my part to be created on the fly like that while my heart was still pounding.

"Then he said he didn't believe me and asked to see the camera. So I just turned the engine on and put the car in gear and drove off. Uh, that was why I needed the big glass of wine when I reached your house."

"Based on your brief encounter with him, what was your impression?" Angela asked.

"I thought his approaching the car and yelling at me was over the top. If I had passed him on the street, I wouldn't have thought anything of it. He looks like an average guy. I wonder how he spotted me. I wasn't in front of his house and I had only been there just under an hour. Maybe his wife said something."

"Why would she say anything?" Jo questioned. "When did you meet her?"

"I watched her pass me on the street and pull into the garage of their home. She had one of the kids in the front passenger seat. Maybe I raised her protective instincts. Would any of you notice a car parked three houses down with a person in it? I know I wouldn't have in my old location. Now that I sort of live in the country, I would notice a lone car parked just because there hasn't been one in the five years I have lived there."

"You know me, I don't notice anything going on," replied Jo. "A car would probably have to be parked at the curb on my street for at least three months before I might notice it."

Angela added, "I live on such a busy street that it would take me several days to notice a car. If they were beyond the inter-section near my house, it might take me a few months to notice."

Marie offered the dissenting voice, "I think I am a little more paranoid then you guys, so I might notice the car the same day."

"The whole incident was just weird," Jill said shrugging. "My heart rate is back to normal, and finally the hair on the back of my neck is sitting down. The video feed should be here soon. Is Jack on his way?"

"He should be here any moment," replied Jo. "Are the detectives coming here as well?

"They'll be here sometime within the hour. They like Jack's technique with the video. Of course they also want the tape and depending on what we find on it, I imagine the Cook County Sheriff might want a copy as well. We'll see what's on the feed. I heard a ping a few moments ago and when I checked my inbox it was the video email. I am dying of curiosity as to what we will see on the feed."

They heard Jack come in through the kitchen door yelling "hello". In his hands was his laptop. He was soon seated at the island counter and began the process of opening the video feed from the satellite company. The four women were peering over his shoulder at the screen.

"They didn't have an absolute time of death," Jill noted. "While there is a time listed on the death certificate, actual death occurred sometime within an hour on the certificate. This will be very tedious feed as first we will have to spot movement in the trees of the Northwoods. Then we'll eventually need some way to identify a snowmobile as that of Dr. Phillips. So Jack, how can we all help you view the video feed?"

"Ladies, you all smell great but it would help if you backed off. I thought I had gained your trust for spotting things on tape after the last video feed. So why don't you go back to your own searches and I'll let you know when I spot something."

With a sigh, they all retreated to their respective computers to continue their searches. The silence in the room was broken by the sound of the doorbell. Marie went to the door to let the detectives inside.

"Detectives, can I get you something to drink?"

"No thanks, we have already had too much coffee."

"Would you like water, soda, or wine?"

"We're fine, we just want to see if you find anything on the video feed. I'm glad to see Jack here operating the system. I'm thinking that this is even more tedious than the last video feed."

"Why don't you have seat here with us? Jack just started reviewing the video and he asked us to back off to reduce his distraction. Jill can tell you about her adventures with Dr. Lewis today." Marie enjoyed stirring the pot for her friend and Jill gave her a look that said she would enjoy ratting her out the next chance she got.

The detectives looked at Jill almost as if afraid to ask, "Why did you interact with Dr. Lewis today?" came the patient question.

"It was boredom that got me into trouble. Everyone else was engaged in their computer searches and I had nothing going on. So I looked up how to do surveillance on the internet. I then went to his street address and parked about three houses away. I was dressed in black with a large brimmed hat."

"That is obviously not the full story so what else happened?" asked Haro.

"I'd been there about ten minutes when I saw his wife and a teenager come home in an SUV and pull into the garage. Then there wasn't any movement, so I started reading my emails. Suddenly, there was a loud 'bang' on my window. When I looked up, I found myself staring into the rather hostile eyes of a would-be murderer. It was quite unsettling!"

The two detectives were giving her pained looks and Van Bruggin added, "It sounds like you were engaged in stalking."

"I wouldn't call it stalking as the only place I was watching, was his home. I didn't follow him anywhere, make contact with him, or send him emails or letters."

"Tell that to a judge," Haro explained. "So what happened when he approached you?"

"First I was startled as I had been concentrating on email, so when he tapped the glass of my car window, I nearly jumped out of my skin. He asked me what I was doing watching his house. I told him I was admiring his landscaping and taking pictures of what I liked. We traded a few more sentences and then he asked to see the camera to see what pictures were on it. I put the car in gear and left his street to return here. End of story."

"Hmm, somehow I bet there is more to the story than you're telling us," said Haro. "Just tell me there wasn't sufficient criminal activity on your part such that he might call and complain about your behavior."

"No detective, nothing of the sort. He said he had my car's license plate number but as my car is a rental that won't get him that far."

After giving her another long look, the detectives looked over at Jack and asked, "Have you found the snowmobile in the woods yet?

"No," Jack replied without further explanation.

Angela spoke up, "Detectives, we have been warned by Jack to stay away from him while he works his magic on the video feed. Why don't you come and join us and tell Jill and I where you are with the investigation? Jo and Marie are still working their own magic with the internet culling out obscure facts, so we should probably move to the living room for our conversation."

The two detectives found themselves being swept up by Angela and moved to another room before they could object. They didn't know why they were persuaded to follow her directions, and looked over their shoulders as if expecting to see what hidden object had moved them forward to another room. If they had thought deeply about the situation, they might have been worried over what secrets they might tell her.

Jill and Angela each had a glass of wine and they relaxed against the cushions of their arm chairs while they stared at the two detectives. Jill opened the conversation with, "Do you have any additional suspects other than those we have already discussed?"

The two detectives, sitting side by side on the sofa, had disconcerted looks on their faces as they reviewed in their minds how they had come to be sitting on the sofa being questioned by Jill and Angela.

"This is an ongoing police investigation and we're not at liberty to share information about the case with civilians."

"I am disappointed with you, detectives," replied Jill. "I thought we were beyond these barriers. Surely you checked out our references with other law enforcement agencies. You know that we will keep any information you share confidential; if we don't stay confidential, my part-time consultancy for a second opinion on the cause of death will be at an end. If you have googled me, you know that I don't hold press conferences. We have shared our leads with you saving you time. In addition, we are probably responsible for the most promising leads you have had for this case. If we get somewhere with the current footage that Jack is reviewing you may have something very big on your hands. So again, do you have any additional suspects? What are your officers working on? Have you uncovered any other relevant information from either crime scene?"

The two detectives looked at each other and, sighed; then Van Bruggin spoke up, "We are not concerned with your confidentiality practices rather you likely have all of the information already. Other than Dr. Lewis, we don't have any additional suspects. There is a real lack of evidence in this case. The footprint casts won't be back for a few days."

Angela probed, "So what is your gut telling you on this case? You guys are the professionals. We have been assisting Jill for five years, and have been closely involved with several cases, but mostly we help her from two-thousand miles away. We have a suspect for this murder, maybe two, but we want to know what your instinct is about this homicide."

Before the two detectives could address Angela's remarks, Jack called from the other room. They were soon gathered around Jack's screen. He turned around and addressed the group.

"I combed through the footage trying to find a snowmobile accident. As I understand, Dr. Phillips suffered a heart attack in the woods, so I was looking for a snowmobile that came to a stop with the passenger slumping over or slipping to the ground. As you know snowmobile trails are managed by snowmobile clubs throughout the state. So I looked on-line to see if Dr. Phillips or Dr. Lewis belonged to such a club. Turns out that Dr. Lewis and his sons are part of a club that maintains the trail we are watching footage on."

Jo was quick to compliment him, "Jack, our investigative techniques are rubbing off on you. None of us thought to look up the snowmobile club memberships. That was brilliant!"

Jack just smiled and continued, "I isolated the footage for an event that looks like it might be a heart attack. Until you take a second look. Watch the screen."

He leaned back as the four women and two detectives peered closely at his screen watching the footage. He replayed it three times. Waiting for the others to see what he saw. He heard no 'Eureka'; indeed all he saw was puzzlement. Finally, he played it a fourth time in slow motion and the lightbulb went on for two of the group of six.

Angela stated, "It's the sequence of events that is off. The snowmobile appears to be having engine problems. It looks like Dr. Phillips is trying to give it more gas, yet the vehicle is slowing down. The snowmobile gradually comes to a halt, like it ran out of gas, and in fact Dr. Phillips gestures to the gas tank. Dr. Lewis gets off his snowmobile and approaches. Meanwhile Dr. Phillips is not clutching his chest rather he is looking and gesturing at the snowmobiles gauges. This next part is smooth. Dr. Lewis approaches as though he is concerned, puts his bare hand on his friend's back. We then see Dr. Phillips turn a sharp look over his shoulder and then he doesn't move much, Dr. Lewis pulls him off the snowmobile and onto the snow. For every public service announcement I have ever on heart attacks, that does not match what the American Heart Association has been telling me. Jill, does that look like a person having a heart attack to you?"

"Jack, you have an awesome observant eye. I can't say I have ever seen a heart attack cause the behavior we see from Dr. Phillips on this tape. It looked more to me that he had sudden and complete paralysis shortly after Dr. Lewis placed a hand on his shoulder. Let's see if we can get more resolution on that hand. They make auto-injector syringes that are quick enough to inject a paralytic agent."

Jack played with the resolution, but they couldn't get enough to tell if anything was in his hand let alone what it was.

"When does he phone for help?" asked Haro.

"He doesn't phone for help, he hops on his snowmobile and leaves after checking Dr. Phillips's pulse. It's quite possible that there is no cell phone reception in that area of the state. Later on in the tape - perhaps another ten minutes you see him return with rescue folks."

"We of course would like a copy of the tape," Van Bruggin remarked. "Jill, that was brilliant to think of that angle. I think we have a few more directions to take. I'd like to verify the cell phone coverage issue in that area. I would also like to get my hands on the snowmobile to see if it was tampered with - I wonder who has the sled? I also want to go over the report Lewis gave to the Sheriff in Cook and see if it matches what is on screen."

Jill added, "I would also recommend a state medical examiner review this tape against the findings on the death certificate and I bet that he or she would request exhumation of the body. If the State doesn't have such a position, I would be happy to consult with the Cook County coroner. I could perform the examination on my own as a forensic expert, but if you end up prosecuting someone, you'll have cleaner lines if you can use a county coroner. Whoever has the body in their laboratory can test for trace drugs and examine the skin to see if there was an injection approximately where Dr. Lewis patted Dr. Phillips on the back. At the very least, I would think they would have to change the cause of death."

"Again Dr. Quint and team, thank you for your help with this homicide," Van Bruggin expressed. "We have a lot of investigative work we need to get in motion."

Marie asked, "Do you have enough information to bring Dr. Lewis in for questioning?"

"The Green Bay police do not have enough information to bring him in for questioning, but I would think that the Cook County Sheriff has enough information. I'm not sure we want to do that at this time. I would prefer to collect answers to the questions we just spelled out before we bring him in for questioning," Haro noted.

They were getting ready to exit the house when Angela asked about Helen.

"She is still unconscious. They have her in a medically induced coma trying to give her brain a rest. They tell us that the earliest she might wake up is still three days away and they really don't know the condition of her brain."

"My thoughts and prayers are with her family. She is lucky to have the excellent and caring supervisor that she does," said Angela.

Haro nodded and the two detectives left.

"Whew! Thanks, Jack, for being so darn good with that video feed. Your diligence in seeing something the rest of us did not, was amazing," Jill said. "The police have all kinds of new clues of potential physical evidence to follow. I wish we could be involved in that. I should get back to what you guys were looking up. Is there any new news there? Anything I can help research?"

"I haven't come across anything yet primarily due to the lack of public information about the personal lives of Dr. Lewis and the Easleys," Jo bemoaned. "I'll keep looking for something, but it's not going well."

"I've been chasing a lot of information about Dr. Lewis," Marie explained. "As a distant observer, his posts on a variety of plat-forms are all over the place. Sometimes he is celebrating an accomplishment, other times he is on a complete tear about someone. Erratic behavior is always a red flag when generally looking at any candidate for employment. He belongs to several gun organizations which I guess is not surprising given his profi-ciency with a pistol."

"Have you discovered any intersection with Michelle? Do their kids hang out together, attend the same church, belong to the same charitable organization?" asked Jill.

"Nothing so far, but I have a lot more work to do on this group of people. Hey, it's coming up on dinner. Do you guys want to eat in or dine out?"

"I love your cooking, Marie, but our last cleansing the brain experience worked well by going to Curley's. I think that Jo should pick another restaurant since she has been successful with her choices so far," Jill said.

She looked around and got nods of agreement from Angela, Marie, and Jack. Jo hated to be put on the spot like this, but she thought about what she was in the mood for and then checked with Angelina's to see if their party of five could be accom-modated.

They were in luck as the restaurant could accommodate their party probably because it was early in the peak dinner traffic period. They were soon driving toward downtown for a delicious Italian meal. An hour and a half later they were again headed back to Marie's house, relaxed with full bellies and mellowed brains.

There was nothing more for Jack to do with the video feed. He had worked the footage with all technology that he was capable of applying and had finessed the pertinent section to its best view. With nothing more to contribute he gave everyone a hug and departed.

"I get the feeling we have done every bit of research we can on this case," Marie noted. "I'm simply not coming up with anything new. We need some feedback from the detectives. It's been several hours, do you think they would share anything with us?"

"Never hurts to ask. Other than my failed attempt at surveillance, everything else we have handed them has been their only solid leads. It's not quite 7pm yet so I don't think it is too late to call."

CHAPTER 19

"Detective Van Bruggin this is Jill. My team is at a standstill as far as investigating leads. We wondered if we could either assist you, or if you would share any new information that you have to see if that causes us to follow a new direction? I know it's later in the evening, but we wanted to give you time to follow-up with the satellite feed of Dr. Phillips' death."

"We don't generally share the results of our investigation with civilians,"

Jill cut off his speech with "Yeah so you told us earlier tonight. If asked, I'll tell anyone that you want, that you were uncooperative with us and didn't share data. Now can we move on and will you share whatever you have uncovered in the last two hours?"

With a sigh on the other end of the phone, Van Bruggin said, "I had a long conversation with the Cook County Sheriff and coroner and they have agreed to re-open the report of the accident. We discussed the next steps which were primarily focused on notifying Dr. Phillips's family. There is interest on the Sheriff's part in meeting you and possibly having you consult during the actual autopsy which would not occur for a few days. We had a discussion about the snowmobile that Dr. Phillips used. Apparently the snowmobile belonged to Dr. Lewis and he indicated at the time of the incident that he would tow it back to his cabin, so they don't think they can examine it without a warrant. We're not sure if it would have told us anything given the six months that have passed.

"The Sheriff was able to put the responding officers on the phone and we listened to the 911 call Dr. Lewis made. His discussion on the phone does not match what we can see on the video feed so the Cook Sheriff is sending an officer to join us in an interview tomorrow. We called Dr. Lewis at home and asked him to come down to the station for an interview. He agreed to our request and asked what this was about. We indicated that we had some follow-up questions about Dr. Phillips's death from six months ago. He'll be at the station at ten in the morning."

"Would you like some medical questions to ask him during the interview?" Jill volunteered. "I can give you some questions to ask. If you have an observation area for the interview room, I could send in some comments based on his responses if he says anything that is not medically accurate."

"We would appreciate your help," Van Bruggin said. "What time does your flight leave tomorrow?"

"I need to be at the airport by four in the afternoon. If the Cook County Sheriff and I reach an agreement regarding the autopsy, I may delay my trip home. I would think the court order for the exhumation would come about quickly and as the ground is not frozen, they could dig up Dr. Phillips's body as soon as the next day or day after. If that is the case, I'll delay my trip home. If the family plans to fight the exhumation, I'll head home as scheduled"

"Detective Haro is on the other line with Cook County as we speak, so he should soon have a reading as to how the widow will respond to our request. Let me put you on hold a moment as I see he is ending the call."

Soon there was a buzzing sound in her ear and she took the hold time to update everyone on the conversation, most of which they had been able to glean from Jill's side of the conversation.

Van Bruggin came back on the line and said, "The family is anxious to have a full autopsy performed on Dr. Phillips. They have a lot of anger directed towards law enforcement at this time, but we're getting what we want. If I had been the Cook County Sheriff, I would have thrown your name in as a consultant to assure the family the investigation would be done correctly this time. Can you send me your biography and contract and I'll forward it to Cook County? Of course, I'm assuming you can stay and provide consulting services."

"I already checked my schedule and if the Sheriff will pay my change ticket fee, I'll be happy to stay and help. Did you hear back on the cell phone coverage?"

"Yes the Sheriff confirmed it is very possible that the cell phone did not get any reception. We're going to check cell phone records to see if an attempt was made. I'd appreciate if you could get me the medical questions by nine in the morning and if you would like to observe; I request that you do not enter the building at the same time as Dr. Lewis as he has already made your acquaintance. There is a back parking lot for employees only. Park there and I'll notify the staff to let you in."

"One more question, would you mind if I brought Angela to the observation room? She is our resident people person and she may think of something I don't, based on his answers."

Another pause while he thought about Jill's request then he said "ok" and they ended the call."

Jill looked at Angela and said, "You're joining me to observe the interview. It will be interesting to get your read of the situation."

"I don't know whether to be excited or bothered by watching this process. I guess Dr. Lewis is innocent until proven guilty and we're getting closer to the truth."

"It's not like they are going to bang heads against the wall; this is strictly a conversation between two officers and Dr. Lewis. I'll be listening to the medical side of his answers and you'll be watching his body language for 'gives' as to his emotions. By the way, do you mind having a house guest for a few more days?"

"Of course I don't mind, we love having you in town. Besides after all of these interactions with the police, maybe we'll all get out of speeding tickets for the foreseeable future!"

"That would be a nice advantage to solving this case," Marie agreed. "Jo always seems to talk her way out of tickets but the rest of us never have that luck."

"Hey, it's Saturday night and we have no more investigating to do tonight," Angela proclaimed. "Jill, you can comprise your question list in the morning. Let's head for a bar. We could start at Libertine and then head for Nines, or we could try Republic as their bar can be quieter than Nines."

The friends were in agreement and were soon heading out in their separate cars so they could leave and go to their respective homes at the end of the evening. They were, before long, seated at a table in Libertine discussing the beer menu. It felt like their trip through Belgium; all the women discussing their beer choices based on taste preferences. All that was missing was the unique Belgium beer glasses. These were boring plain glass beer pint tumblers. Part of the fun in Belgium had been the unique glass for each beer. They had been able to compare beer flavors along with glass designs.

They were engrossed in a conversation of where to travel next with their heads bent together when Angela caught a movement out of the corner of her eye.

"Jill, keep your back to the door because Dr. Lewis just walked in. I recognize him from the picture on the murder board. He is coming this way. Marie and Jo, why don't you stand on either side of Jill, to block the view of her."

Soon everyone was in place as he got closer. He briefly eyed the patrons before stepping up to the bar, leaning in and giving his order. Angela motioned to Jill to stand up and head to the exit, keeping her face averted from the position of where he was standing. Marie and Jo stayed at her back further blocking the view and as they had five inches on Jill's height, it wasn't hard to do.

Angela wandered up to the bar next to Dr. Lewis to settle their tab. He looked over at her and she smiled back at him in her usual friendly manner, but he did not smile back. He soon got a beer and headed over to the table they had just vacated. Angela closed out the tab and headed for the door.

Her friends were huddled down the street about three store fronts away and Angela walked the distance to join them.

"He got a beer and is occupying the table we just left. I smiled at him, but he didn't smile back. What should we do next?"

"Let's see if he meets anyone for a drink," Marie suggested. "We can give it thirty minutes. Let's go into Fox Heights and the three of us can take turns checking the bar to see if he has met up with anyone. Jill, you can stay here out of sight and not participate in our little adventure!"

"Okay that is just plain mean-spirited, you know I like to be in the thick of things."

"You dodged enough danger in your life, now it is time to stay out of sight, while your team mates put their capes on to save the world," Angela said with a laugh.

"Should we keep someone posted there and replace them every five minutes or should we just check in the windows every five minutes?" Jo asked.

"I would vote on a surveillance method but since I obviously failed this afternoon, my view doesn't count," Jill murmured.

"Let's try checking the window every five minutes, we don't know who, if anyone, he is meeting," Marie suggested. "What if it is someone that we recognize? That could get sticky if we are inside observing rather than walking by the window."

"Good point," Angela agreed. "I'll take the first shift, and I'll set the timer on my phone to signal every five minutes. If you guys see anything try to take a picture with your cell. Turn your flash off before you take the picture and if you have to, do a selfie with your back to them to capture them in the background."

"Great advice from our resident photographer!" complimented Jo. "I'll order a beer for you to drink upon your return. Do you want a Stillmank Wisco Disco? I believe that is your most recent favorite beer."

"Yes, thanks, see you in a few minutes," and Angela left the bar.

"We have the strangest adventures together," Marie noted. " When my assistant asks me how my vacation was, she'll look at me with incredulity when I tell her about the murder, the investigation, our surveillance. I've told her enough about other investigations that she'll believe me, but she'll still be shaking her head."

"I know what you mean. I get the same response from friends and family," Jo agreed. "Jill, you don't even tell your mother about these cases unless it makes national news. Nathan takes our adventures in stride especially since he has had the opportunity to participate in them. Let me grab our beers - Marie, do you want a Stella, and Jill, a Guinness?"

To accompanying "yeses", Jo approached this new bar for drinks. She returned to the table just as Angela re-entered the bar.

"He is still sitting there alone, watching the doorway, so I think he must be expecting someone. I took a picture as I walked by just to make sure it was doable. Let's take a look."

They all leaned forward to look at the cell phone screen that Angela was holding. It was indeed a great shot of Dr. Lewis. Angela had got him looking down at his watch, so it was nice that the practice picture wasn't seen by him. Her phone timer then vibrated so, Jo stood up and went for a walk. The rotation continued until Marie's second and final surveillance trek. She was so surprised by what she saw that she quickly took a selfie, back to the bar's exterior window and then immediately crossed the street to get well out of view of the bar inhabitants. A few minutes later, she returned to the bar with her friends.

Marie's dimples were in full force as she grinned at her friends, "Here take a look at this cell phone picture. Isn't it an interesting selfie?" Her friends looked at the picture then returned her smile with equal mirth.

The picture was indeed interesting. It had capture about a third of Marie's face with the other two thirds devoted to the bar scene behind her. There at the table were Michelle and Dr. Lewis sharing a pint of beer.

"What an interesting picture. Why would Michelle risk being seen out in public just days after her husband has been murdered? It is nearly ten at night, I can't imagine this is a meeting to go over fabric choices for the patio furniture," Jo commented.

"I can't pretend to know what it is like to lose a spouse, and I hate to be judgmental, but I have to agree with you, Jo, that I would not be away from my children at this hour of the night so soon after their father's death," Marie agreed. "I wouldn't have even behaved that way about my ex-spouse."

"Let's go somewhere a few blocks from here so we can chat about this some more," Jill requested. "I am a little uneasy being so close to them especially since I had that encounter this afternoon."

Marie checked to see that the sidewalk was clear and the couple appeared to have no intention of exiting the Libertine in the next few moments. They walked over the bridge to Titletown Brewery to strategize some more with little conversation along the way. Once inside, Jill felt less vulnerable at being caught by Dr. Lewis.

"Let's talk about Michelle. We all thought that there was something a little different about her last night when we interviewed her at the winery," Angela reminded them all. "Do you think she could have conspired with Dr. Lewis to kill her husband? We know he potentially has a problem with his work product that may be big enough to give him a motive for murder. Was there a secondary motive here with him wanting to get Dr. Easley out of the picture for Michelle? What do we think we saw with Michelle when we interviewed her?"

"Good questions, Angela, and I'll add a few of my own," Jo said. "Have we heard from anyone that there were problems with their marriage? What was Dr. Lewis planning to do with his own wife? Did Michelle financially benefit from her husband's passing? There is also the puzzling question of where Lewis blows his money. Is it drugs and that is perhaps, what is impacting his work? How much do illicit drugs cost anyway? Can you spent say fifty-thousand dollars on cocaine or meth or heroine?"

Jill asked to see the picture again. She studied the picture of the couple but in the end decided it was wishful thing - wanting to imagine something there that wasn't.

Jill said, "If we thought this was a planned murder between the two of them, how would we go about proving Michelle's role in it? Merely meeting a man for a beer alone on a Saturday at ten is too thin of a piece of evidence to do anything with."

"Detective Van Bruggin said they were pulling Dr. Lewis's phone records to see if he tried to make a call from the site where Dr. Phillips collapsed," reminded Marie. "Might we ask him to see if there were frequent calls to Michelle?"

"At the moment, we are holding back two details from the police," Jill noted. "One is the issue of his performance at the hospital and the other is this relationship with Michelle. I think we should keep his hospital performance to ourselves. Since we acquired the information illegally, we need to direct the police to a way to find it legally. However, for the situation with Michelle, I think we should discuss our findings with the detectives tomorrow when we meet them for the interview."

"Should we go back to Libertine to see if the two of them are still together or perhaps Michelle has left and returned home? Again, I can't imagine leaving her two daughters alone at this time." Marie said.

"Why don't I make a run back over the bridge and see if the two are still together?" offered Jo. "After I get a look in the window, I'll text you with what I see. Then I'll go ahead to my car and go home. I'll keep my schedule open tomorrow for whatever you need me for but at this point we don't have any new research to do. Do you agree, Jill?"

"Sadly, I do agree with your plan. I don't recall being so blocked from following up on clues about a case. Oh well, at least the police are blocked too and the main clues that they're following up on are our ones that we've dug up. See you later!"

Jo exited the brewery and walked over the bridge. Turning right on Washington Street, she saw Dr. Lewis and Michelle exit the bar together. They weren't holding hands or hugging or kissing but there was something in their body language that said 'couple'. Jo took out her cell phone and took a picture. She stopped to text the picture to her friends while keeping an eye on the departing couple. She increased her pace after the text was sent to close distance with them. Dr. Lewis escorted Michelle to the driver side of the car and she got in and took off.

Unfortunately Jo had gotten too close to the couple. Dr. Lewis shifted his gaze and focused on Jo.

"Can you tell me which way St. Brendan's is? I thought it was at this end of the street."

He pointed over his left shoulder as he said, "it's that way, about a block and a half."

He then turned and seemingly made his way back to the bar. Jo knew she needed to keep going until she entered Saint Brendan's. She would make a bathroom stop there and swing back to where her car was parked so she could go home. Just before she entered the pub, she made a call to Jill.

"Where are you?" asked Jill.

"St. Brendan's. I followed our infamous couple until they reached Michelle's car. After she left, he looked over at me seemingly wondering what I was doing there. Perhaps it was my own suspicious mind. So I asked for directions to St. Brendan's acting like I was on the wrong end of Washington Street. So I figured I better come down here. Now I need to go back in order to get my car to go home. He headed back toward the bar so he may still be inside Libertine."

"Wow, quick thinking on your part to head to St. Brendan's! Marie's going to walk over the bridge and look in the bar window to see if he's there and then head home. If you're creeped out, she could meet you and you could walk to your cars together."

"That sounds like a plan. I am going to use the bathroom here and then I'll meet her at the parking lot by the sculpture at the corner of Cherry and Washington. See you later."

"Take care" Jill said as she ended the call. "It seems like we're all getting creeped out by our encounters with Dr. Lewis. He has spoken to me and Jo, he has refused to return Angela's smile, and we'll have to assume that he hasn't noticed your face yet, Marie. Can you and Jo text me when you get home? I just want to make sure that nothing else happens on this strange night."

"Jill, why don't you stay here at the brewery and I'll walk across the bridge with Marie. Since we're all parked together we can all get in our cars at the same time and leave. I'll swing back around and pick you up here. That way we won't be forced to play hide and seek."

"That sounds like a brilliant plan, Angela!"

Fifteen minutes later, Angela notified her that she was waiting outside. Jill paid the bar tab and left the brewery to join Angela, who was driving her rental car."

Jo, Marie, and Angela had had no further adventures on the way to their cars. When they walked by the Libertine's window, they could not spot Dr. Lewis at a table. The two friends chatted a while longer upon arriving at Angela's house. Jill, an early riser, would create questions for the detectives in the morning. All was quiet on a Saturday night in late spring in Green Bay, Wisconsin.

CHAPTER 20

It was a Sunday morning and Angela had dropped Jill off at Starbucks on her way to Mass. Jill sat in the café sipping her Americano coffee and composing a list of questions for the detectives. If she were able to conduct the interview, the first question she would ask Dr. Lewis to describe the scene as he best remembered.

She would then move on to questions without telling Dr. Lewis that they had a satellite surveillance shot of the incident. What caused Dr. Phillips to stop the snowmobile? Was he experiencing chest pain? What did he say? What were the symptoms that Dr. Lewis could observe? Did Dr. Phillips clutch his chest? Did he rub an arm? What was his coloring? Did he lose consciousness? Did Dr. Lewis attempt CPR? Did the county coroner ask him as a licensed physician to pronounce Dr. Phillips dead?

Depending on the answers, she might ask more questions during the actual interview process. Otherwise if she had no questions, she would wait for the detectives to show him the satellite picture and ask him again to describe what happened as it unfolded on the screen. She would then compare his statements to those that he made earlier about what happened at the scene of Dr. Phillips's death.

She looked up to see Angela walking toward her table. She had been so engrossed in thinking about the potential murder of Dr. Phillips that they saw on the tape, and making sure that the right questions were asked of Dr. Lewis, she had not noticed that an entire hour had passed. They were due at the police station in about thirty minutes. They debated staying in the café or going home. In the end, Angela got a cup of tea and looked over Jill's questions. She couldn't think of anything additional to add so they set out for downtown Green Bay with the plan to wear wide brimmed hats and dark sunglasses until they entered the back door of the police station. You never knew who would pass you on the street inside a car. The last thing the two of them needed was to have Dr. Lewis spot them on the street. As planned, they entered through the back door of the police station and took a circuitous route to an observation room. The interview room was empty as there were still about ten minutes before the interview was to take place. Jill was interested to see if Dr. Lewis showed up with an attorney to represent him. Shortly, Detective Van Bruggin, and an officer from the Cook County Sheriff's department, Deputy Payne, and Dr. Lewis entered the interview room. Detective Haro join them in the observation room. Dr. Lewis stared at the one-way glass as though trying to decipher who was observing this conversation. He had no attorney with him, which showed confidence on his part. Soon, the interview was underway.

"Dr. Lewis, we appreciate you taking the time to meet us here this morning. As I mentioned on the phone yesterday, Deputy Payne has some follow-up questions. I am here for the interview as the legal representative of the city that both you and Dr. Phillips reside in. This interview will be recorded and as I advised you last night, you are free to bring an attorney to this conversation."

Dr. Lewis nodded but said nothing.

"Dr. Lewis, would you please recount what happened on the snowmobile trip in which Dr. Phillips died approximately six months ago?" asked Deputy Payne.

"Randall and I were colleagues at Our Lady of Guadalupe Hospital. I have a cabin in Cook County that my family uses for hunting, fishing, and snowmobiling. I invited Randy to the cabin for a snowmobile vacation. He had never been snowmobiling before and as I keep four sleds at the cabin it was a great opportunity for him to try this activity. We had planned two nights at my cabin. We drove up after work on a Friday, reaching the cabin in the evening. It is about a three hour drive from Green Bay. The next morning we planned to spend the whole day snowmobiling. We drove through the woods in the morning and stopped at a restaurant for lunch. We went out again after lunch. We had been in the woods for about an hour when Randy started slowing his snowmobile. He came to a halt as did I behind him. I got off my machine and approached Randy to see what was wrong. I thought he was having a mechanical problem with the snowmobile. However when I got to his side I saw the classic symptoms of a massive heart attack. Using my cell phone I dialed 911 but unfortunately I was in an area of no reception. I carry a first aid kit on my snowmobile but I knew it included nothing for heart attack. There was no aspirin or nitroglycerin in the kit. I assisted Randy to the ground as he was beginning to lose consciousness from the effects of a heart attack. Once I had him flat on the ground, I opened his jacket and checked his carotid artery for a pulse. There was none and I started CPR. I knew the odds were poor that I could save him. I continued CPR for twenty minutes and as I still had no pulse and he was quite blue, I knew my efforts were futile and I stopped. I then hopped on my snowmobile until I found cell reception and could call for emergency help.

"About seven minutes after I made the call, the first responders arrived. I used my snowmobile to ferry the first responders to where Randy lay. They agreed that Randy was dead and so the snowmobile was used to take him back to the first responders' vehicles. About three hours later, I received a call from the coroner and I recounted to her what had happened in the woods. I think that was pretty much it. Did I leave anything out from the statement I made at the time of Randy's death?"

"Thank you, Dr. Lewis," Payne acknowledged. "What you described correlates well to your statement six months ago. Did Dr. Phillips have a history of heart disease?"

"I wouldn't know. We were work colleagues and I had not heard of him having heart disease. Sudden death in someone Randy's age is usually the result of a fat deposit or blood clot blocking the major arteries of the heart. Even if I had had a defibrillator in my first aid kit, it would not have saved him as it would not have removed the fat deposit or blood clot. The only thing that would've made a difference is if he had had this heart attack while standing outside a cardiac catheterization lab."

"Would you describe Dr. Phillips's symptoms when you approached him on the snowmobile?"

"He was in severe pain and breathing fast because of the pain. He got a few words out but then rapidly slumped into unconsciousness. I would guess that from the time I approached him to his becoming unconscious that perhaps sixty seconds passed."

"Based upon the symptoms you observed, you diagnosed sudden death by heart attack and passed that information on to the County coroner, correct?"

"That is correct."

"Did you advise the coroner to do an autopsy to verify your diagnosis of the situation?" Payne asked.

"I did advise the coroner that in my physician's opinion and from being on the scene that a heart attack was the clear-cut cause of death of Randy. I thought the family would appreciate if Randy was not cut up during an autopsy just to verify my recommended cause of death. The coroner agreed with that recommendation.

"Gentlemen, I'm not hearing any new questions or any new information regarding Randy's death," Dr. Lewis advised. "What was the purpose in having me come down to the station to answer these questions?"

"We just wanted to verify your statement of the events that took place at the time of Dr. Phillips's death," replied Deputy Payne. "We'd like to show you some new details concerning this case. Detective Van Bruggin is going to play a short video for you to watch and comment on."

Soon the video of the snowmobile scene was played on the laptop monitor that Van Bruggin had sitting on the interview room table. Dr. Lewis remained motionless and expressionless throughout the seven minute video.

Van Bruggin asked, "Do you want to watch that again?"

"No," replied Dr. Lewis. "Where did that video come from?"

"There are a variety of satellites in the sky primarily used for military or security purposes. We asked for a copy of the video feed for the time around Dr. Easley's death on the golf course. After we reviewed that tape and learned of another physician death at the same hospital, we went back to the satellite company and asked for the video feed for the time of Dr. Phillips's death."

Dr. Lewis asked, "What did you learn about Dr. Easley's death from the video feed?"

"We learned many things including that the shooter hid out in the forest behind the second hole for several hours until it got dark," replied Van Bruggin.

Deputy Payne asked, "What you observe about Dr. Phillips in this video does not match your statement both from the day of the event and what you retold this morning. Do you want to change anything that you told us today?"

"No I have nothing to add. Is this interview over? I need to be somewhere in a few minutes," replied Dr. Lewis as he stood up and got ready to leave the room.

Both detectives were so nonplussed by the response that they momentarily said nothing; so Dr. Lewis just opened the door and walked out of the interview room and out of the police building.

Jill asked Haro, "Aren't you going to detain him?"

"On what grounds? People lie to the cops all the time. I need more evidence to charge the good doctor with anything."

"But," said Jill as she paused for a moment thinking of charges and then closed her mouth. Detective Van Bruggin and Deputy Payne joined them in the observation area.

"I am sure we will find evidence, it just takes time," said Payne. "What we didn't tell him is that the body is being exhumed tomorrow morning. If you have a moment, I would like to go over constructing an agreement to have you consult on the autopsy. Detective Van Bruggin indicated that you would be available to assist our coroner."

Jill's mind was still arguing inside her head about letting Dr. Lewis go free. It took her a moment longer to put it in gear and acknowledge the deputy.

"Yes, I can help with the autopsy and I'm very easy to work with on a contract. I'd like to charge the county for two things - one, the cost of changing my airline ticket home and two, I would like to have my autopsy kit overnighted to Green Bay. Can Cook County cover the cost of those two requirements?"

Payne smiled, "Ma'am, I was sent here with more purchasing power than you have asked for. If we can get someone to type those requirements onto a page that you and I sign then we are good to go. Let's move on and talk about what will happen with the autopsy. We have made arrangements to use the medical examiner facilities in this building. Our coroner who is a nurse by background will be listed as the person signing off on the autopsy. You may work with our coroner or conduct a separate autopsy of the victim. Whatever works for your examination. Regardless, I'll be in the room for one or both autopsies."

"Thanks Deputy Payne. I would prefer to work side by side

with your coroner and do a single autopsy, but it will depend on the communication skills between the two of us."

"Our coroner has read your bio and looked up some of the high profile cases you have helped police agencies solve. She is very much looking forward to 'working and learning from Dr. Quint' was her statement. I'd like to set your mind at ease that you will not feel any friction from our end. We think we're pretty lucky to have you to guide us through the examination."

Jill had forgotten how welcoming and friendly people were in Wisconsin. She was starting to have high hopes that the exhumation would go well tomorrow. Then she thought of a question.

"Have you ever had an exhumation before in your County?"

"No ma'am, I haven't and I looked at the County records and this is the first exhumation in the history of the County. Given the grief that we are putting the family through, they want to get it right this time. Once the family agreed yesterday during our telephone call I was able to get a judge to sign a court order to begin the process. In my ten years on the force, we've never had a murder in the County. So if this proves to be a homicide, it will be something we don't have much experience with in the County and we appreciate all the help we can get finding the right answers and assisting Dr. Phillips's family during this terrible time."

Jill was impressed and pleased to be working alongside such good law enforcement officers. She had no complaint about anyone she had worked with on this case. Everyone was cooperative which made her job so much easier.

"That's great news. If you'll excuse me, I need to step out to have my autopsy kit shipped to me if it's going to reach me by the time of the autopsy tomorrow."

Jill stepped out and made a quick call to Nathan. She kept a flyable kit in her car's trunk and he could easily drop it off at a shipping company office before noon California time. When they had spoken that morning, she had warned him that she might need his help in getting the kit to her. She then returned to finish the conversation with the deputy.

"Your coroner probably has all the right instruments, but we really want to provide the family with answers as soon as we can. Often I'll fly or drive specimens to my own lab for processing. In this case, I assume there's some kind of reciprocity for Cook County with Brown County to use their contracts to process blood work and pathology samples from the autopsy itself?"

"Yes, we have such an arrangement for other DNA evidence, so we'll handle it the same way here," replied Payne.

"What is your turnaround time on results usually?"

"Depends on what it is. If it is a blood alcohol level, then it can be as soon as an hour. I am thinking that you have more sophisticated tests that may take longer."

"Detectives, do you have your own crime lab in Green Bay or do you send out tests to a regional crime lab or to a hospital?"

"Blood alcohol gets processed by local hospitals, everything else goes to the crime lab."

"What I would like to do is to take double samples of everything worth sampling during the autopsy. I'll fly back to California in the evening after we've completed the autopsy. I'll process the specimens in my own laboratory which will get you the results much sooner. You'll still want the results from the state crime lab should the case go to trial, but I can give you a jumpstart on the results."

"That sounds like a plan. By the way, Mrs. Phillips would like to talk to you at the end of the autopsy," remarked Deputy Payne. "Will that be a problem for you?"

"It shouldn't be. If you get Dr. Phillips's remains to us by noon, we'll have time to do the autopsy, speak with Mrs. Phillips, and for me to make my flight home. It would only be if we run into the problems with the autopsy that I might be forced to cancel on Mrs. Phillips in order to make it to the airport to go home. If that happens, I could set up a video conference call with your coroner and Mrs. Phillips from the Minneapolis airport while I'm changing planes."

"Great, it sounds like we're done with arrangements for the autopsy," Angela noted. "Can we go back to the interview for minute or two?"

Angela received nods of approval from the deputy and detectives.

"In my opinion, I believe that the entire story that Dr. Lewis told this morning was a lie. If you go back and look at your interview tape he had completely different body language when he was confirming his name, address, and his presence near Dr. Phillips last winter. Nearly everything he said after that personal information verification, I believe he knew to be a lie. Watch his eye motion, his lip motion, and his right hand. At the end of the interview, when he uttered his final sentence, his behavior returned to that of the beginning of the interview when he was asked for his full name and if he was present at the death of Dr. Phillips. He is a really easy read, but knowing that he is lying doesn't do you much good since you knew that already through the video feed."

"Yes, we did know he was lying, but it helps to have your clues on his body language," Van Bruggin noted. "I think today was the first of several conversations we'll be having with Dr. Lewis. We were respectful this time during this interview; we won't be the next time."

"I think we're done here," Jill observed. "Deputy Payne, if you have an email address for your coroner, I would like to reach out to her later today to discuss our approach on the autopsy."

"If you'll give me your email address, I'll perform an introduction and the two of you can take it from there. Here is my card."

"Great, I'll email you right now," Jill said, pulling out her phone and hitting a few keystrokes.

They turned and started to go when Angela turned back and said "there is one more thing we should tell you about."

"Yes?"

"We were out at the Libertine last night around ten when Dr. Lewis arrived. After the poor interaction Jill had with the good doctor yesterday, we figured it was best to get her out of there before she was seen and Jo and Marie did just that. I paid our tab and we soon settled in at Fox Heights bar a few doors away. Dr. Lewis acted like he was waiting for someone, so we decided to do surveillance on him by checking the bar every five minutes."

The three law enforcement officers were staring, slack-jawed, at Angela and were all wearing the same expression of curiosity about what would come next in her narrative. Angela could see their distress at the thought that the women had, once again, placed themselves in a potentially dangerous situation.

"Seriously you guys shouldn't play poker as your faces are so easy to read. You need to stop worrying about whether we will sabotage your investigation or become victims ourselves. Someday you'll fully appreciate our contribution to this case."

"Since you know what we are thinking, can you just put an end to our curiosity of who met Dr. Lewis at the bar?" urged detective Haro.

"Sure. He met Michelle Easley at the bar about twenty minutes after he arrived."

"What? Are you sure? At ten in the evening?" asked Van Bruggin.

"Yes we're sure. Even though Michelle hired us, we have had a weird feeling about her from the beginning. Besides we interviewed her for an hour one evening so we are sure as to identification."

"I am afraid to ask this next question for what you'll tell me, but what did you ladies do next? In my short acquaintance with you, I would predict your behavior was not to leave this meeting alone, so I am sure you did more. What happened?"

"Marie got a selfie of herself standing outside of the bar window and you can see the two of them in the background. We weren't sure what to do next - whether to observe for a while longer or leave. We just felt a need to get out of the immediate neighborhood. So we walked across the bridge to Titletown Brewery to huddle there. After another half an hour, Jo was ready to call it a night, so she walked toward the Libertine as that was where her car was parked. As she approached her car, Dr. Lewis and Michelle left the bar and strode down the street in front her, so rather than going to her car, she continued to follow them at a distance. Michelle got into her own vehicle and left. Jo continued down the street to where Dr. Lewis was standing and asked him which way to St. Brendan's. That was the last we saw of them. We were just surprised that the night before her husband's funeral, she is meeting a male friend at a bar at ten o'clock at night. This relationship may have something to do with this case... or it may not."

"I guess I am like you ladies in that I don't know what to make of this information. My immediate thought is that they needed Dr. Easley out of the way for their own relationship, but then what has Dr. Lewis done with his wife?" Haro observed.

Angela suggested, "When you pull the telephone records for the time around Dr. Phillips's death, I thought you might look at the possibility of calls between him and Michelle. Again that doesn't give you proof of anything, but it would be interesting to know."

"Good point and I'll do that once I get the records," Haro replied.

With that the group split up and went their separate ways. Angela and Jill discussed what they wanted to do for the remainder of the day.

"Do you want to go golfing again?" asked Jill. "We never got a full round in the other day."

"That sounds like a great idea. Let's see if Marie and Jo are available for a two o'clock tee time at Coyote Creek. We haven't played that course this year and it's always so lovely there."

Jill called Marie and then Jo, while Angela was heading back to her house so they could change clothes. Soon they were driving to the golf course. They hadn't had time for lunch yet, so the plan was to grab something to eat at the golf course bar and by the time they finished it would be tee time. After a great late lunch, they exited the bar to head over to the first tee where they were expecting to tee off in ten minutes.

Once Jo and Marie walked over to the tee box, Jo asked, "Now that we have some privacy, what happened this morning at the station? Did Dr. Lewis confess?"

Angela described their morning including the lack of confession by Dr. Lewis. She then went on to add, "Jill is staying an extra twenty-four hours as the Cook County Sheriff has hired her to be an expert consultant during the autopsy of Dr. Randall Phillips. The family is in agreement with exhuming the body and Jill's expecting to begin the autopsy tomorrow about noon. I also relayed our chance meeting with Dr. Lewis and Michelle last night."

"So what did our erstwhile detectives make of that strange meeting?" asked Jo.

"They didn't know what to make of the two of them getting together," replied Jill. "Angela suggested they look at the phone records when they get them to see if there were calls to Michelle."

"Let's forget about this murder investigation for a few hours and just enjoy some girlfriend golf," Jo proclaimed. "I'll buy the first round of drinks from the drink cart when it arrives. The sky is blue, there are flowers blossoming, there are no bugs yet and I am with my best friends. What could be better?"

With that thought, they all stepped up to the tee box on the first hole. Taking turns, they all had their usually disastrous first shots with the exception of Angela. Her shot was straight on the fairway, one-hundred yards ahead. Marie, Jill, and Jo all spread out to chase their wayward first shots. The first hole was about 256 yards long, so they had plenty of time to improve their swing by the time they reached the green. Jill looked over her shoulder and saw no one behind them on the fairway. It was a nice feeling that they could take as long as they wanted to study and swing at each shot. The group in front of them came into view once, so they had a nice feeling of having the golf course all to themselves that day.

They were walking the course rather than using golf carts. They got better exercise with walking so that was an important part of the game. The second hole had everyone's tee shot going much better. They all ended up on the fairway, but this hole was long at 414 yards. They all eventually made it to the green, but had lost count of their shots by then. Good thing they weren't keeping score. By the time they were on the seventh hole they could see they had someone behind them on the fifth hole, as the course wrap around at this point. He was playing by himself, using a golf cart.

Jill pointed him out and commented that they would have to keep an eye open for the gentleman and let him hit through their group as he would be faster than they were. Angela stood still, squinted at the man, then took her tee shot. After she was done she pulled out her camera which had a zoom feature. She used that to focus on the gentleman playing by himself.

"Uh oh. I think that is Dr. Lewis in that cart behind us. Do you think it is coincidence that he is playing behind us?"

"I don't know," said Jo, worried. "How would he know we were playing this course at this time? We made a last minute decision to come here. What should we do next? Call the detectives or head back to the clubhouse by cutting through the eighth hole?"

"He is not under arrest so even if we called the detectives, what could they do?" Jill commented. "I can't think how he could have followed us here when he doesn't know any of us by name. Let's pick up our balls and head to the next hole. Create some distance between us and then see what he does. Marie, it would be good if the three of us kept our backs to him and you did the face to face looks since he hasn't met you."

"Let's check our cell reception in case trouble happens," said Marie. "There can be dead zones where you can't get any phone reception and we don't want to be there if we need help."

As they walked toward the eighth hole, they all checked their reception. Angela had the best reception, while Jill, Marie, and Jo's reception wavered. They all knew the ninth hole was down a hill and isolated from the rest of the course. Depending on what move Dr. Lewis made next, they would either skip that hole entirely and head right to the clubhouse or, if he wasn't creeping up on them, they would finish out the nine holes. None of them carried weapons, but they knew of his marksmanship skills. There were plenty of large trees to take cover behind if they saw him pull a rifle out of his golf bag.

"You know, my friends, I will admit that I am scared of this guy," Jo's voice sounded stressed. "Let's just walk up this fairway to the clubhouse and skip these last holes. He has me so rattled, I really doubt I could make contact with the ball."

"Okay let start walking back to the clubhouse, but let's walk close to the trees," Jill suggested. "That way we will have cover if necessary, while we walk the five-hundred plus yards of this hole. Who has the best eyesight to observe what he is doing? It seems like it's you, Angela."

"I'll keep watch while we walk. I am also trying to think of his awards in those shooting contests. Do you remember the maximum distance that he competed in? I think it was three-hundred yards."

"Yes it was three -hundred yards and I think we thought the shooter that killed Doug was about fifty yards away," Jo agreed. "Okay that means he has to get closer to us to reliably shoot. I wonder if he wants all of his dead or just one of us?"

"If he is intent on shooting us, then he'll want all of us dead," replied Jill. "If he is out playing a round of golf, then none of us needs to be dead."

"He has drastically picked up his pace. He just rounded the

corner from the seventh green to the eighth fairway. He has both hands on the steering wheel and he is heading this way without stopping to tee off at the eighth hole."

They had all been walking fast with their golf bag pull carts while Angela had kept up her narrative. Jill was steering their group closer to the woods where there lots of thick tree trunks they could duck behind for protection.

Angela looked over her shoulder and said he has stopped about fifty yards away and he is digging for something in his golf bag. "I think it is time to leave our bags here and jump into the woods."

Angela's last glance confirmed the worst. Dr. Lewis had abandoned his golf cart and was moving swiftly on foot, with his rifle in hand.

They abandoned their carts and took position behind a tree each. Jill called out, "I have no reception here. Can anyone use their phone to call 911?"

She could hear everyone trying to make a call, but they had all lost reception.

"Let's head farther into the woods now rather than waiting until he reaches us. Maybe we'll get reception if we move." Marie took off in a light jog with the others following on her heels. The foliage was thick and Jill hoped that ticks and snakes were not in their vicinity. They made good distance in a short time. They stopped their trek, panting, all trying to dial 911 but still no reception. They all listened for sounds of pursuit and heard it.

"Let's keep going, we need to keep distance between him and us. Maybe we can circle around to the clubhouse," Jill urged.

Marie again took off in the lead. She was the faster runner of their group, so the best person to have in the lead, Angela didn't run, but she could speed walk fast enough to keep up with them in this terrain.

A bullet flew by their heads and lodged in a tree to their right. Given the shooting skill that their pursuer had, it was likely only their movement that was saving them. Jill urged them to be erratic in their running motion, moving side to side. They continued with even greater speed, and then they could hear Angela talking to the 911 dispatcher behind them. Her phone had found a cell tower.

Angela gave the report of a shot fired into the woods of the eighth hole, who their pursuer was, and ask the dispatcher to message Detectives Haro or Van Bruggin. Then she stopped talking.

"Darn, I lost cell phone reception again. At least I warned them that this might happen. I was worried that they would think this was a crank call because it sounds so far-fetched."

Marie had been doing a good job guiding them toward the clubhouse; they could see it up ahead on a slope.

CHAPTER 21

Then they ran into a dead-end. A huge smooth sandstone rock stood in front of them. None of the women were rock climbers had they been so inclined, but it also seemed to be a bad idea to expose themselves to a shooter by climbing up the face of the rock. Marie plunged to the left of the rock to keep them moving. The direction moved them away from the clubhouse, but there was really no other option. They couldn't go back the way they came or turn right at the rock as both options would put them closer to Dr. Lewis. They heard another ping off the rock just as Angela, the last person, turned left at the rock. These bullets were a little too close.

A siren sounded in the distance and they hoped it was coming to their aid. Their legs and arms were scratched from weaving haphazardly through the brush and trees. It was worse for Angela who was walking fast in flip flops that she had grabbed off her golf bag before they had set out. If she hadn't had the foresight to do that, she would now be running on bare feet. If that had happened, her feet would likely have been bloodied by now. As it was she had poor traction and cold feet from the wetness of the floor of the woods.

Suddenly, Jill's phone rang. She continued jogging while answering it, recognizing Van Bruggin's telephone number.

"Hello, we need your help like ten minutes ago. Where are you? Are you at Coyote Creek golf course?"

"We have officers that have arrived at the golf course, my ETA is still another four minutes away."

"Dr. Lewis has shot at us twice, narrowly missing," Jill yelled. Then she heard a third gunshot ring out and a cry of pain from Angela. "Dammit, Angela has been hit. Where are the officers? Tell them we are being chased through the back wooded side of the clubhouse."

Jo had turned back to Angela, and had taken her by the arm to urge her on. Jill took a close look at Angela who was pale but otherwise able to maintain her walking speed. Her arm was bleeding, and it looked like more of a graze wound then being shot through the arm.

They heard a PA from the back deck of the clubhouse. "This is the police, you are surrounded, put your gun down and come out with your hands in the air."

The announcement slowed their gunman down long enough that they made it to the side of hill, where police officers were scrambling down the hillside to reach and provide protection for the women. Using riots shields and blocked by officers in bullet proof vests, they continued their climb and reached the safety of the door of the lower level of the clubhouse. They nearly fell upon each other in their haste to get inside and out of range of the gunman.

Jill immediately began to examine Angela's arm. One of the patrolmen fetched a first aid kit from his car and soon the bleeding was stopped. They sat against the wall, away from the windows, legs stretched out in front of them.

Then Jo looked at her friends and began to laugh, "Sorry for the laughter" she got out in a garbled fashion as the laughter was interfering with her pronunciation, "but the sight of us would not get us on the cover of Vogue magazine this month. Marie, you have a branch in your hair, Jill, your cheek and legs are bleeding, Angela has a bandage on her arm big enough to cover up an encounter with a machete, and God knows what I look like."

Angela smiled back and added, "Could we appear on the cover of Ducks Unlimited Magazine, then?"

Soon her friends were joining in the laughter which was where the two detectives found them moments later. Sitting on the floor, wearing parts of the woods, scratched and bloody and laughing like children watching a cartoon. The detectives recognized immediately that the laughter was a substitute for hysteria, a way to deal with the adrenaline rushing through their systems. On their heels was an emergency medical services crew for Angela. They stepped aside to allow the squad into the room. The laughter died very quickly as they all returned to business mode.

Jill joined the two paramedics, identifying herself as a physician. "I examined the wound and it appears to be a grazing injury from a bullet. I don't believe that it will require stitches, but it should be cleaned and wrapped with appropriate dressings. We made do with a first aid kit. Angela, when was your last tetanus shot?"

"I had one last year at the same time as my flu shot, so I am good. My arm bled a lot but I agree with Jill that I only need cleaning, some ointment, and a smaller dressing."

Marie looked at the detectives and asked, "Do you have Dr. Lewis under arrest? We can identify him as our shooter and I believe that Angela got him on camera."

"Actually, we haven't found him yet. We have many officers scouring the woods looking for him," replied Haro.

That announcement wiped any remaining humor off the women's faces.

"Look we need to find a new location to sleep tonight with police officers guarding us," Jo demanded. "This Dr. Lewis has lost his mind and he is very dangerous. He has terrific shooting skills.

We can't figure out how he knew where we were. We decided to go golfing about forty-five minutes before we showed up to the course. It's not like our name was on the tee time book for more than an hour or that we talked about it in town."

"Yes, we have been wondering how Dr. Lewis found us. We have never been introduced to him. Even when I was caught by him during my surveillance yesterday, I didn't give him my name. If he looked up my license plate he would have only found the rental company."

"Did you drive your car to this golf course?" asked Van Bruggin. "What is the make and model, I'll go inspect it."

"It's a silver Ford Escort," replied Jill. "I would give you the keys but we left our golf bags on their pull carts over at the edge of the eighth fairway before we disappeared into the woods. We'll need to retrieve those carts for our car keys and wallets."

"I'll send some golf course personnel to bring your carts over here. This golf course has been closed as we search for Dr. Lewis."

"He is going to escape," Marie speculated. "He probably exited the woods and into a getaway car just like last time. When his third and final shot grazed Angela, I think that he stopped chasing us, as you could easily hear the sirens getting closer to the golf course. So I would look in that area. Certainly you should be able to recover the shell casings of the three shots."

"Do you remember exactly where you were standing when you were shot?" Van Bruggin asked Angela.

"I wasn't standing still when I was shot, I was walking fast and had just cleared the big rock face and was plunging back into the woods. To tell you the truth, I don't know if I was grazed from a direct shot or if I was hit by a ricochet off the rock."

"We have men searching the woods and a K-9 unit out there with them," Van Bruggin said. "Dr. Lewis may be able to elude the search and escape in a vehicle, but it's only a matter of time before he is captured. Someone mentioned, Angela, that you took his picture as he was approaching you with his gun in hand. I would like to have your camera for evidence and it will be returned to you, but that's a pretty clear piece of evidence that we can use to charge him with attempted murder. While in our custody, we will be able to link him, hopefully, to the other two murders."

Angela reached over to the detective with her good arm to hand him her camera. She'd had the camera strap around her wrist when they entered the woods.

A couple of golf course employees entered the room with their golf bags and carts. Jill walked over to her bag and dug out her car keys and handed them to the detective.

"Let me know if you find anything on my car. Like I said, it remains a mystery as to how Dr. Lewis tracked us down on this golf course."

A police officer entered the room and told Van Bruggin that the woods were clear and they had not found Dr. Lewis. The detective looked over at the women and asked, "Are you ladies able to walk us through the woods to indicate your path and point out where you think shots were fired?"

"Of course we're able to walk through the woods. We've already scratched our legs so I suppose it can't get any worse," said Marie. "Angela, can you walk through the woods with your flip-flops? I know that was a pretty difficult pace given the shoes you had on your feet."

"On our return to the woods, it will be a leisurely pace," Angela said. "At that slower pace both my wounded arm and flip-flop shod feet will be fine while we search for bullet casings."

"How does your arm feel my friend?" Jo asked.

"I've had flu shots in my arm that have felt worse than this injury. I could play golf with my arm; especially since the emergency personnel greatly reduced the size of the bandage," added Angela, with a smile.

"Hey, are you commenting on my doctoring skills?" Jill questioned. "I had hoped a gigantic bandage would add to your status as hero since you took one for the team."

A crime scene tech returned to the room, having examined Jill's car. He spoke with the detective first and then came over to Jill.

"Ma'am, we found this device placed under the rubber molding around the back window of your rental car. It's a simple GPS tracking device that you can find at any electronics store. We contacted the rental car company to see if they used such a device to track their cars, and the answer is no. I'll take this back to the lab and see if I can track it to a computer IP address which will tell us who placed it on the car."

"Was it on the driver or passenger side of the back window?" Jill asked.

"Driver side."

"Hmm, it might have been Dr. Lewis. He approached my car from the back and as I was looking down at my iPhone, I didn't see him until he banged on my window. He could have placed it there without my noticing the movement."

Both detectives gave her a pained look shaking their heads at her lousy surveillance technique. Jill caught the motion, grinned, and said "I really do suck at surveillance. I'll have to give thought to getting some training since doing an internet search on surveillance techniques failed to provide me with the necessary skills."

"Ladies, are you ready to go back to the woods and direct us on our search?" asked Haro.

"Our suspect is an excellent shot. Are you sure, he is no longer in the woods?" Jo asked.

"I'll admit that we didn't search tree branches to see if he is hiding up in a tree, but our K-9 unit followed a scent to the end of the woods and beyond to a road, where the scent ended for the dog. That suggests he entered a vehicle and left. However, if you would feel more secure, we can provide you with bullet proof vests to wear while we search."

"I'll take you up on that offer," Angela agreed.

Soon all four women were wearing vests not designed for their more slender frames. The weight was heavy, and Jill and Jo were soon perspiring as they returned to the path they had taken.

"This is a reminder to never gain five pounds," Jo noted. "I'm amazed how sensitive I am to the burden of this extra weight."

"It is amazing and, while I appreciate the protective qualities of this vest, I don't like the smell of body odor left behind by the last wearer," Angela said her nose wrinkling.

"Yeah, that too," Marie added.

Soon they were at the large rock where Angela had been grazed by the bullet. In addition to the two detectives, a crime scene tech was with them. After many questions about the location, they finally had Angela in the position according to her memory of when she had been struck by the bullet. It was a recreation of the crime scene.

As the rock was sandstone, it was prone to chipping. By the position of Angela's arm when she was grazed, they were able to determine that she took a direct hit by the bullet rather than a ricochet off the rock. That led the crime scene tech on a path with a metal detector to locate the bullet, which she quickly found. While she photographed the scene of the bullet's location, the detectives and the women moved on to the two other points that they had heard gun shots. The first shot fired was able to be dug out of the tree into which it had lodged. The bullet that had pinged off the rock had not been located yet. The detectives would have a second crime scene tech go over the location later, but with two bullets in hand already, they had powerful evidence.

Three hours after their original tee time, the women were wrapping it up with the detectives at the golf course. Dr. Lewis had still not been found. Officers had visited his home, but found only his wife and children who were shocked by the appearance of the police with guns drawn and pointed. After the shock had worn off and the officers questioned the family, it was clear that they had no knowledge of his actions. In fact, his wife had not known about her husband's snowmobile trip during which Dr. Phillips died. Mrs. Lewis had been on her annual visit to her sister in Florida and had taken their children with her for the long week-end. The Cook County Sheriff checked the property that Dr. Lewis owned in the county, but there was no sign of him there. The cabin was a good three hour drive from Green Bay though and so they would make a few more checks to the property.

There was also a 'be on the look-out' issued for Dr. Lewis. He seemed to have a series of cars to help him escape. He had arrived at the golf course in one car and escaped out the backside of the course in another car. That car was found abandoned about ten miles away by a Sheriff's deputy and it was unknown what vehicle he was currently using. The first two cars were owned by him. The police searched the family home for cars registered to him and they were all accounted for.

"Can you have the officers check the cars registered to Michelle or Doug Easley?" Marie suggested. "Perhaps Dr. Lewis doesn't know that we saw him out last night with Michelle. Jill, did you have your daily communication with Michelle today?"

The detective stepped away to make those inquiries.

"Wow, for the first time in my career as a consultant, I've forgotten to contact the client as planned," said a pained Jill. "Thank goodness she isn't paying for our services or I would feel really bad. She is also the client that I have sat on the fence the longest with as far as guilt or innocence of involvement in a homicide. I'm tempted to avoid contacting her until Dr. Lewis is captured. I am afraid she might want to meet us in person and Dr. Lewis would show up and shoot us." She observed the other three shudder and thought she best keep her thoughts to her herself.

"That brings us to the next question," Jo said. "How do we protect ourselves until he is captured? I really think we need to stay together and have police protection while Dr. Lewis is roaming free. He was just too skilled at finding us on the golf course for me to feel comfortable with this situation."

"We could get a suite at a local hotel and stay together," Marie suggested. "The detectives haven't mentioned police protection so I think we'll have to ask for it."

Detective Haro stepped back to the women and said to the group, "All of Dr. Easley's cars are accounted for. They have two cars and both are parked on their driveway."

"Are you planning to give us police protection until Dr. Lewis is captured?" asked Jo.

"Yes, we have requested resources to guard you, ladies. We would like to move you to a single location. Both to get you away from your known residences and conserve our resources by locating you all to one place."

"We were thinking the same thing," Marie agreed. "Do you know if any of our local hotels have a suite that could give us three to four bedrooms?"

"I don't think any hotels have suites that large, but we could easily put you in two side by side suites."

"I need to go to work tomorrow. If the police will escort me to the office, I should be safe as our building has the front door locked and I could work out of an empty cube so he can't shoot me through a window." Jo grimaced and added, "I can't believe I am thinking like a criminal."

"Better to think that way, than be a victim," replied Haro. "We'll escort you to work and we can have a conversation with your workplace security personnel if necessary." He then looked at the other three and asked, "Anyone else need to go to work?"

He got nods and made arrangements for Marie and Angela to be secure at their workplaces. Marie worked for a large company and there would be a conversation with her on-site security people by the police. Angela had work to do in her studio before heading out to a client's house for a photo shoot.

Jill said, "I'll have a few hours free in the morning, then I'll drive to your justice building to supervise the autopsy, and then I'll be heading to the airport. I could turn in my rental car now and allow you folks to courier me everywhere, but if you capture Dr. Lewis in the next hour or so, I could be left without transportation. So, like the others, I'd appreciate a police escort between locations."

Arrangements in place, the women parted company to head to their respective homes with a police escort for Marie and Jo separately, and for Angela and Jill together to pack for a stay at a hotel. Jo, Marie, and Angela might be stuck at the hotel for several days. Jill would cease to be under their protection the moment she boarded the plane at the Green Bay airport. An hour later, they met up at a local hotel. Despite the graveness of the situation, they were all taking it in stride. They felt secure in the protection of law enforcement. They would order room service for dinner. Fortunately, Marie had brought a couple of bottles of wine with her which they would all enjoy. It was their last night together as a team as Jill would fly back to California the next day.

They were planning a vacation to the United Kingdom in the fall. While Jo, Jill, and Angela had been to London before, only Jill had explored Wales and the English towns outside of London. Angela had visited Scotland as had Jill. For Marie, the vacation was wide open and full of new places to see. They would rent a car and stay at a variety of Bed and Breakfast establishments wherever they traveled.

They also needed to have a discussion about Michelle. Jill was still vacillating on whether she was a co-conspirator or not to her husband's murder. They needed to discuss the body language between Dr. Lewis and Michelle that Jo was able to observe last evening, when they exited the bar. Jill also wanted to give some thought to the records of Dr. Lewis's hospital performance. At this point, there appeared to be no motive purported by the detectives for Dr. Easley's murder or potentially Dr. Phillips's murder if that was the finding tomorrow during the autopsy.

Was being identified as having difficulties with your technique as a surgeon worth murder? They had to be something more to it than that. After seeing Dr. Lewis walk towards them on the golf course, gun in hand, there had to be a psychological diagnosis to label him with. Jill did not remember enough of her psych rotation as a resident to begin to figure out what was troubling Dr. Lewis. She checked her watch and noted that she had enough time to give Nathan a call and see what was new in his world.

"Hey, thanks for taking my autopsy case to UPS for shipping. I probably could have made do with the instruments here, but I haven't seen their autopsy area and I plan to fly specimens back home to analyze them in my lab and it's much easier to get the entire case through airport security, than individual samples in a zip-lock bag."

"No problem, babe. I didn't even have to go anywhere; they stopped for a delivery and the case went from your car trunk to their shipping truck in a matter of seconds."

"Cool, glad you weren't inconvenienced. I should be at your house by about eleven tomorrow evening. I have the autopsy in the morning. If I have time, I'll meet Dr. Phillips's widow in person, if not, I'll call her from the Minneapolis airport."

"How did the interview go with Dr. Lewis? Wasn't that supposed to happen this morning?"

"It didn't go well," Jill summarized. "The detective and the deputy asked him to recount his experience and he repeated what he said to the police just after the event. When they showed him the video, he again told them he didn't want to change to his original statement and then he stood up and left."

"Wow, he is a pretty cool customer...or a psychopath."

"Even though you have no training in psychology, you're dead on the money on that one. We decided to play golf this afternoon, thinking we would finish the golf game that got cut short due to Dr. Easley's murder. On the seventh hole, we noticed Dr. Lewis two holes behind us because of the way the course is set up. Jo wanted to return to the clubhouse, as he made her nervous. That turned out to be a good call. He followed us in his electric golf cart, pulled out a gun from his golf bag, and followed us on foot into the woods lining the golf course."

"What!?"

"We couldn't make the clubhouse for protection, so we had to plunge into the woods," Jill began to rush through her explanation. "We had no cell coverage for a while or we couldn't call for help, but we did eventually get through. Marie led our group and Angela brought up the rear. Angela's arm was grazed by a bullet and now we are in a hotel under police protection as they have not located Dr. Lewis yet."

There was a long silence on the other end of the phone. It went on for so long, that Jill thought her connection had been cut. She pulled her cell phone away from her ear to see if the call was still connected and then she said, "Nathan, are you still there?"

After another pause, he said, "Yes, I am here. How is Angela? Were you hurt?"

"Angela is fine. It truly was a graze, she has a large Band-Aid on the wound; it didn't require a trip to the hospital. I'm fine. When you're the short person of the group, you're harder to hit with a bullet."

"Was he chasing you in particular?"

"I don't know. Since the police have not captured him yet, they don't have Dr. Lewis's explanation for his actions. We wondered how he found us at the golf course. A crime scene tech searched my car and found a GPS tracking device on it. He could have placed it on my car yesterday while I was doing surveillance."

"Surveillance? So you took my recommendation on doing some surveillance?"

"I didn't tell you about my surveillance experience? It must've been because I was embarrassed that I was so bad at it. I wanted to be useful, so I drove over to Dr. Lewis's house planning to watch it for a few hours. I had done my own internet search to define good surveillance techniques. Despite reading about it, I had little success with my first attempt at surveillance.

"Jill went on to explain her failed attempt at surveillance and concluded with, "We are speculating that Dr. Lewis placed a GPS tracker on the molding of my back window without me noticing because I wasn't paying attention."

"You're kidding; you told him you were taking pictures because he had great landscaping?"

"Nathan, I can hear you shake your head over the telephone line."

"No, what you're hearing is silent laughter on my end. You sound like half of Abbott and Costello doing surveillance. So none of you were hurt?"

"Other than Angela's injury, the worst the rest of us incurred was scratches from the bushes growing in the woods."

"Now you're in police custody in a hotel. It sounds like you should be safe up to the point you get on the airplane to come home."

"I think so. We all feel safe at the moment even though Dr. Lewis has not been captured yet. Hey, I just heard room service delivering our meal so I got to run. I'll text you from the two airports tomorrow so that you have confirmation that I'm on my way home. Love you"

"Love you back. I would appreciate a call or text in the morning so that I know you've made it through the night," said Nathan with a serious tone to his voice.

Jill rejoined her friends in one of the two suites' living rooms. It looked like room service was laying out a delicious meal. Angela was uncorking a bottle of wine and pouring it into the little plastic cups supplied by the hotel. Not at all an elegant way to drink wine but no one cared. Soon they were alone in the room.

Jill raised her plastic cup for a toast, "To Angela" and there was the sound of plastic rubbing against plastic as they brought their cups together.

Angela added, "All for one and one for all!" Again they smashed their plastic cups together.

"Nathan asked how your arm was doing. He was a little shocked to hear that you were hit by a bullet. I think this is the first time that any of us have actually been injured during one of our investigations. I am very grateful, Angela, that you have such a small dressing on your arm."

Soon there was a group hug and then they sat down to eat. They sampled each other's dishes and in the end everyone was happy with their dinner choice. Once they finished, they put the room service materials outside of their suite and then took their cups of wine and settled into the sofa and chairs of the living room.

"Let's talk about Michelle and her role in this murder mystery. I am really puzzled by her behavior. Jo, when you watched Dr. Lewis and Michelle leave the bar last night, was there anything lover like in their relationship? Were they holding hands? Did they stare into each other's faces? Did you hear any conversation between the two of them?"

Jo was replaying the events of the previous night like a movie in a dark theater. As the movie rolled, Jo said, "No hand holding, no kisses, and I don't remember them walking close to each other as a couple does. I wasn't close enough to hear a single word of any conversation between them. As for staring into each other's eyes, it was too dark and I was too far away for me to tell if there was any staring going on. I do remember at the time thinking that something about the two of them said 'couple', I just can't put my finger on what it was."

"Marie, did you see anything when you peered in the window?"

"No"

"So what do we think of Michelle?" Jill mused. "Did she have a relationship with Dr. Lewis or is she an innocent bystander in this whole situation? It's not like any of us know her well enough to tell if the behavior we saw in the interview was normal for a grieving widow or whether something truly was going on."

"I am going to choose to believe the best of Michelle," Angela stated. "I think we do not know her well enough to understand her behavior at this time in her life."

"Like you Jill, I can't make my mind up about Michelle," Jo affirmed. "I think it's very weird that a night before her husband's funeral, she is in a bar with a member of the opposite sex late at night. That's a big red flag for me. However, with all of the internet searches we've performed, we're unable to find any connection between Michelle and Dr. Lewis other than the decorating job she did for him and his wife."

"I guess we'll just have to leave the issue of Michelle's guilt or innocence as undecided," Jill said. "Let's move on to a discussion about quality and whether Dr. Lewis is a problematic surgeon. We were able to read some reports that Nick obtained for us in an illegal manner. I wonder if he could find any more material for us that spells out what actions the hospital was planning to take in regards to his performance."

"I think there will be far too many documents for Nick to search through," noted Jo. "I don't know enough about cyber security to understand if there is a huge risk to him personally for dabbling in that database for us. I think that they may not have labeled any planned actions as a 'quality problem with Dr. Lewis'. It's more likely buried in some generic report or memo which means that Nick would be looking for a needle in a haystack."

"Maybe we best leave that up to the detectives when they capture Dr. Lewis," Angela suggested. "I bet they could lead him to a point where he complains about the unfair actions of the hospital, then they would have enough to get a warrant for digging into that area of the records. However, we need to warn them first, as for all we know they could be in the process of arresting Dr. Lewis as we speak."

"Good point, Angela," Marie said. "How do we provide this

information to the detectives so they don't have grounds to arrest us for illegally obtaining the information?"

They all contemplated a scenario where they could avoid prosecution, yet still pass on the useful information. After a moment, Jo floated an idea.

"How about if we tell the detectives that one of the people we interviewed mentioned that there were rumors about the quality of Dr. Lewis's work? Given the attack on the quality manager, Helen, at our Lady of Guadalupe there are signs pointing to the fact that he may have quality problems. We could then provide some suggested questions to ask him during the interview process. What we need to think about is what his reaction will be to being asked those questions. If he is narcissistic, he will deny everything. At that point, the detectives could ask him about his complication rate and see what happens next."

"I like that idea," Angela agreed. "I think we should send an e-mail to the detectives with a list of questions to ask Dr. Lewis. We could just say that we don't remember who told us that there were issues but that it would be worth exploring during the interview."

Soon they had a script written with questions for Dr. Lewis followed by secondary questions depending on what answers he provided to the initial inquiry.

"Unless you need some help with the autopsy, Jill, I think we should move on to planning our fall vacation." Marie added, "This is the last time we will be face-to-face until we arrive in merry old England."

"Sad but true," Jill agreed. "So I think I have the most travel experience around the United Kingdom of the four of us. Personally, I have a castle fetish and I have to think that I have viewed close to twenty castles throughout Wales, Scotland, and England. I would be more than happy to go on that same journey."

"We could do a poetry and literature tour," Angela proposed. "We could visit the regions of Shakespeare, Brontë, Austen, Chaucer, Dickens, and Keats. Read great stuff along the way."

"Could we shop from the southern tip of England to the North of Scotland and West to Wales?" Marie asked. "I am a shopaholic and I'm sure I could find lots of things to buy."

"I don't like to have a very planned itinerary," Jo declared. "How about if each of us picks one place that we want to visit in each country? That would give us twelve things to see and do. We could pick our lodging around those twelve things and rent a car or take the train between these attractions."

The other three women smiled and nodded their agreement.

"One month from today, let's all share with each other the three places we want to go. That way I can build our lodging around these places. Let's all agree that no one has to name London as we all want to see that city. Perhaps we give it two days before heading out to the countryside?" Jill suggested.

Again they nodded their agreement and soon their group broke up to head for bed. With the thought and a prayer for a quiet night, they all relaxed into their respective beds. Their wish was granted as they awoke incident free the next morning. Jill stayed out of everyone's way while they got ready to go to work. She would grab a shower after they left as she had two hours before she needed to meet the coroner for the autopsy. She got hugs from everyone as they departed for the day, police escort in place as Dr. Lewis had still not been located, knowing that they would not see each other again until that fall vacation.

CHAPTER 22

*J*ill left the hotel with her police escort. It was a short drive to police headquarters where the medical examiner laboratory was located. Jill met the coroner from Cook County at the laboratory. She was a nurse by background with special forensic training. Deputy Payne had to return to Cook County and was unable to attend the autopsy as he had planned.

"Hello, Dr. Quint, it's nice to meet you. The police received your autopsy suitcase and it's waiting in the lab for you along with Dr. Phillips. It's nice to meet you in person after the email introduction provided by Deputy Payne."

"Hi Jane, it's nice to meet you in person as well. Please call me Jill. As you know, I am not licensed in this state, so you will be the official of record for this case. You have seen the satellite feed of this death?"

"Yes I have and I'll be searching for evidence in regards to the event."

"How do you want to divide up the autopsy? We could do two completely separate examinations. Just before you close up the Y incision, I'll follow in your shoes and perform a second autopsy.

Or, if you don't mind me serving as a supervisor, I could watch what you do and offer suggestions. A third approach we might take is, I could do the autopsy and have you supervise me."

"Jill, I have never performed an autopsy on an exhumed body so I don't know what to expect. If you don't mind taking direction from a nurse, I would like to run with your last suggestion and supervise you. I will learn the most, Dr. Phillips will get the best autopsy, and I'll be able to sign the death certificate as the coroner as long as I closely observe and agree with what you're doing."

"I don't mind at all taking direction from a nurse. I went into the business of consulting to provide a second opinion on the cause of death just so families could get at the truth of a loved one's death. I want the best autopsy with the least challengeable results because that is what the family wants."

"Great let's get started on this."

After putting on protective gear, Jill and Jane wrestled Dr. Phillips out of his burial clothes. Having been embalmed and dead for about six months, his rigor mortis was long gone. He was well preserved as the ground had been frozen for most of the time he had been buried. Some bodies, based on temperature and the amount of embalming fluid, were well preserved upon exhumation; others had the skin beginning to decay. Jill began the autopsy. She spoke aloud for both Jane to hear and to record her findings.

"I am beginning with an examination of the skin. I am using a magnifying lens to view any imperfections. Normally, I start from the feet up, but given what we know, I am going to start with his back side beginning at the head."

With Jane's help, they turned Dr. Phillips onto his face, and began their search. Jane had her own micro-goggles and they both looked for and found the injection site suggested by the video feed on the snowmobile incident.

"Let's take pictures and sample the tissue around this injection site. I'd also like to take tissue samples from the leg muscles and the diaphragm to look for the presence of a paralytic agent. Since Dr. Lewis was a surgeon and would have access to certain drugs, I recommend doing a toxicology test for the paralytic agents of anesthesia," Jill said.

"For all the autopsies that I have performed as the medical examiner for Cook County, I've never had a homicide discovered or confirmed as a result of my autopsy," Jane noted. "Certainly, Dr. Lewis's willingness to declare Dr. Phillips's cause of death from a witnessed heart attack greatly influenced my decision not to autopsy him at the time of his death. Even if I had performed an autopsy, I am not sure I would have discovered this injection site or collected any tissue samples for paralytic agents as it's not routine."

"Don't be too hard on yourself. Even if you had autopsied Dr. Phillips at the time of his death, you would probably look for evidence of a heart attack. We don't know what was in that injector that Dr. Lewis used on Dr. Phillips, but suppose it contained potassium? His death would look like a heart attack and again unless you were suspicious, you would not normally perform toxicology tests for the presence of excessive potassium."

The two women continued with the autopsy for another hour and a half. They looked for evidence of death by asphyxiation. If the diaphragm was paralyzed, then the lungs could not move air in and out. This would lead to death by asphyxiation or the lack of oxygen for the major organs of the body such as the heart and brain. Jane duplicated every sample that Jill collected to analyze in her own lab in California. Jane would send her specimens to the contract lab of Cook County for analysis. Until they got results back, all the two women could conclude is that it was a suspicious death. Soon they were finished with the autopsy and they contacted the funeral director for preparation and reburial of Dr. Phillips's remains.

After Jill cleaned up and was back in her street clothes, she and Jane had a conversation about her decision not to perform the autopsy at the time of death. Jill was convinced that Jane wanted to do a good job as her county's coroner. It was a once-in-a-life-time snap decision heavily influenced by Dr. Lewis. She would never make that mistake again – trusting a fellow member of the medical profession while carrying out her duties as coroner.

Since she had time, Jill contacted Dr. Phillips's widow Emily, to see if she was available to meet. Emily was pleased to be able to meet Dr. Quint in person. She lived in Ashwaubenon and thus Jill could visit her on her way to the airport. The police weren't taking any chances though and stood guard inside Emily's house while they spoke.

"Hello, Dr. Quint. Thank you so much for stopping by on your way to the airport. What can you tell me about Randy's death?"

"Please call me Jill. Let me tell you what we did today first so you understand my credentials and the legal proceedings of this case. As you know I am a licensed and trained forensic patholo-gist. My license to practice medicine is for the state of California therefore any autopsy that I render an opinion on anywhere in the nation fails to meet the legal standard of the medical examiner outside of California. Therefore I must work in tandem with the coroner of the jurisdiction that the death occurred in. So in this case I performed an autopsy under the supervision and approval of the Cook County coroner. She must sign off on your husband's death certificate. I do not have that privilege in this state.

"The Cook County coroner issued a death certificate for your husband based on the witnessed medical event that your husband suffered while snowmobiling. She was within the letter of the law to do that. She will be revising the cause of death on the original death certificate to 'deferred pending further investigation.'"

"I thought you were doing this autopsy to determine Randy's cause of death; why are you now saying that it's deferred?"

"Unfortunately until we have all evidence in front of us, and that includes test results from specimens that were sent out to Wisconsin labs today, we can't label Randy's cause of death to anything but 'deferred'. Once all the lab tests are completed, I would expect that we will change Dr. Phillips's cause of death to homicide. I have duplicate specimens that I'll be processing in my lab in California, but the results must be confirmed by the Wisconsin lab."

"What test results are you looking for specifically? How will they tell whether Randy was murdered? Hasn't it been too long since his death to find something and does embalming fluid change test results?"

"Emily, those are all really good questions. Let me answer the last two first. Embalming fluid does impact test results. If I wanted to detect if someone had been injected with excessive insulin and that caused this person's death, then I would find insulin in the tissues. The embalming fluid might dilute it, but it would still be measurable. In regards to your first question, did the police talk to you about the evidence they had that caused them to want to exhume Dr. Phillips?"

"They told me they had new information from where they found Randy that was suspicious, and therefore they wanted to do another autopsy. Since I had never believed that Randy had a heart attack, I readily agreed."

Jill thought for a few moments about what to say to the widow. She was surprised somewhat that they hadn't provided a better explanation and no one seemed to have interviewed her yet about her husband and Dr. Lewis. Well, they had their opportunity, and now it was hers. She wouldn't hesitate to question the widow about Dr. Lewis.

"Emily, I was visiting friends in Green Bay when Dr. Easley was shot. My team and I began work on that murder investigation and in doing so came across the fact that Dr. Easley and Dr. Phillips had occupied the same leadership positions at Our Lady of Guadalupe. That was too much of a coincidence for me, so we briefly looked into the circumstance of your husband's death.

"We really didn't do any more work on it than that. One of

the clues we were looking at in the case of Dr. Easley's murder was satellite video feed. There are companies around the world that have placed satellites in orbit around the Earth. They are used for entertainment and surveillance. The American military uses them to spy on other countries and I assume that other countries spy on us as well. I contacted one of those companies to see if we could get the footage of the woods around the golf course where Dr. Easley was murdered. We were provided with footage that gave us some clues about the shooter but no solid evidence.

"We had pretty much run out of clues, when I thought of your husband's death last winter and so I worked with the Cook County Sheriff to get the geographical coordinates of where he was found next to his snowmobile. In watching that video, you can see some behavior that might lead you to believe that this was not a heart attack."

"Do you have it with you? You obtained it so you must have a copy in your possession," Emily urged.

Again Jill paused to think before saying something hurtful to this widow.

"I do have it with me on my laptop. Let me send one of the officers out to my car to fetch it."

So saying Jill stood up, walked to the living room door and asked the officer if he would retrieve her laptop from a carry-on bag in the trunk of her car. A few moments later he returned with the computer. Jill powered it up, glancing at the time, as she walked over to sit down next to the widow.

"I need to head to the airport in about ten minutes," Jill observed. "If I don't answer all your questions by then, we'll have to talk by phone later. Let me caution you, I'm about to show you footage of your husband's death. Is there someone close-by that you would like to have come over and view with you?"

"No, let's just get this over with."

Jill shrugged and hit play on the video and Jill narrated the events as they unfolded on the video, she could sense the sadness, disbelief and finally, anger, emanating from Emily.

Other than the sound of Emily's tear splashing on the laptop keyboard, there was no sound in the room. Jill moved the laptop out of harm's way and began to power it down, wanting to give Emily a little time to her thoughts.

"Is this why there is an all-points bulletin out for Dr. Lewis?"

"No, not for your husband's murder yet. That was why we needed to exhume the body. He was questioned yesterday morning, shown this video, then he said he had no changes to his original statement. The bulletin is because he tried to murder my friends and me at Coyote Creek Golf Course yesterday. We believe he has a role in the deaths of Drs. Phillips and Easley, as well as the attempted murder of Angela Weber, a member of my team."

"Why would he do anything like this? He is a respected surgeon and father."

Jill thought she had dumped enough information on the woman, so she would leave the murder's motive for the law enforcement to discuss with her.

"I don't know and I need to get going to the airport in a few minutes. Is there someone I can call for you to come over and keep you company?"

"No, despite the tears, I'll be fine. I'd like to have a gun to go after Dr. Lewis myself. Randy felt badgered to go on that snowmobile trip by Dr. Lewis. He had mentioned once in passing that he would never allow his family to be cared for by Dr. Lewis. When I asked him why, he said the guy had problems in the OR. I think over our twenty year marriage that was the only criticism of a fellow physician that I heard Randy make and at that he didn't elaborate."

Emily had given Jill valuable information that she could use to pass on to the detectives. Maybe Emily's comments could be used to direct the detectives to get a subpoena for those hospital records. Still she thought it might be better to use the comment on Dr. Lewis during an interview, and see if his temper might cause him to give up information.

"Emily, if you don't mind, I am going to pass your comments on to the detectives, I think that once I get some definitive test results that they will be on your doorstep with questions for you about Dr. Phillips's relationship with Dr. Lewis. Use this next twenty-four hours to think about any comments over the years that your husband may have made about Dr. Lewis."

"Would you call me tomorrow, once you have some test results back? I understand that they are not official, but it will give me a preview of what is coming. Thanks for stopping to talk with me, I really appreciate it. If I can ever provide you some assistance, please let me know."

Jill was soon out the door and on her way to the airport, her police escort tailing her. She dropped the rental car off at the agency and proceeded inside the airport. They stayed with her until she boarded. The airline was made aware of her situation, and boarded her first, the police escort took one last look at the departure lounge and left. Thirty minutes later the plane taxied to the runway and took off. Jill heaved a sigh of relief and then felt guilty. She was out of harm's way but her friends were not. At least they were being protected by a solid law enforcement agency. Jill had been impressed with the way they had protected her during her visit to Emily's house. After a change of planes in Minneapolis, she flew home to California. She arrived at Nathan's house at eleven in the evening. Fortunately, he was a night person and was wide awake. Trixie was overjoyed to be reunited with Jill.

CHAPTER 23

*A*fter a long embrace, equally long kisses, and a very pleasurable hour spent in Nathan's bed, they were laying naked, covers over them, glass of wine in hand. Arthur was curled up on a chair near Nathan's side of the bed while Trixie was asleep on the floor near Jill.

"It's nice to have you home where you're safe," Nathan said. "Why are the murderers after you now, when you had four peaceful years as a consultant?"

"I've had a few cases in the past year that weren't dangerous," Jill replied. "I think the dangerous cases are when I am dealing with someone who thinks they got away with murder. In their mind, they planned the perfect murder and I come along and spoil that opinion of themselves. Rather than agreeing that they didn't plan the perfect murder, they try to stop my voice saying they failed. That would be my pop psychology explanation for what has occurred."

"Hmmm, so what are your plans for the next few days?"

"Since I just came back from vacation, I won't be going anywhere for a while. I have a bunch of tests to do in my lab tomorrow and several discussions with the team, the detectives, and Dr. Phillips's widow. When I get through all of that, then I'll be concentrating on the vineyard. I probably have some grape bunches that need thinning out. I hate to remove fruit, but then I can't have broken branches or small grapes as we march towards harvest time. How about you?"

"I need to drive over to a client vineyard in St Helena."

"The wine glass dude?"

"Yes, exactly. I have a few designs to show him. I just love the 3D printer. For those customers unable to envision the true genius of my design, they can see it with their own eyes to help them make a decision. I don't know Andrew well enough yet to know how good he is at imagining things."

"Are you going tomorrow?"

"I was going to. Why? Do you want to join me?"

"Yes I would like to see his situation. In some ways it mirrors my own. Some day when I open a tasting room, I won't have much traffic that just happens to drive by and decide to come in and taste my wine. I'll need something to make it a destination and so it would be good to understand his business growth. It seems like he is about four years ahead of me in the life of a business. Would you be able to reschedule the visit for a few days from now? I would love to spend the whole day with you, I've missed you."

"Hey babe, I missed you too," Nathan said reaching over to give her another kiss. "Andrew said he was available all this week. I hate to visit the Napa area on Friday because it is filled with tourists. Do you think you can clear your role in your current investigation by Wednesday night? We could then travel on Thursday."

"That should be doable," Jill said and then glancing at the clock she added "it's three in the morning Wisconsin time, I need to go to sleep now."

As usual she was up the next morning shortly after dawn. She would need a nap later that afternoon, but she couldn't sleep anymore despite only being asleep for five hours. Nathan, her polar opposite, would sleep deeply for at least another three hours and then it would take another forty-five minutes after that to get his head in gear. She would pack up Trixie and head home to begin work. She left Nathan a note suggesting they meet for lunch or dinner at her place today. She called Angela, Jo, and Marie to check on their safety and to see if Dr. Lewis had been apprehended. According to Angela, there was still no sight of him.

Shortly, she was making the turn through her gates to her vineyard. She loved seeing the sign for Quixotic Winery. Trixie was whining and wagging her tail, recognizing that she was home. Jill spent a quick hour filling up her dirty clothes basket with her vacation gear, and glancing through the pile of mail awaiting her. She didn't see anything that needed her immediate attention. Thus she began unloading and processing her specimens. While she had many tests to process, she was most interested in looking for any trace of the paralytic agent near the injection site, or in the muscles of respiration. This was also her favorite area of pathology - toxicology.

She kept a supply of commercial kits that contained antibodies directed toward common drugs of abuse. A paralytic drug was not a drug of abuse, so she would be using her gas chromatograph to test the blood. It was rather like the testing performed for therapeutic drug monitoring. An hour later, she had her first answer. She contacted Jane by phone to deliver the news and then moved on to the detectives. She dialed their office number first; soon Haro and Van Bruggin had switched their phone to speaker mode so she could talk with both of them at once.

"I just completed the preliminary analytical test for the presence of a paralytic drug in Dr. Phillips. My tests were positive for the presence of a drug called Pancuronium, a common drug used in the operating room by anesthesia. You'll need to wait until your lab in Wisconsin produces the results in several days for legal reasons. Have you located Dr. Lewis yet? I thought it might be useful information if you had him in interview."

"We have quite a manhunt going, but we still haven't found him," asked Haro. "Did you notify Deputy Payne about your test results?"

"No, but I did notify the coroner, Jane. I am amazed that Dr. Lewis hasn't been located yet. He must have had an escape planned in case he was ever in a tight situation. By the way, I have a call scheduled with Michelle today. Is there anything you do or don't want discussed with her?"

"Why are you speaking with her? She is a suspect." Van Bruggin stated.

"I normally have daily conversation with my clients on my investigation. With her, I have let the rule go by the wayside for two reasons. One, as you noted, she is a suspect of sorts and two, we are doing this investigation gratis as a favor to Angela. Before I forget to ask, is there any word on Helen? Has she regained consciousness yet?"

"We heard that her brain is beginning the awakening process and we're hopeful that we'll be able to talk with her within a few days," Haro replied. "As for Michelle, let's discuss this a moment. There are three potential explanations for Michelle's behavior; she was a conspirator in her husband's death, Dr. Lewis was a friend and she wanted comfort, or she was pressured by Dr. Lewis to do something. Can you think of anything to add?"

"No, you have it covered. Have you spoken with her since the manhunt began for Dr. Lewis?"

"No, why would we?" asked Van Bruggin.

"I would ask her if she knows where he might be, since the two of them were seen together two nights ago in a bar. I don't think there is a downside to asking the question. If she is a friend, she should be shocked by his behavior. If he is forcing her to do something, then perhaps she'll come clean, and if she is a co-conspirator, she'll pass your questions onto Dr. Lewis, but so what if he has the information. I plan to tell her about Dr. Phillips and the search for Dr. Lewis."

"When are you speaking with her?" Van Bruggin questioned.

"In a few hours. Why, do you want to interview her first?"

"Yes, now that you've suggested a link between Michelle and Dr. Lewis's manhunt, we feel duty bound to seek her out and interview her," said Haro. "By the time you chat with her in a few hours, we will have informed her of the link to Dr. Phillips's death as well as questioned her about where we should look for Dr. Lewis."

"Okay I'll plan on talking to her in a few hours unless I hear from you that something has changed on your end," Jo remarked. "I originally called to notify you of the test results for Dr. Phillips and now I need to get back to my lab to work on some more specimens."

After they ended the call, Jill returned to processing specimens. She guessed that she had another six solid hours of testing in front of her. Nathan planned to drop by for lunch; or she should probably say Nathan was bringing lunch since she had been on vacation for a week and had not restocked her refrigerator. Supplies were scarce at the best of times and she feared if someone looked in that appliance now they would find mayonnaise, pickles, yogurt, and hopefully some non-moldy bread. Unless her plan was to feed her man a pickle sandwich, her man would need to stop somewhere and grab lunch for the two of them.

After a few more hours of processing specimens for analysis, she heard Nathan then knock on her laboratory door. When she looked over at him he was carrying a bag from her favorite take-out café. Jill needed another five minutes and then she could break for lunch. Nathan left the lab and walked toward her house planning to grab utensils. As he walked across the yard, a reflection off of something metallic in the vineyard caught his peripheral vision. Catching a second, stronger look, he was sure that he was looking at a reflection off of a rifle. In milliseconds, he was sorting through his options.

Should he drop to the ground?

No, he would just be a nonmoving target.

Where could he find cover?

Jill's front door was about twenty feet away.

The oak tree was on his left about five feet away.

His car was about ten feet on his right.

Perhaps he should drop to the ground and crawl toward the car.

He would soon be out of range of the gun, but he also would not be able to see shooter's movement.

Was this Jill's suspected murderer - Dr. Lewis? Jill said he had won marksman's awards for distances of three-hundred yards.

With all those thoughts speeding through his head, he decided he would do best to duck behind the tree. He moved quickly and made sure his head and vital organs were protected by the trunk. Then he pulled out his cell phone and made two calls.

"Jill, I think there's a shooter in your vineyard."

"What?!"

"After I'm done speaking with you, I'll call 911. I just wanted to make sure that you stayed inside your laboratory. I've taken cover behind an oak tree in your front yard. I'll call 911 and get back to you."

"911 operator. What is your emergency?"

"This is Nathan Conroy and I am at the home of Dr. Jill Quint. We have a shooter in the vineyard and I am requesting assistance from the police."

The operator asked for Jill's address and asked Nathan to stay on the line. He said he would but he would put the operator on hold while he conferenced in his girlfriend who was in another building on the property. Soon all three were connected. The ETA of a sheriff was expected to be another five minutes. As both Nathan and Jill were protected and Nathan was occasionally seeing metallic flashes in the vineyard, he felt had a handle on the situation. Nathan began speaking with Jill with the emergency operator listening.

"Jill, this Dr. Lewis that you were worried about, what was his shooting award for?"

"Three-hundred yards with a rifle. But how could he have followed me here? I thought they had notices everywhere to stop him from getting through airport security."

"Who else has tried to kill you in the last few days other than Dr. Lewis? That puts him on the top of my list of who is sitting out there in your vineyard with a gun."

"You're right! Operator, can you warn any incoming law enforcement that the person with the gun may be wanted for murder in the state of Wisconsin. Furthermore, he has won shooting tournaments for his rifle target accuracy. I would advise that any sheriff's deputies arrive in bullet-proof body armor."

"One moment please," said the operator and they could tell that they had been placed on hold while she hopefully talked to the officer on its way to her house.

She came back on the line and said, "This is the emergency operator. I have been asked by responding officers if the suspect is on the move?"

Nathan slowly leaned around the oak tree and looked at the rows of grape vines. At first, he had a hard time locating the shooter, than he found him and said, "He's moved forward about ten yards."

"Is he continuing to move forward or is he stopping and adjusting his aim before moving forward?" asked Jill. "How far is he from you or the entrance to my lab?"

"He's about sixty to seventy yards away from both of us, and he is stopping and aiming."

Again the emergency operator put them on hold to relay the information to the sheriff.

Then they heard the sirens in the distance.

"He is on the move again rapidly," said Nathan in a quiet voice. "He's heading for the house rather than your lab. He must think you're inside your house."

"Good, let him waste time searching for me there. Hopefully before he finishes, the cops will be here. Can you get a good look at the shooter?" asked Jill.

"No, the person was completely covered up including a ski mask over his face."

He looked around the tree to see two county sheriff cars turning into Jill's driveway. He could see the first officer and noted it to be Deputy Davis.

"Hey Jill, your favorite cop is here - it's Deputy Davis."

"This is the emergency operator, has the sheriff's deputy arrived on the scene?"

"Yes, ma'am," replied Nathan.

"Okay, I'll end this call now."

The shooter was in Jill's house so Jill thought it was safe to peek through the door to lab. When she saw Deputy Davis taking cover at the back of her car, she made the quick jog to her squad car trunk and she was offered a bullet proof vest and helmet. Nathan was still stuck behind the oak tree, but at least he was safe from any flying bullets. A second car had pulled in behind Deputy Davis' car and the deputy joined Jill and Davis.

Davis was a sharpshooter in her own right. The tall African-American woman was smart, quick, and an awesome shot. She had saved Jill on a previous case with her shooting skills.

"How did I luck out, that you were the responding officer to my house?!" Jill exclaimed.

"How did I get jinxed enough to have to answer your call of distress?" replied the deputy with a smirk. "It's really annoying to have so many people always wanting to kill you. Would you just move to another county?"

The second deputy was watching the exchange between the two women in mild alarm. Jill noted his expression and said with a laugh. "Don't mind Deputy Davis, without me she would never have the opportunity to use those fine shooting talents of hers. Last time we worked together, she took out a group of black ops thugs that shot up your station."

The second deputy continued to look alarmed while Davis broke in and asked, "Who is the shooter and why does he want you dead this time?"

"The shooter is covered up so we have been unable to make a positive identification. Before I left Wisconsin, a physician tried to kill me and my team on a golf course. He got away and they have a manhunt in progress to capture and arrest him. I figured he followed me here. He participates in a group called the U.S. Practical Shooting Association and has won several awards for marksmanship. His distance of choice seems to be three-hundred yards."

"Ok, I'm going to give Deputy Rawlings an opportunity to get to the back side of your house, than we're going to have a conversation over the PA to see if we can get him to give himself up without any shots being fired."

With this, Rawlings ran from cover to cover until he was out of view. A minute later, Davis got a text that he was in position. She checked in with Nathan to see that he remained covered by the oak tree.

Turning on her car's PA speaker, Davis announced "This is Deputy Davis of the Palisades Valley County Sheriff's Office. Please come out of the house with your hands up in the air."

The deputy waited, heard nothing and so she repeated her instructions. Again, no movement around the house. A third law enforcement vehicle pulled up and Davis now had two fellow officers to charge through the door with.

The three officers entered her house and soon they could hear a lot of shouting. Nathan took the opportunity to leave the protection of the tree and join Jill behind the sheriff's car. After a brief hug, they crouched down behind the car awaiting action from inside her house. Ten minutes later, they appeared to be leading the shooter out of the house. Jill and Nathan rose to their full height and both gawked for different reasons at the person being lead down her front steps.

CHAPTER 24

*N*athan was surprised because it was a woman, Jill because she recognized the woman.

"Michelle, what are you doing here with a gun?" Jill could have kicked herself for not having anything more intelligent to say.

"You know this woman?" asked Deputy Davis.

"Yes, I have a contract with her to investigate her husband's murder in Green Bay, Wisconsin. Her name is Michelle Easley. Michelle, why are you on my property with a gun. Were you planning on killing me? Couldn't you have just fired me instead?" again Jill thought what an inane thing to say. Aargh.

Michelle's hands were handcuffed behind her back. One of the deputies was carrying a rifle with a scope on it and a black ski mask. The deputies were escorting Michelle to the back seat of the third squad car. Deputy Rawlings had returned from the back of the house as well.

"Jill, we have a crime scene team on its way here to record her actions inside your house. I ask you to stay out of your house for now. Nathan, if you could direct the tech as to where you first sighted Michelle on the hill and her subsequent path that would be great. Deputy Rawlings and I would like to take separate statements from you two and then we'll need to have a joint discussion."

"Deputy Davis, once again thank you for protecting my life. This might be the third or fourth time that you have saved me. Can I offer you unlimited bottles of Moscato wine from my vineyard? I can't think of what other favors a forensic pathologist can do for you."

"Actually, I do have a favor in mind, but let's talk about that at a later time. I would like to get your statements."

"Before we start, would you mind if I notified the police in Green Bay, Wisconsin? When I spoke with them about an hour ago, they were going to be seeking Michelle out to interview her. I think it would save them time if we could tell them she is in custody. How about if I call and hand the phone over to you?"

Davis agreed that was a good plan. She liked the idea that she might be saving her fellow law enforcement brethren time on an investigation. Besides she had a feeling they would be speaking a lot over this connected case.

Jill dialed Van Bruggin and the call went to voicemail, so then she dialed Haro and he answered.

"Detective Haro."

"Hello Detective, it's Jill Quint. We have had some activity in California related to the case. I'm going to put Deputy Davis on the phone to speak with you."

She passed her phone over to the Deputy who stepped away from the group and conducted a longer than expected phone call. Jill was shifting her weight from one foot to another waiting. It was hard to keep still after the adrenaline rush of the last thirty minutes. Finally, Deputy Davis ended the call and returned the phone to Jill. Jill looked expectantly at Davis, but she only shook her head and said "Interesting that I am not the only cop trying to keep you alive."

She and Deputy Rawlings split up Nathan and Jill to take their statements. Nathan had to describe the path that Michelle had taken. Jill had not witnessed Michelle on her property until her capture, so her interview was focused on the ongoing murder investigation occurring in Green Bay. Nathan joined Jill wrapping an arm across her front and having her lean against him while she finished describing the complexities of the Wisconsin murders.

"For a vineyard grower, you sure lead an exciting life," commented Davis." I bet you have had more people take shots at you, than I have, in this uniform. Have you thought of retiring?"

"Yes, but I have stopped some people from getting away with murder and that's pretty heady stuff," Jill asserted. "Besides two of my recent dangerous cases happened while I was on vacation. I must be walking around with an invisible target on my back that says 'murder close to this person', or something."

"Again, please stay out of your house until notified by the crime scene tech that it is safe to enter," Davis admonished. "Nothing looked broken or damaged inside, so all you have to clean up is fingerprint dust. Detective Haro and I exchanged contact information so we'll be in contact with each other."

"I would love to be a part of the interview of Michelle or to at least observe," Jill requested. "As I know so much about the connected case in Wisconsin, I think it would be helpful to have me in attendance. One of the first questions I would like answered is where is Dr. Lewis? It would be nice to know if he was also in California and likely to come after me."

"Dr. Lewis?" Davis questioned.

"Dr. Lewis was our prime suspect in the murders of Drs. Easley and Phillips, and the attempted murder of a woman named Helen. The Green Bay police has a warrant for his arrest after the attempted murder of my team two days ago. Angela Weber was grazed by a bullet and we have him on camera approaching us, rifle in hand. Michelle has some kind of relationship with him - we have yet to figure it out."

"Let me check with my supervisor, but it sounds like if you were an observer that you could add to our interview questions,"

Davis commented. "I'll give you a call as soon as I know. I am going to walk your vineyard just to make sure no one is hiding in your vines, and that there aren't any cars filled with gun toting strangers."

Nathan grabbed their lunch that he had dropped at the foot of the tree when the action began. The food was all in covered containers so fortunately no ants had joined their picnic. With nothing more to do outside, they headed into Jill's lab to eat. Trixie had been barricaded inside the laboratory while all the activity was going on. The last thing that Jill had wanted was the dog shot. Once Trixie had seen and smelled the bag of food in Nathan's hand, she had quickly lost the desire to assist Deputy Davis in her walk around Jill's vineyard.

Fifteen minutes later they were working through the food on their plates when Davis returned. They offered her their selection of appetizers and finger foods but she passed.

"I walked to the top of the hill up your vineyard rows. There is a rental car parked with no owner in sight, it may be Mrs. Easley's car. There is no indication that there was ever a second car parked there."

"Good, hopefully that means that Dr. Lewis stayed behind in Wisconsin." Jill noted.

"You are welcome to join us in the observation area during this interview. Right now, I'm heading back to the station and I plan to have a conversation with the two detectives in Green Bay. I estimate that we'll get to Mrs. Easley's interview at about three this afternoon. So far she hasn't asked for an attorney, if she does this afternoon, then we'll be required to delay the interview."

"So noted, I'll be there at three. Again, thanks for the rescue and let me know about the favor I can do for you."

Davis nodded and left. Nathan stood up and cleaned up their lunch while Jill took a look around at her analyzers trying to decide what to do next.

Nathan asked, "I thought you had your property wired with

loads of security and cameras. Why didn't Michelle trigger any alarms?"

Looking chagrinned, Jill replied, "Because I forgot to set the alarms. I often don't set my alarms during the day because I don't feel threatened."

"Can you set them from out here in this lab?"

"Yes, but with the crime scene folks coming, I'm afraid to do that."

"Can you turn on pieces of the system; for example access to your laboratory and the cameras on the vineyard?"

"Good idea. I can do that. Give me a minute," and she pulled up software on one of her lab's computers. Soon she had a view of the hillside.

"I'm going to go back to my house and get some work done. Dinner at eight? Until they catch this Dr. Lewis I think we should stick together as much as possible. Don't waste your breath by telling me you don't want to inconvenience me."

"Okay, I won't. I appreciate your help," she added with a smile.

Nathan left and Jill went back to work on her tests. The crime scene tech was still over at her house collecting evidence. She had additional test results in from Dr. Phillips's autopsy, confirming her theory of suffocation by muscle failure. She emailed those results to Jane.

She took a few minutes to jot down some questions for the sheriff to ask Michelle. How did she find Jill? How did she travel to California? Where are her two teenage daughters? What was her motivation for killing Jill? Where was Dr. Lewis? Did she kill her own husband? Why did she want him dead?

When she was satisfied with the list, she printed it out and threw it into her purse to give to the sheriff. She checked in with the crime scene tech and put Trixie in a side yard where she could chase squirrels until she returned. She then drove down to the sheriff's office where she was shown to an observation area. Jill had brought paper with her to write down questions to send in to the interviewer whom she didn't recognize.

Deputy Davis joined her in observation, "That is Deputy Gibbs. He is our go-to guy for interviewing. We swear he could squeeze state secrets out of a spy without breaking a sweat. He'll read her the Miranda Rights a second time and then pause to determine if she waives her rights. He has your questions as well as my own."

The interview went on for two and a half hours, before the Deputy called it quits for the night. According to Michelle, she had woken up from a trance-like state while in the process of being arrested. She had no explanation of what had caused her to travel to California to kill Jill. She was shocked at her behavior and worse still, she was horrified at the harm her actions would inflict on her children. She asked to have her blood tested for drugs and wanted to take a lie detector test to prove she was unaware of her behavior. She was so visibly and vocally distressed that Gibbs decided to end the interview even though he had made little progress in understanding her explanation for her behavior. At the end, she had sobbed to be released to see her children. It was all very ugly to watch. She heard and felt the woman's distress, but she had tried to murder Jill and she had cried so much during the interview that they didn't have answers to their questions. Detective Haro was also on his way to California so he could interview her about her role in her husband's murder.

Other than Michelle's capture, Jill felt like they really had not made much progress that day in understanding Michelle's and Dr. Lewis's role in the murder of the two physicians. Michelle's interview had been nothing but weeping and sobbing for over two hours. Jill had no sympathy for the woman. Her arrival on Jill's property was not a single moment of insanity; rather it required planning to travel from the Midwest to the west coast. There was a ten day waiting period to get a gun in California, so she must have checked it into her baggage or somehow brought it with her. Even Nevada had a three day wait for a background check.

While she was at the Sheriff's station she had received word that the crime scene tech had finished. It was closing on six when she made the turn into her driveway. Trixie was usually a pretty good barometer of whether a stranger was near-by. She did not get that read from the dog, so it would appear they were fine with no Dr. Lewis lurking in her area.

Jill had expected to pass an uneventful day in her lab. Instead she had lost several hours to Michelle's capture and interview. She still had a week's worth of mail to review, vacation clothes to be washed, and now a house that needed fingerprint dust removal. She passionately hated cleaning, so on the way home she called her cleaning service to find out if they were available for some emergency clean-up of her house. Fortunately, they had agreed and were due to arrive at any moment.

She had called her friends earlier and they were all sad at Michelle's actions. No one was totally surprised, but still Angela had taken pictures of her twin daughters and they felt so bad for the kids. She had also put a call into the detectives and spoke with Van Bruggin. There were still no sightings of Dr. Lewis and so her friends' lives were severely disrupted from being under police protection. They had agreed to leave the hotel and stay in Jo's house. They had Jack on the inside for protection and cops on the outside. Living with Jo was better than being in a hotel, but Angela and Marie would have been happier in their own beds.

She took stock of her own immediate future. She had no consulting jobs on the horizon and if called for one, she would likely have to turn it down until Dr. Lewis was captured. While she hoped he was still in Wisconsin, he could have crossed into California if he was driving a car, so she wasn't safe yet. She had no thought of trying to fulfill the contract with Michelle after she tried to shoot her today.

It was time to start the washing machine and begin sorting her mail. Thirty minutes later she could hear the washing machine agitating, the mail had all been sorted and her recycling bin was now full of lots of junk mail, and she could hear the cleaning service cleaning up the black dust used for fingerprinting. She was happy to see that Michelle and her capture had not resulted in any damage to her walls or furniture.

Nathan would arrive in about an hour with dinner in hand. Now that there was some semblance of control, she could go back to her lab for an hour and perhaps finish the last of the tests from Dr. Phillips's autopsy. It would be nice to get that done and a final report sent to his widow, the medical examiner, and the detectives. Nathan found her there an hour later.

"What are you doing out here?" Nathan asked.

"I lost so much time today thanks to Michelle's arrival that I wanted to see if I could finish up the autopsy findings on Dr. Phillips. If you'll give me another twenty minutes, I can send off a final report to all of the interested parties in Wisconsin."

"I need some cooking prep time so that works. What is that other car in your driveway?"

"It's my cleaning service wiping up the mess left by the crime scene tech. Next to my lack of passion for cooking is my lack of passion for cleaning. I called them up after the interview with Michelle and they agreed to do a special cleaning for me. You shouldn't have to cross paths with them as I noted no crime scene gunk in the kitchen."

"Great, see you in twenty then. Don't lose track of time," Nathan said as he kissed her and left.

As Jill predicted, she had completed her paperwork on the case within her projected time. There was no point in doing a final report for Michelle. After she tried to kill Jill, she lost all rights to whatever information Jill collected. From her perspective, the case in Wisconsin was complete. The police had enough information to convict Dr. Lewis of Dr. Phillips's death and once they arrested him, they would have the right to search his properties for the weapon or any other evidence. As for motive, she hadn't figured out how to direct the police to request hospital records on the doctor's quality. That was probably her last loose end with the case. Now she would put aside the whole thing and join Nathan for a wonderfully cooked meal accompanied by a perfect glass of wine.

"Was Andrew upset that you rescheduled your visit by a few days?" Jill asked.

"I wouldn't say upset so much as disappointed. Even though he has seen pictures of the wine glasses, he can't wait to see them in person. You delayed his pleasure by a few days."

"Whoops! I'm glad you moved the visit as I think that Michelle might have cornered me eventually in the lab. I don't know if she would have looked for me out there when she didn't find me inside the house. Your alertness saved me this afternoon. Thank you," and Jill leaned in to give Nathan a hug and long kiss. He had to break off the kiss when he smelled something unpleasant coming from the stove they were standing in front of.

"Whoops again, now I am causing you to burn dinner!" said Jill with a laugh.

Nathan was making several quick moves with the spinach he had been sautéing. It looked like he was going to be able to save the vegetable.

"You need to make that up to me in your bedroom tonight. I haven' burned a vegetable for twenty years. Your kisses are a big distraction to a chef!" Nathan added with a raised eyebrow.

"Seriously I'm sorry I've caused you problems with cooking dinner; I really love when you cook in my kitchen. As for later tonight, I'll do my best to make you feel like you have reached out and touched a live electrical wire. That's a promise!"

"We could skip dinner and just move on to playing electrician," Nathan offered.

Jill scoffed at that and Nathan returned to completing the

cooking of the meal as well as plating it such that it was a culinary work of art.

They enjoyed the meal and soon retired to play electrician and Nathan lived through the experience to awake to another day in glorious California.

ABOUT THE AUTHOR

I reside in Northern California with my rescue dog and cat. I love to travel, play sports, read, and drink wine and beer. I enjoy the diversity of the world and I'm always watching people and events for story ideas. All of my stories are generated by my imagination, I don't use AI to write books.

If you would like to sign up for my bi-weekly blog and announcement of new books, please follow this link: https://www.AlecPecheBooks.com

While you're waiting for the next story, if you would be so kind as to leave a review for this book, that would be great. I appreciate all the feedback and support. Reviews buoy my spirits and stoke the fires of creativity.

Readers that sign up for my blog receive a free prequel novelette for the Jill Quint Series.

ALSO BY ALEC PECHE

Discover my other books:

Jill Quint, MD Forensic Pathologist Series

Time's Up (prequel short story)

Vials

Chocolate Diamonds

A Breck Death

Death On A Green

A Taxing Death

Murder At The Podium

Castle Killing

Crescent City Murder

Sicilian Murder

Opus Murder

Forensic Murder

Return to the Scene of the Crime (short story)

Embers of Murder

Ashes to Murder

Mint Death

Damian Green Series

Red Rock Island

Willow Glen Heist

The Girl From Diana Park

Evergreen Valley Murder

Long Delayed Justice

Michelle Watson Series

Now You Don't See Me

Where Did She Go?

How Did She Get There?

Dog Humor

Eat, Play, Poop: Letters to my parents from camp

New Urban Fantasy Series

The Awakening at Lake Tahoe (short story)